Murder in the Miracle Room

Micah S. Harris

MINOR PROFIT PRESS

DEDICATION

To my mom, Merle Swanson Harris,
who has always loved a good mystery.

Other works by Micah S. Harris

Novels and Collections
The Eldritch New Adventures of Becky Sharp
Ravenwood - Stepson of Mystery: Return of the Dugpa
Slouching Toward Camulodunum and Other Stories
Jim Anthony - Super Detective: The Hunters (with Joshua Reynolds) 2nd ed.

Graphic Novels and Comics
Heaven's War (with Michael Gaydos) 2nd ed.
Lorna, Relic Wrangler (with Loston Wallace)

Audio Books
Jim Anthony - Super Detective: The Hunters (with Joshua Reynolds) 2nd ed.

Forthcoming from Minor Profit Press: **The Frequency of Fear**

Murder in the
Miracle Room

Chapter 1

Angels were said to hover about the vaulted ceiling and well swept corners of the comatose woman's room. And although Twyla was in April Gurley's room five days a week, she could neither deny nor affirm this. Twyla *thought* she glimpsed them sometimes, but only peripherally.

Nor did the angels offer any aural confirmations. Rather, they seemed to take care that even their folded, trailing wings only whispered over the floor, hushed, as though April merely slumbered and could be easily awakened. Of course, it was possible April *was* conscious, or on another level of consciousness. Who really knew? Maybe her spirit flew about the room with the angels, straining against the ceiling for the freedom of more celestial environs.

But she remained anchored to this world by her body.

April hadn't always been in a coma, of course, and Twyla knew about her long before her home health care job would bring her into almost daily contact with the small town saint. April had gained notoriety early on, at age twelve, when her palms began to spontaneously bleed during school one day. Word had quickly spread through Tar Forks that she bore the stigmata.

Twyla was in April's class and witnessed the onset of the miracle. Twyla had, in fact, also started to bleed the same day as April, though Twyla's was a much more private hemorrhaging, and a natural one, in contrast to April's paranormal palms.

Those remarkable hands had now come into Twyla's care. While most of her ministrations to April were typical home health care duties such as bathing her, combing her hair and dressing her, the hands presented one chore that was peculiar to her sacred charge. Every morning, she changed the bandages that wrapped April's stigmatic palms, applying by cotton swabs an antibacterial fluid to the wounds that continued to spontaneously bleed.

The thought had occurred to Twyla that maybe such sanitizing represented a lack of faith. Certainly, no benign wound from God would become infected. Still, when it came down to it, she reasoned such precautions would be expected as part of her job, and it couldn't *hurt* anything to apply the antiseptic. After all, Jesus had his disciples pick up leftovers after miraculously multiplying the loaves and fishes. That set a precedent, as far as Twyla was concerned, for being practical, even in the face of the supernatural.

She had failed, however, to be sensible regarding the strange turn of her own life that began with the bizarre death of her aunt and ended with the demise of what Twyla once had believed would be her only chance for true love.

Chapter 2

Answering a 911 call from the distraught husband, authorities came upon what had been Twyla's Aunt Grusilla, now reduced to a greasy smear of ashes and burned body fat coating the cushion and backrest of her favorite recliner. The only unspoiled remains, still perched on the chair's outstretched footrest, were her feet.

Appearances could indeed be construed to mean just what Grusilla's husband Tate claimed: his wife had spontaneously combusted.

"She knew she could go at any time," a tearful Tate told the Tar Fork's volunteer rescue squad and police.

As evidence for his claim, Tate presented to the authorities Grusilla's collection of *National Expose* clippings, as well as a video tape labeled in her handwriting: SHC doc. On the tape was indeed a program from the Discovery Network on the phenomenon of spontaneous human combustion.

"She'd done a lot of her own research," Tate said, "and come to the conclusion she fit the classic profile of a spontaneous combustion victim. That it was just a case of 'when,' not 'if.' Well, she just got on with her life as usual. Groo was always one of them 'the glass is half full' people."

Indeed, the elements of the death scene suggested Grusilla at her leisure: the most recent copy of *The National Expose* lay on the end table by Groo's easy chair. A video tape was in the VCR, filled with a week's worth of *Days of Our Lives* episodes. Even the remaining feet were clad in comfortable shoes – a well worn pair that one might retain for kicking back at home. All evidence indicated the deceased had just settled down for a catch-up marathon of her favorite soap opera when she was suddenly overcome by constitutional conflagration.

All the classic anomalies were there: for instance, the tabloid pages, apparently so close to flame so intense it had reduced even Groo's bones to ashes, were not even curled by the heat. And the only intact remains, Grusilla's feet, were typical of a victim's extremities coming through the roasting unscathed. All and all, virtually a Fortean textbook case of spontaneous human combustion.

Occam's razor sliced it another way. Namely, Tate had murdered his wife and set her on fire after coming up with the spontaneous combustion story. He based it on the tabloids he – not Groo – had read and the Discovery Network special *he'd* seen. He'd probably even cold bloodedly asked Grusilla to label that tape for him, to get her handwriting on it. "The poor woman never knew she was in the process of covering up her own murder," the prosecution concluded.

Twyla had fond memories of her Aunt Groo. She was a plump, good-natured woman who always called a midget an "elf," but in a quite innocent manner, inoffensive to even the most politically correct. The prosecution brought in Twyla as a character witness for her late aunt.

Ironically, the power of her testimony rested on the only physical remains of Groo left unscorched – left because the killer had considered them incapable of incriminating? If so, he was wrong. Fatefully so.

Twyla related a story from her aunt's past, how once she'd gone to the mailbox in her big, fuzzy orange bedroom slippers, and, while on the side of the road, nearly been hit by a car.

"Aunt Groo personally related to me her only thought as she looked certain death in the face was, 'They're gonna find my body with these fuzzy orange slippers on me.'

"After surviving that near fatal encounter," Twyla had continued, "she wouldn't even go to the mailbox without wearing her strappy pumps or having her face on. 'cause she'd learned you never knew when your number would be up.

"Your honor, the shoes she wore at the time of her death were an unflattering old pair of high top Converse she wouldn't of even wore out in inclement weather."

"And your point is?" the prosecution had asked.

"The point *is* ... if my Aunt Groo *had* studied this thing out, like Tate says, and knew that she could light up at any moment, and if she believed that there was even the remotest chance her only earthly remains would be her feet, she would *not* of been caught dead wearing them ugly shoes!"

During her testimony, Uncle Tate's eyes had fired daggers at her in comic book style. No matter Tate's intentions toward his niece, any implied threat proved as serious as anything from a cartoon. He was sentenced to a minimum of fourteen years imprisonment. And that should have been that.

Of course, given Twyla's luck, it was not.

Chapter 3

Twyla suffered an obsessive compulsive disorder about fire. The behavior initially manifested itself in the typical "did I leave the burner on or not" worry that prompted a double check. But less than an hour after leaving the trailer, she found herself wondering again if she had indeed turned it off. It was that element of doubt that exacerbated the obsessive compulsive behavior, of not being able to be sure . . . . what if she were wrong, and the trailer burned down with her boyfriend Dwayne in it?

Soon she was coming in late for work because of turning around and driving back to check the stove. This happened enough that she was finally reprimanded by her boss. That had been something of a wake-up call, and Twyla's pragmatism finally reasserted itself.

What she did was buy a little athletic counter that she would click over from 0 to 1 after checking the burners. When uncertainty had put her synapses in a tug-a-war of "did I or didn't I," she would pull out the counter, see that number 1, and relax. She always clicked it back to 0 when she returned home to find everything okay. And she had successfully put her fear of burning down the house in the back of her mind –

– for a while. Then another uncle, Aunt Groo's brother Cephas, who was known to smoke in bed, had burned up one night after falling asleep with a lit cigarette. At least, that was the theory. It hadn't been proven conclusively. The fact was, there were no other cigarettes in the house, and friends reported he had claimed to have stopped cold about a month before his death.

"Most have gone off the wagon," the detective in charge had concluded and that closed the book as far as the authorities were concerned.

They didn't know, of course, Uncle Tate's claims about Twyla's aunt's death. All this flashing of incinerating incandescence among the branches of her family tree made Twyla wonder if her Aunt Grusilla had indeed discovered she fit the classic profile for spontaneous human combustion, just as her uncle had claimed. And if Groo's brother Cephas had gone up in smoke as well? Was it a family thing? If so, Twyla believed she could be next.

So she went to see the one person who could resolve her worries: Uncle Tate. She knew better than to tell him what had given rise to her doubts, and she hoped he hadn't heard about the circumstances of his former brother-in-law's passing for fear that he would figure out why this was so all-of-a-sudden important to her. If he knew he could torment her by keeping her guessing, she had no doubt he would enjoy inflicting revenge on her.

Twyla had never been to a prison before and had uneasily dropped her keys in the drawer that slid out and then back in to the cubicle where the entrance attendant would keep them. Giving up her keys made her feel vulnerable, a disconcerting loss of autonomy. Even though she knew they would be given back to her when she left, it all felt a bit too final. The sudden, angry hornet buzzing of electrical voltage that announced the opening and closing of the magnetically sealed doors only increased her feelings of menace, not security.

She approached her uncle in steps that were near faltering as he waited for her behind an unbreakable window. There was no possibility of his being able to touch her, but she still could feel his hate-seasoned appraisal as she walked up.

"Well, well," Tate said as she was seated across from him. "So I finally get a visit from one of the Chaynes. You people sure don't know how to treat kin."

We treated you like a murderer deserves, Twyla thought, but she did not say that. She didn't want to antagonize Tate; she was there for his help, she reminded herself. So with an obviously forced smile, she said, "How you been?"

"How do you think I've been?" Tate asked, one side of his upper lip curling. "I been in prison for years! You should know that. I only agreed

9

to see you 'cause I'm hopin' you've come to tell me you changed your mind about your testimony – even though it's eight years too late!"

Twyla swallowed. She said, "So, you're still holding on to that spontaneous combustion story, huh?"

"What else do you think I've had to hold on to in here?" Tate asked, but in that same instant she saw Tate's eyes move over her in a quick glance that made her feel like running home immediately and taking a shower.

"Look, I just would like to know, did Aunt Groo really spontaneously combust? Had she really researched it out? Did she believe that she was a candidate for that to happen to her?"

"Why? Are you changing your testimony about how Groo wouldn't have had them ugly shoes on if she thought she could light up at any time? Are . . . are you thinking about getting them to reopen my case or something?" Tate leaned forward.

"No, no," Twyla said. "Tate, you weren't convicted on my testimony alone, okay? I know my speaking up didn't help you any –"

"Turned the last nail in my coffin," Tate said, tightening his lips and leaning back.

"I think you would've been convicted anyway."

"Oh, so you just had to get your two cents in, too, just for extra, huh? Spiteful! Your aunt was the same way. I guess it's a Chayne family trait."

"I can't help you . . . Uncle Tate. I just need to know . . ."

"Oh, so it's 'uncle' again, now that you want somethin'."

"Did my aunt really go up in flames in her Lazy Lady recliner gettin' ready to watch her stories?" Twyla abruptly barked, making herself look Tate dead in the eye. She was no longer begging him for anything. Even though she didn't have anything to back her up, she was *demanding* now.

Of course, she expected that she had only made him mad and that he wouldn't tell her now, not for anything. Surprisingly, Tate smiled, leaning the chair back with him so that only the back two legs were on the floor and the two front ones, along with his feet, were raised into the air.

"Gettin' a little bossy, huh? You looked just like your aunt when you said that . . ."

His voice trailed. Twyla wondered: *is he having a moment of regret? Was he actually still capable of a tender moment?* Because she realized if he was, if he saw a chance to at least make the gesture of making it right with his wife by helping out her niece, he might –

". . . always turned me on," Tate said, his eyes level with her breasts as he slowly licked his lips and brought the chair completely back to the floor.

Twyla immediately shoved her own chair back from the cubicle and rose to her feet. "Go to hell," she said.

"Now, hold on," Tate said, waving her back. Twy stopped, cocking her head at him in a way that said "If you give me one ounce of crap, I am *so* out that door."

"*Quid pro quo,*" Tate said, smiling. "I give you something; you give me something."

"You don't need to translate – I saw *Silence of the Lambs*, too," Twyla snapped. "Do they actually show you guys movies like that in prison? What – is that supposed to inspire you for when you get out?"

"Nobody gets something for nothing – this is America," Tate said. "I'll tell you what you want to know –"

"Yeah?"

"If you'd come back and ask me again in a little, tight skirt."

Twyla rolled her eyes, turned on her heel and walked away without another word.

"Hey!" she heard Tate shouting from behind her. "You gotta understand – I'm tryin' to hold on to my masculinity in this place!"

Chapter 4

So she could never be absolutely sure whether she was a candidate for spontaneous combustion or not. The possibility remained an itch she couldn't completely reach, and thus one which could never be satisfactorily assuaged. There was medication for obsessive compulsive behavior, of course, but it was expensive, and Twyla had no medical coverage from her job.

At first she thought she might bring her pragmatism to bear on her fear of bursting into flame. Thus, she'd assiduously set about perfecting her technique of "stop, drop, and roll." And that should have been that.

But –

What if it were not enough? She would, after all, undoubtedly suffer burns before she smothered the flames by rolling on the ground. Maybe she couldn't handle it alone.

So she'd brought a fire extinguisher into the mobile home she shared with Dwayne Woolard: an "A" labeled issue, which, as was written on the cylinder itself, meant it was appropriate for fires involving trash, wood, and paper. She would coach Dwayne, drilling him mercilessly:

"Dwayne, hold it upright, pull the ring – the ring, Dwayne – now back away ten feet. That's what the instructions say. But don't it seem like you oughta be running toward me? Oh, I guess that's for *your* safety . . . well, *I'm* the one on fire. Get over here – in close, now. C'mon! Your love potato's baking over here! Now squeeze the lever and sweep from side to side."

Then the critiques would begin: "Congratulations, Dwayne. If this had been a real case of spontaneous combustion, I'd be in the burn ward now. And that's the best case scenario. Worst case: we're talking a closed casket for your sweet thing, so step it up, okay, sug'?"

(A frustrated, irritated Dwayne had once scratched in the world "trailer" in front of "trash" on the cylinder of their home extinguisher, telling Twy, "There! You should feel covered now").

Further, whenever she started with a new home health care client, the first thing she did was find out if there were a fire extinguisher in the house and where it was kept – and if a home didn't have a fire extinguisher, she brought in her own.

Well and good – *if* she erupted into flame during her waking hours.

But what if she were asleep at the time she went up? That could have been what got her uncle. But *he* hadn't known what to expect. Twyla did.

So she then insisted on flame retardant bed sheets and asbestos pajamas which were far from comfortable. That was when Dwayne, ill from restless nights and a rash from the asbestos, had first moved out.

Desperate now, Twyla decided she would try playing Uncle Tate's game. As soon as he gave her an answer – any definite answer – she would be free to cut bait and flee. It wasn't like he could come after her.

So she arrived at the prison to see Tate again. The short skirt she wore raised an eyebrow of the big boned female guard at the plexi glass encased booth where she left her keys.

Blushing, Twyla turned and walked quickly on past.

A satisfied leer settled over Tate's features as he saw Twy coming. She sat down in the chair before him, knees pressed firmly together.

"Oh, yeah," he said. "Now that's more like it. But . . . Twy . . . would you cross your legs now? So that your skirt rises up on your thighs?"

"Look, Tate. I did what you asked. I'm here – feeling like a 'ho' every second that goes by. So will you please tell me, did Aunt Groo really spontaneously combust?"

"I'm feelin' my heat register risin' if that means anything," he said with a grin.

"I don't care what you're registering! I don't want to hear none of that. I just want to know if my aunt –"

"And I want you to cross your legs, okay? Why is that such a big deal? I mean, you're here, you got on the skirt –"

Twyla expelled a puff of breath, narrowing her eyes as she held Tate in a gaze of contempt. Then she crossed her legs.

"Yeah," Tate said, licking his lips. "Now that's what I'm talkin' about."

"Okay. So. Did my aunt spontaneously –"

"Now, hold on now. Not so quick. That's been a while, you know. I gotta think."

"I'd think you'd remember your wife suddenly bursting into flames!"

"I know, I know. It's just that . . . if you could just, like, stand up, turn your back to me, then pretend like you dropped something and bend way down –"

The fact that she caught herself – even momentarily – actually considering bending over for Hannibal Cracker made Twyla realize in a way she never had before that, *yes, I have a problem*. She knew before she came that giving into Uncle Tate's demands would be like giving in to a terrorist, and yet she'd come anyway.

Well, there was a self-respecting way to deal with her obsession, expensive though it was. Unfortunately, while her reaction to the medicine was enough to ensure she wouldn't be exhibiting herself to Tate back in prison, it failed to completely still her worries. She managed to hide this from Dwayne when he moved back in; thanks to the medication she could usually wait until he'd gone out of the room to scratch her particular itch.

Then one evening, when she'd gone to pick him up at the local Oro Boro Loops factory where he worked as a security guard, she couldn't resist checking out the issue and expiration date of a fire extinguisher on the wall. When she turned around, after giving it her intense scrutiny, there was Dwayne. He'd been watching her for five minutes he said, holding up the wrist on which he wore his watch and tapping the crystal.

After that, the tension around their mobile home was palpable, as Dwayne watched her, expecting to see her cave in at any moment. This, along with the financial drain incurred from Twyla's continuing to take medication – whose effects were not completely satisfactory – only put more strain on their relationship.

And in the end, Dwayne's love had not endured.

Chapter 5

Regardless of having her personal fire extinguisher at her hip, fire was not foremost on Twyla's mind *this* morning. She had a secret scheme to enact while alone with the stigmatic April, though for the most part, things would follow standard procedure.

Every morning after tending to April's bleeding palms, Twyla would turn to more routine matters of hygiene without missing a beat. She changed April's diaper, which also served as her sanitary napkin. Or it *would have*, but there was no blood. Not *there*. Twyla often wondered if April's menstruation had only stopped after the coma inducing accident she'd suffered, from some kind of shock, or if it had ceased back when she was still conscious. If somehow God or nature had compensated her for the inconvenience she endured from the bleeding of her palms every day by ceasing the inconvenience and discomfort of her monthly cycle.

There were other burdens that April had carried in her waking life as well. As though manifesting the stigmata were not enough, her alleged visitations from the angel Gabriel began shortly thereafter, bringing with them visions and revelations she was responsible to share. At her local church first, then over the Internet on her web page. That's when the pilgrimages began from all over the world to her home in Tar Forks, North Carolina.

Those pilgrimages continued even to this day: for despite her coma, people still believed April remained connected to a higher power. Besides the rumors of angels, there were more tangible paranormal phenomena: after the comatose April was returned home, her followers had crowded her room with religious icons and pictures of Mary, Christ, and the saints to show their support. And all of these images and statues began to bleed or weep oil in April's presence.

The ultimate icon in April's room was, of course, April herself. Unconscious, hooked up to a respirator, she was still regularly presented to her disciples who were initially allowed into her bedroom a few at a time for a moment or two of prayer and meditation. The Gurley house was huge, the only mansion in Tar Forks, and so April's father Vernon, and her late mother, Kyra, had dutifully gone about remodeling a wing of their house to serve as a chapel in which a bedded April could continue to be viewed – from behind glass – by her devoted followers.

There were those, of course, who envied Twyla's daily ministrations to their saint, her immersion into the miraculous which they could only behold apart at an impersonal space. But for Twyla, who was there to do a job, tending to April was a part of the daily grind, and she had no time to be sidetracked by supernatural distractions. It was more like, "Okay, so it's miraculous around here. I still have a diaper to change, and I don't hear any of the heavenly host volunteering to do it for me, so – ."

Again, all pretty much routine.

And this day she was determined that all *seem* to go as usual, that no one would know what she was doing with April.

Chapter 6

Twyla arrived at almost 7:00 AM, running thirty minutes behind her regular time. *Today of all days,* she thought as she let herself into the Gurley's house. She actually apologized to April when she entered her room. Twyla *always* talked to April throughout her morning preparations, in case she could hear her. A morning didn't go by that Twyla didn't think about how bad it would be to have to lie there with no one ever speaking to you – talking *around* you but never *to* you, like you were just a piece of furniture.

"'Bout time for a new manicure, ain't it, girl?" Twyla asked, regarding the nails of one of April's miraculous hands. "I'll fix you up pretty, I promise – tomorrow. Any other day, I'd take the time, but I've got something more pressing. Actually, I hope you'll be able to do something for *me* today. How 'bout that?" she asked, smiling at her unresponsive charge.

Twyla's one-sided chatter with April was typical, but there was an undercurrent of nervousness in her voice this particular morning, and she actually hoped that April wasn't conscious *this* time and wouldn't notice what she was about to do. Twyla didn't want to have to explain herself if April ever came out of her coma.

Normally she found the time she cleaned up April calming, meditative even, with all the icons and images of Christ and Mary and various saints that were about her. Twyla would look over them while she combed April's hair, softly humming a religious standard from the old blue hymnals that were always laid out before service on her church's

17

cushioned pews. She kept a mental, informal record of how long it had taken the new pictures and statues to start weeping oil and dripping blood once they had been placed in April's room.

While these icons had been brought in to be taken out by their owners once they began their own paranormal precipitation, there was one bleeding statue that always remained in April's room, one that was always left behind her door. This was the icon of Saint Anthony, which depicted the saint holding the Christ child in his arms. Saint Anthony was said to aid in the recovery of health, and his icon, in its special location, reportedly warded off danger.

Twyla regarded him a bit warily today. Not that April needed protection from her, of course; she wasn't doing anything to hurt her charge. But her actions could be misinterpreted –

Her hands trembled as they approached April's. This deviation in routine would only be for a moment. But if the nurse on duty walked in at that instant –

Twyla quickly removed the bandage from April's right hand. There was the dark stain of the blood that had dried there, and the vivid scarlet of the fresh that welled up in the center of April's palm even as Twyla peeled away the gauze.

Usually, she would drop the bandages into the trashcan she had lined with a special waste disposal bag. Today, however, she placed the quickly folded gauze into a plastic sandwich bag she had brought, sealed it, and slid it into one of her smock's pockets. Barely just in time, for in the next moment the nurse on duty came in through the door that led into the main house. That morning, the R.N. was Janice Sasser, one of Twyla's friends.

"Hi, Twy," Janice said, trying to stifle a yawn.

"Hi," Twyla said, turning her attention to removing the remaining bandage on April's other hand.

"You doing all right?" Janice said, checking April's vital signs.

"'bout the same," Twyla said. "Well, Mr. Gurley and I had a few words yesterday."

"Oh yeah? Did he not like something you're doing with April?"

"No. Nothing like that. I just reminded him – for the third time – that his fire extinguishers in this wing were overdue for inspection. Well, you'd think he'd want them to be in top shape – for his own protection. And his daughter's. He seems to think it's like the shelf date on a gallon of milk, you know, like you've got a grace period. But I don't think so. I've been lugging my own in here this last week. Which is ridiculous, since there's one on the wall right outside the door. But I'm not taking any chances."

"I should say not."

"So, how's Jocy?" Twyla asked.

"He's fine," Janice said and yawned – widely this time.

"Having trouble sleeping, hon'?"

"I sleep like a rock – when I get to. Joy has been out with strep, so I've been picking up some extra hours for her. The agency wanted me to do it again tomorrow, but I told them I just can't anymore and stay alert on my own shift. They want me to be in at 5:00 AM again tomorrow, which would add another two hours to my work day before it's supposed to begin. I just had to put my foot down. My boss was tenacious, but I know she's under staffed, she's not trying to be a bitch. She finally told me she would have to inform Mr. Gurley and let him know his daughter wouldn't have a nurse on duty for two hours.

"I told her you'd be here at 6:30, and she could tell Mr. Gurley that if she thought it might make a difference. Even if you aren't a nurse, you are a care giver. I hope that was all right?"

"Yeah. Sure. I'm going to be here anyway."

"Oh, that's great. Because she's already talked to Mr. Gurley, and it turns out he was very understanding. So as long as the nurse who would be leaving at 5:00 would make sure everything was in order before she leaves, so they'd hear the alarm on April's respirator if it went off – then, yeah, that would be okay since you would be here at 6:30. But I wanted to ask, Twy, since you're usually here by 6:30 anyway, maybe you wouldn't mind being here a little earlier at 6:00? So you could check April's vitals? Then April'll still get checked on the hour. It's not like I'm looking for anything out of the way to happen; April hasn't been having health problems or anything. I'd just feel better."

"Yeah. Sure."

"My boss can't know; she probably wouldn't approve it because that could make her liable if something happened. Not that anything is *going* to happen. Thank you, hon'. I'll buy you some gourmet ice cream, mint chocolate chip or something. Hey, when I left, you and Dwayne were going to have lunch. How'd that go? You two didn't get back together or anything, did you?"

"No. Not in this life time," Twyla said, keeping her attention on dressing April and making a point not to make eye contact with Janice for fear she'd give herself away. "We just got together so I could return some house keys to him. He's getting the trailer."

"I'm sorry," Janice said. "I shouldn't of said anything."

"It's okay. I'm definitely not wasting time worrying about Dwayne Woolard," Twyla said as she stretched over April to adjust the gown she had been working her into. Twyla's smock that served as her home health care uniform rode up a bit to reveal she wore a midriff baring blouse underneath.

"Well, you're looking good, girl," Janice said. "I like that little belly shirt you're wearing. Just a peek of stomach. Just flirtatious enough without looking slutty. But you better keep that smock a little tighter on you," she teased. "I mean, the effect is sort of lost on me and April, but you're going to be raising the blood pressure of your male clients if you don't stay covered up."

Twyla blushed and pulled her smock back down.

"I assume you got a hot lunch date?" Janice pried with a smile. "Or somebody you're going to be seeing right after work that you want to impress?"

"No, actually. I just haven't done laundry in a couple weeks. It was either this or Sunday-go-to-meeting clothes. I figured I'd pull the smock over it, and who'd know?"

"Well, you oughta shed that smock and go to happy hour, just as you are. You won't be lacking for some male attention, I guarantee you that."

"I don't do the bars anymore, Janice. I thought you knew that."

"I'm just saying you oughta dress like that more often and don't hide it under a smock. Go to where men will appreciate it. They're not gonna do that at church."

Twyla was insisting she dressed to please herself and that she wasn't looking for a new man when Apostlette Shametrice Prayer walked in.

It was her usual time, 7:15 AM. Apostlette Prayer was always bright and early, though she would not be needed to direct the flow of the pilgrims who would come to see April until 10:00 AM. In addition to her moderator duties, Shametrice also maintained the website dedicated to April. The computer was in a small room right across from April's, and Shametrice used the early morning hours to work on the site.

The middle-aged, heavy-set African-American woman also pastored a small interdenominational church in Tar Forks, the *Open Door Ministries*. Keen as she was on the ecumenical movement, she had accepted – as had April's Pentecostal Holiness parents – the peculiarly Catholic milieu created by the numerous icons of saints in April's room and the precipitating miracles that spontaneously generated around her.

Right after Twyla's break-up with Dwayne, Shametrice had offered her a sympathetic ear. The two women had bonded, and Shametrice had become something of an unofficial mentor to Twyla. As it turned out, Shametrice had also suffered the termination of a long-term relationship. Though in her case, it was a marriage that had foundered, leaving her a single mom.

"How are our ministering angels of mercy this morning?" Shametrice asked, smiling. She didn't mean the angels that were said to hover about the room, but Janice and Twyla themselves. "God's ministering angels" was Shametrice's pet name for all the nurses and home health care aids who tended to April.

"Just fine," the young women said together. While the laptop that April had used was still booting up, Shametrice had walked across the hall to where April lay and placed her hand on the comatose woman's forehead. Squeezing her eyes tightly, she mumbled something at length which was always unintelligible to Twyla and Janice. The only part they ever understood was the very end when she was slowing down: "In Jesus' name I pray, Amen." This was also part of Shametrice's daily routine: her morning prayer and laying on of hands in hope that she would one day summon April Gurley to full consciousness.

And although her prayers remained unanswered, Shametrice never lost hope. She believed, as did many, that the weeping and bleeding pictures and icons were signs that God had not abandoned April Gurley, and that she would one day emerge to continue the ministry that had been disrupted by her tragic accident.

By this time the computer was up and running. Shametrice was soon busy reviewing the website, preparatory to combing the e-mail for prayer requests that would be placed on April's web page. There was also news to be posted about the upcoming ground breaking on the multi-million dollar prayer and meditation park April's wealthy father planned to build in honor of his daughter.

As Twyla was packing up her things to go, she kept an eye on Janice and Shametrice across the hall who remained unaware that she had taken one of April's bandages. She was going to get away with it, and that was going to be it.

Nevertheless, she felt her heart beat quicken when Shametrice suddenly turned.

"Twyla, don't you go a step further."

Chapter 7

"Yes?" Twyla asked.

"These are trying times for our faith," Shametrice said. "You don't know who to depend on anymore, who is really trustworthy . . ."

"Yes?" Twyla asked again, swallowing. Shametrice had arrested Janice's attention as well.

"Just have a seat in my office. Both you girls, while I've got you here. You need to be aware of something."

When Twyla and Janice had done as she asked, Shametrice began:

"You heard about Vatican World? It's a theme park over in Italy, designed to teach kids Catholic history in a fun way."

"Yeah," Janice said, "we had a little Catholic girl in our neighborhood selling chocolate bars to raise money for a school trip over there."

"Well, April's homepage is linked with Vatican World's, and, do you know the exhibit they have over there, the 'Hall of Popes'? Animatronic mannequins that can move and talk, like the presidents in Walt Disney World? But these are selected popes, going back to Peter. Well, someone broke into Vatican World, into the 'Hall of Popes,' and arranged them around a table with playing cards, like they were all enjoying a friendly game of poker. It's irreverence, that's what it is!"

"That's terrible," Twyla said, unable to keep from smiling. Under normal circumstances, she would have been able to conceal her mirth for Shametrice's sake. Today, however, she was nervous. Fortunately,

Shametrice was too intent on what she was saying to really notice.

"There have been other instances, so we just have to be careful, my angels," Shametrice said. "The most sacred of sanctuaries is no longer considered inviolate. We don't want nobody getting in here and painting a clown face on our precious April, or doing any other kind of desecration in her room."

"You're not suggesting that Janice or me or –" Twyla began.

"No, no," Shametrice was quick to inject. "All you angels are precious. And trust worthy. But these break-ins have come along right when the security cameras on the grounds and at the gates are having their computer hard drive replaced."

"What happened to it?" Twyla asked.

"Something that stops it from recording. But it's only 'til day after tomorrow. The cameras can still work – like scarecrows – as long as it don't get out they ain't working. These are the last days, and wolves in sheep's clothing may seduce even the righteous, if it were possible. Listen: just be careful who you put your trust in."

"No problem here," Twyla said with a sigh. "My ex taught me all about getting your trust abused."

Then Shametrice looked Twyla in the eye. "Honey, you take care you don't have an unforgiving spirit. Remember, if you want to be forgiven, you have to forgive, too."

What does she think I need forgiving for? Twyla thought. *Is she letting me know she knows I've taken something? Who does she mean I need to forgive? Dwayne?* She knew Shametrice claimed at times to "operate a spirit of discernment" as the lady preacher called it.

But whatever Shametrice meant, she obviously intended it to remain opaque. For that morning at least. And so, smiling, Twyla Chayne collected her things and walked, unchallenged, out the door with her prize.

Chapter 8

From a window in the wing of the mansion opposite the one that housed April, someone watched Twyla with keen interest as she crossed the backyard. This was the residential section that Twyla – like most people – never got to see. Her watcher had just emerged from the wing's elaborate private gym, having undergone a taxing morning workout.

Twyla's presence at the mansion was no longer desired. But she couldn't simply be fired. A reason would have to be given to her employer, and since the truth certainly couldn't come out – then what? Even an evasive but truthful "I'd rather not say" might put Twyla's job in jeopardy. These days, even the hint of health care workers abusing their clients was taken very seriously. And if it got out that Vernon Gurley had become, for some reason, dissatisfied with Twyla's treatment of his beloved April, who else in Tar Forks would feel comfortable with her services?

The big hope had been that Twyla herself would request to be reassigned when that fire extinguisher went past its inspection date, and it became clear her protests about getting it checked were being ignored. Ah well . . . . The plan had been a good one. Who knew that Twyla would go so far as to lug her own extinguisher around with her?

If only April would die . . .

It was a horrible thought, but it would solve so many things. April would be better off, for one . . .

And then there'd be no more need for Twyla at the mansion.

No more divided loyalties.

Chapter 9

Five miles away from the Gurley's there was a roadside picnic area with a couple of sheltered tables. The woman was already there even though Twyla was early for their meeting. She rose before Twyla's car had even come to a stop.

"Did you —" she began as soon as Twyla was out of her car.

"I got it," Twyla said immediately with a smile, not wishing to keep the woman in suspense a moment longer.

"Oh, thank you, *thank you*," the woman said, tears suddenly spilling from her eyes. "I know it doesn't have any power, but it helps my faith to have some point of contact with the miraculous. And ever since Tommy, Junior's cancer went out of remission. I thought— "

Twyla blinked back her own tears at the woman's mixture of pain, hope and despair. She could have lost her job or been penalized for her actions, but at that moment, it was worth it. Although she wondered what would happen now, if the cancer still didn't go away —

"Just don't stop with the chemo, okay?" Twyla said as she passed the bag with the bandage from April's hand to the woman. "Remember, you promised you wouldn't if I got you this."

"Yes, I promise. I do."

"And no word to anybody about where you got the bandage – or that you even have it – outside of your husband. I'm glad I could do this for you, but I don't want people asking me to get bandages from April on a regular basis. Already someone has been selling bandages from other stigmatics over the Internet, and I can't look like I'm involved with that. It'd be the end of my job, understand?"

"Yes, I –" Suddenly the woman looked up, over Twyla's shoulder. Twyla turned around. Another car was pulling in right behind Twyla's, as though to block her. And then she felt her heart bolt:

The person behind the car's steering wheel was wearing a priest's collar.

As the car came to a halt, Twyla turned back to the woman and told her, "Get that bag in your purse and get out of here. Don't stop to talk to that person if he speaks to you. Just act like you don't hear him and go. All right?"

The woman nodded her head, and made for her car at a quick pace. Twyla sat down at one of the roadside tables. With any luck, he'd just go away.

She heard a car door open, shut, and then the crisp sound of gravel underfoot.

"Excuse me." Twyla could no longer ignore him, she turned and looked up –

– to see, above the cleric's collar, an astonishing set of blue eyes. And the way he was looking at her made it obvious this meeting was not accidental.

Chapter 10

"Hello," the man said. "You are one of the home health care technicians who tends to April Gurley, right?"

"Who wants to know?"

"Please, if you just left the Gurley mansion, I've been following you . . ."

"Whoa, hold on . . . . You were following me?" Twyla asked, wanting to keep him on the defensive until she could come up with some answers that were not incriminating but truthful just the same.

"You better tell me who you are and what you want, or that collar aside, I'm going to start screaming. And if you try to grab me, I will bite and scratch —"

The man in the cleric's collar smiled and stepped back from her.

"I'm sorry to frighten you. I only followed you because you left the Gurley house before I could catch you. One of April Gurley's followers pointed you out to me as you were driving off. I am Father Andrew Paton, and I am investigating the phenomena around April Gurley for the Vatican. *Are* you April's home health care technician?"

"Yes, one of them," she said after a moment.

"I followed you to ask your help," he said. He smiled again. "May I ask your name?"

"My name is Twyla," she finally said, rising and simultaneously remembering she was wearing a belly-baring shirt. Immediately, she began tugging at the bottom of her blouse with one hand, hoping to stretch the material at least another half-inch or so.

She had left her smock in the car because she didn't want to wear anything that might associate her with her home health care job in case anyone happened by and saw her passing the bandage off. And although her abdomen was only exposed to just above her navel, she felt very underdressed to be meeting a priest.

But this priest maintained eye contact (with his startling blue eyes) and successfully acted as if he hadn't noticed at all. Had he actually *not*, though?

"Bad Twyla," she mentally chided herself. She was terrible – disappointed that she hadn't distracted a priest by inspiring carnal thoughts. Then again, the thought that she didn't possess the material to make him reconsider – even momentarily – his vow of chastity left her feeling even *more* ridiculous in her belly shirt.

All this ran through her mind, but what she said was: "Why would you want to see me, and not Mr. Gurley?"

"Believe me, there is a reason I followed you out here, why I am trying to be secretive, and if we could just talk? I hope I didn't interrupt your meeting with your friend." He nodded in the direction of the departed car of the woman with the bandage.

"No, no. That's okay. We were done. But I've got appointments all morning, and I'm pushing being late for the next one," Twyla said. Being approached this way was becoming exciting in a *good* way now, much more so coming from *him* than the woman from her church who had instigated her previous covert operation that morning. Still, she would have to work any further intrigue into her schedule. "I have a break at 1:00 for lunch," she offered. "Where would you like to meet?"

"Where were you going to have lunch? I don't wish to interfere with your plans too much."

"What about Wahl-Mart? Do you need directions?"

"I'll find it."

"At the Rednek Grill? Their little restaurant?" she said, all the time knowing that she was only going to pick over her food. *Of all days to wear a belly shirt . . . .*

"Great. I will see you there, then," Father Paton said, flashing bright blue eyes and giving her a little wave of the hand.

He began to enter his car, and Twyla saw him pause to read her bumper sticker that said "God Is My Co-Pilot." That *had* to win her points she thought, and then saw him squinting to read her *other* bumper sticker; the one that, before the sun had faded it, read "Drink Until He's Cute." At least she *hoped* it was as illegible as she'd insisted when her mother had told her she could *not* use her car with *that* sticker to deliver meals to their church's shut-ins last Thanksgiving.

As soon as she was behind the wheel, Twyla's pager started fluting. "C'mon, I ain't late yet," she mumbled, then saw the phone number was not her next appointment's, but her home phone. Home, for Twyla, had been with her folks for the last year, ever since she'd moved out of Dwayne Woolard's trailer.

Twyla used her cell phone to answer the page.

"Chayne residence, hello," a female's voice answered.

"Hi, mama, it's me. What's up?"

"Hey, sug'. Could you run by Wahl-Mart on your lunch hour and carry a couple of gallons of fat free milk over to the house? We're out, and Daddy couldn't have his bran this morning–"

Because I used the last to mix up my glass of chocolate diet shake, Twyla thought. She felt bad enough to spend her lunch break fetching the milk home and just wolfing down a sandwich and diet cola on the road, but today, of course, that was out of the question.

"I can pick it up later this afternoon, but I'm meeting someone for lunch."

Silence over the receiver. Then her mother asked: "A boy?"

"A *man*, mama. And it's not a date, if that's what you're thinking."

"Well, it can all start casual-like. What do you know about him? Does he attend church?"

Twyla smiled into her phone. "Regularly, mama."

"*Our* church?"

"No, mama. He's not Pentecostal Holiness."

"Well, as long as he's a Christian . . ."

"That's a vast improvement over my last boyfriend, I know. Look, I need to get back to work. Can daddy wait for the milk? I was going by *Bill's* to pick up some kitty litter after work any way."

"I'm looking in the fridge again . . . . The date on what's left of this whole milk is still good. I guess he can use it this time. You get on back to work, now. Love you."

Twyla clicked off her cell phone, thinking, *you still don't trust my judgement, do you, Mama? I admitted shacking up with Dwayne was a major mistake, I prayed through at church and I really repented. Haven't missed a Sunday in nine months and I actually enjoy the services now. Trust me.*

Though if her mother knew what Father Paton's eyes had got her thinking . . . .

Chapter 11

Twyla met all her appointments that morning, but all the time she was thinking about why the Vatican was approaching her instead of Mister Gurley, and debating whether she should try to run home and slip on another blouse (but that would be so obvious) or run by the gym for a few stomach crunches. In the end she had time for neither. Despite her anxieties, she thought it was cool having a little mystery going and nice to have something to look forward to at lunch. Even though it wasn't going to be much of a meal. That was all right. She didn't get much excitement.

She had arrived a little before schedule to check out the Wahl-Mart fire extinguisher, the one closest to the Rednek Grill, before Father Paton arrived. She didn't want to have to explain that quirk to a date – but it wasn't a date. That was silly, she knew: the man was a priest.

Anyway, the fire extinguisher was fine, she'd known all along that Wahl-Mart would be up to grade. She was just nervous. That was all.

Still, she now had time to look over the tabloids and magazines. There was Twyla's favorite, *The National Expose* along with the *World Weekly News* and the *National Enquirer*, full of what was going on out in Hollywood, or "Holly*weird*," as Shametrice Prayer called it. And there were the little booklets the tabloids marketed at the check-out lane, little paperbacks with titles like *100 Bible Names for Your Spirit Guide, Psychic Cats*, and *True Stories of Angelic Encounters*. Fun, diverting stuff to look over on a lunch hour alone.

Then, between the latest issues of *People* and *People En Española*, she saw that someone had stuck an issue of *Hot Rods*. Posing on the cover before a sports car, clad only in a tiny bikini and high heels, was Twyla's old high school friend, class valedictorian, former head majorette, and Miss Tar Forks 1999, Lorna Doone Delongpre.

They'd been pretty close, even double dating with their boyfriends. Boo Wallace was Lorna's and Twyla's, embarrassingly, even back then, was Dwayne Woolard. Then Lorna had gone off to college and neither Twyla nor Tar Forks had seen her since. The last thing anyone had heard of Lorna was when the local paper ran a "local girl does good" story that said she was doing graduate work at some university, and starring in a direct-to-video science fiction movie.

There had been nothing more – until about nine months ago. Twyla, perusing the magazines at Wahl-Mart for something to read over lunch, was surprised to see her old friend posing provocatively in front of a shiny sports car. Since then, Lorna had popped up on various car magazine covers in a variety of bikinis.

Lorna Doone Delongpre had never had to agonize about how she looked in a belly shirt, Twyla thought, noting Lorna's flat stomach. Lorna's long hair was blond, her breasts large, her height statuesque. Twyla was a mousy brunette, with a modest bosom, and a petite stature. She found she couldn't help but compare herself to Lorna, even twelve years out of high school, when all that superficial stuff wasn't supposed to matter. *Right.*

Back in high school, she had maintained a friendship with Lorna because she didn't want to be petty and discriminate against her because she was lucky in the gene pool. Still, over a decade later, she could feel a guilty bit of satisfaction to see that the now in her thirties, would-be movie star had obviously failed out there in the entertainment business. Twyla didn't know much about the industry, but she was certain posing on car magazine covers represented its lower drawer. Lorna had entered a realm where stunning girls were a dime a dozen. Maybe she'd found out what it was like to move around in a world where you were just average.

Yet Twyla found the cover not only jealousy inducing but sad. Along with her show business disappointments, Lorna had also obviously *not* finished her graduate work – Ph.Ds, as a rule, did not pose for hot rod magazines. And it wasn't like Lorna had been *completely* without disadvantages during her days in Tar Forks.

Twyla remembered how her jealousy had been tempered by Lorna's family situation. She'd had to come of age in a white trash trailer park with a mother who had been losing her mind all along during Lorna's apparently charmed high school career. Darla-Lu Delongpre had become convinced that a demonic entity – what had she called him? – "Lucifer Vesuvius," that was it. She'd become convinced that something named Lucifer Vesuvius had killed her husband when Lorna was still a child.

Lorna finally had been compelled to commit her mother to a mental institution only a few months before graduating at the top of her class. Valedictorian honors aside, she'd had no family at the ceremony to cheer her on – and more than an envious few believed the blonde beauty had bedded her way to the prized position.

"Them ain't real, you know," a voice announced from over Twyla's shoulder. She looked around to see her friend Myra, who worked at Wahl-Mart and who occasionally took her lunch breaks with Twyla, nodding at Lorna's boobs.

"No," Twyla said, putting the magazine back in the rack. "Unfortunately, those are." Her one-sided rivalry with Lorna was now quickly pushed to the back of Twyla's mind. She had really wanted to avoid Myra today because she knew what she was going to bring up.

Myra was a squat five foot two, more than fifty pounds overweight, and, for the first time in her life, feeling beautiful. She had her first-ever steady boyfriend, whom she'd met at the Flea Market that had set up in the old, abandoned Nichols department store. Myra worked her uncle's booth there on weekends where he sold wrestling and racing memorabilia. Her uncle's space was right next to "Miguel's Mexican Video Rental" booth, an extension of his brick and mortar store, and it wasn't long after Miguel noticed there wasn't a wedding ring on her chubby finger that he was regularly taking his break the same time Myra did to accompany her for a cola and some pork rinds. Steady dating and an engagement soon followed.

In contrast to Myra's suddenly active social life, Twyla had not had a date in over a year. Myra was always wanting to fix her up with one of her friends and lately had been bugging her about this guy named Jesus. Twyla knew you pronounce it "Hey Zeus" but it was still spelled "Jesus" and going out with – let alone kissing – somebody with that name, well . . . it just seemed sacrilegious.

"Well, look," Myra said and Twyla knew it was coming. "A bunch of us are headed out to Jack's Neck this weekend. There's a reproduction of Our Lady of Guadeloupe on display at the Catholic church there. They say it weeps tears of holy oil."

"Myra, I see holy oil dripping off of icons around April Gurley all the time. In fact, it's starting to get monotonous. And who's 'a bunch of us'? Will 'Hey Zeus' be there?"

"And Rodriqo and Miguel and Esteban –"

"No thanks."

"We'd all be driving up in Miguel's Mexican HQ."

"His what?"

"Miguel's Mexican HQ – that's what it says on the license plate. It's his *van*, girl. He's got it fixed up with these little curtains around the top of the windshield on the inside of the cab, and it's all Mexican décor inside."

"I'll pass," Twyla said. She was not going to be used by one of Myra's friends as a means for obtaining a green card. If Myra wanted to risk that, it was her business, though Twyla was afraid she was going to be hurt.

"Oh, come on, Twyla," Myra whined. Twyla sighed, groping for another topic to divert the conversation. She noticed that Myra was wearing a necklace with the image she recognized from behind April's door: Saint Anthony, Christ child in hand. She nodded at it. "Not feeling well, Myra?"

"Huh? No, I'm fine. Why?"

Twyla fingered the necklace. "Saint Anthony. He's the saint who's supposed to help recover your health."

"Miguel gave it to me," Myra said. "See, Miguel practices Santeria. They use some of the Catholic saints to represent their gods. For them, Saint Anthony is Eleggua, the god who controls doorways. He –"

"Wait. A god? Other than the God in the Bible? Myra, are you sure you know exactly what all you're getting into?" Twyla asked. "Our church's Spanish outreach minister told us something about Santeria. Aren't there animal sacrifices and people getting possessed by spirits and stuff?"

"It's a peaceable religion," Myra said. "I've been reading about it over the Internet. It's really cool."

Of course. "Peaceable religion" was not the sort of phrase Myra would have come up with on her own. She's talking herself into it, Twyla thought. Okay. Myra's an adult. It's not my problem, and I'm really going to be late for my meeting with Father

35

Paton if I don't go now.

"Just be careful. I gotta go," she said.

"Do you not want to get something to eat?" Myra asked.

"Actually . . . I'm meeting someone for lunch."

"Someone? A guy?" Myra asked. And Twyla realized that here was the opportunity to get Myra off her back about fixing her up with one of her Mexican friends.

"Yep," Twyla said. "Guess I'm busted. See you later, girl." She then headed for the Rednek Grill and her meeting with the priest. Myra would be sure to check them out, she knew, and she hoped that whatever angle she took obscured Father Paton's clerical collar.

Thankfully, Twyla saw, as he stood at the entrance to the grill, he had removed the collar. In fact, he had changed clothes to a more casual attire. No one – meaning Myra – would think he was a priest. *And maybe,* Twyla thought, *I could forget it for the next hour.*

Chapter 12

"Hello, Twyla," Father Paton said. "Thank you so much for coming. I hope I haven't put you out."

"No, that's okay. I eat lunch here a lot with a girlfri – ," Twyla choked back the last word. "It's no big deal," she said quickly. Why was she having difficulty telling a priest that she usually ate here with Myra, that she wasn't regularly meeting a guy instead? She didn't want to come off as a loser, though, presumably he'd think of her compassionately if he thought she was lonely. But she didn't want him to feel pity for her.

And why did he have to have such blue eyes?

After they'd gotten their food, Paton asked her, "So, how long have you known April Gurley?"

"If you mean how long has she been one of my clients . . . two years now. Since the car accident that put her in the coma."

"I've read the news reports about her accident, of course, and I've talked with Mr. Gurley, gotten his point of view," Father Paton said. "But I'd like to ask you what *you've* heard about it."

"Me? I'm only her home health care tech."

"Well, when I say 'you' I mean 'you all.' What have the people of Tar Forks had to say that maybe wasn't printed in the newspaper accounts? Anything that's not officially documented."

Twyla frowned slightly, thinking of the tabloid magazines she'd just perused at the check-out counter. "You are a priest, aren't you? I mean, you're not looking for sensationalistic dirt to run in *The National Expose* or something?"

His brow furrowed a bit, and he made a little wave with his hand as though to dispel her suspicions like so much cigarette smoke. "No. No nasty rumors –"

"Because there ain't none."

"I'm glad," he said and smiled.

"Mr. Gurley and his late wife have always been good people."

"I neither have any reason or desire to think otherwise. What I mean is, do you know of any details about the accident that you've heard about, that were not in the newspaper articles?"

Twyla relaxed, then smiled apologetically. "I hope I didn't offend you."

"No, not at all," he assured her. "I think it's commendable that you care about your employer's personal reputation."

So you're saying I'm special? Twyla beamed at his appraisal, then reminded herself it wasn't even the equivalent of a peck on the cheek, more like a little foil gold star stuck by her name on the Sunday School roll.

"One thing you probably didn't read was how strange it was for April just to be out in a car, period," she said. "She had become so thronged that she couldn't even finish public school for the attention she attracted. April would always take time to pray with people who stopped her on the street, and eventually it got so bad that there was no point in her even leaving the house. So, she completed high school at home.

"After that, no one saw April unless they were allowed into the house for an audience, or when she came out to announce what the angel had shared with her. Then she would retreat back into her house, and she *supposedly* never ventured out until after the next revelation. In fact, most people were almost as shocked that April had been on the other side of town as they were to learn that she was in a coma."

"And the reason she was out that night? I've never read –"

"No one knows, except Mr. Gurley. And the detectives on the case, I guess. All that got out was that April was being sneaked out occasionally, for secret meetings. But the public was never told with whom. Poor Mr. Gurley. It really hangs over him that he escaped with only a mild concussion and some bruised ribs while April went into a coma."

"Are you and April the same age?"

"We're three months apart. We were in the same class. I was there when she started to bleed for the first time."

The priest raised an eyebrow. "Really? I haven't talked with any witnesses of the initial stigmata. What can you tell me about that?"

"I can tell you I learned that day the sight of blood didn't make me sick. I remember Miss Musgrave asking, 'April, girl, what have you *done* to yourself?' Nobody believed her at first, of course, that she didn't know what made her bleed. And it was unusual, a wound in each palm, neatly in the same spot. It looked like they'd been planned. But there was nothing that she could have used. A number 2 pencil I guess, but that was about the only thing on her desk that wasn't bloody. There was no graphite in the wounds themselves, when they were cleaned. And then they wouldn't stop bleeding. It was a miracle."

Father Paton smiled. "Actually, that hasn't been decided yet. Not officially. That's why I need your help."

"What exactly do you want me to do?"

"It's simple." Here he paused and leaned toward her from across the table. "Okay, Twyla," he said. "Can I trust you with what I'm about to say?"

Twyla leaned forward, eager. She thought, "Is it possible his eyes are getting even more blue, now? Darn it!" But what she said was, "Okay, sure."

Father Paton smiled. "Excellent. Part of the process of ascertaining whether what occurs around April Gurley should be authenticated by the church involves the examination of the alleged miracles. Her stigmata, of course, but also the weeping and bleeding icons."

"Right. Well, you already done that. The Church, I mean. They put in their own icons and pictures and they started bleeding and weeping, too. I thought you were looking for something else."

"Yes, I know. But you see . . . I don't want to sound like I'm bad-mouthing her parents, but the fact is, they knew the Church was coming to investigate. And so it's possible, that if her parents have been pulling a hoax, they had time to set us up."

"No. Mister and Mrs. Gurley aren't like that. I mean, she *wasn't*, before she passed. And he's a community leader and an Exalted Turban in the Mystic Fez Lodge. Why would they want to pull a hoax, anyway?

It's not like they're profiting. Mr. Gurley has money. His family holds major shares *in Oro Boro Loops.*

"You know, Oro Boro, the Breakfast Imp?" Twyla asked when Paton shot her a blank look. "He's the mascot. Kids call the cereal 'hoop snakes.' The main cereal factory's here in town, employs a lot of people in the county. And that's just the home plant. I think there are ten more around the South. Anyway, the Gurley family is a major contender with the breakfast cereal companies in the mid-West. Believe me, they don't need money."

"But there may be motivations other than monetary ones," Paton pointed out. "We have to consider every possibility. We have to be one hundred per cent sure that there is no hoax being perpetrated. And that's why I need to get into April's room without her father – without anyone – knowing. I want to see you take those bandages off her hands and bag them myself. I want to bring in my own icons and see if they start to weep oil and blood."

"I don't know . . . ." Twyla said, leaning back in her chair.

"Twyla, a lot of people look at what's happening around April Gurley for hope. I just want to ascertain that their hope is not misplaced. So that the church can confidently confirm their belief. Or point them elsewhere."

"How do you know that I'm not in on the hoax?"

"It's a possibility I thought of, of course, but why would the Gurleys include you, unnecessarily? If you're trying to pull off a hoax, you keep the secret confined to as few people as possible."

"But it's kind of insulting to Mr. Gurley. And the memory of his wife. And it could lose me my job."

"Not if no one finds out. I'm assuming that you have your own key."

"Well, yeah . . . ."

"Couldn't you get me in at a time when you wouldn't be jeopardizing your job?"

Twyla sighed, then thought. "Look, before we go any further, do you have any credentials you can show me? I only have your word that you're with the Vatican."

"Certainly." Father Paton pulled out his wallet and presented her with some cards with the Vatican seal. They looked official enough, at least. "And . . . ," he said, and Twyla saw him reach into his coat pocket and start to pull out his cleric's collar.

Immediately she looked around. Yes, there was Myra peeking around aisle 15, household appliances, watching Twyla and her "date."

"That's all right," she said, anxiously waving for him to put the collar back before Myra could see anything. "You can put that away. I believe you." She slid his wallet back to him.

"Okay," she said. "Tomorrow, then. I normally get there at 6:30 in the morning, but it turns out I'll be going in a half-hour early tomorrow, and it should just be you and me in the wing for almost the whole six o'clock hour, although you'll need to be done probably by a quarter till 7:00. We don't want to push running into the nurse that will be coming in on the hour."

I could try to bring him in a little after 5:00, after the nurse who'll be getting off after checking on April has had time to leave. But I don't know if Janice's boss will have found somebody to cover that hour, or if they've got the nurse who is supposed to be leaving at 5:00 to stay longer. Janice would surely call me if I didn't need to come in early after all, but a change in scheduling at the last minute is always possible, and I'll need to go in alone at first and make sure the coast is clear before I let Father Paton in.

"April's followers are not out there that early in the morning, but we'll be going in the back way anyhow, so we shouldn't have to worry about someone seeing us from the outside. There *is* a security camera at the gate, and cameras monitoring the grounds, but you're lucky: their hard drive is being repaired, so you can't be recorded. There is also a camera in April's room that has a monitor that, as far as I know, is still recording on its own hard drive. Its monitor and hard drive are both at the nurse's station. Before I can bring you in, I'm going to need to go there and unplug the power to the hard drive.

"So, will that be enough? Because I don't think I'll be able to get up the nerve to do this again."

"That sounds good."

"And if we *are* caught —"

"— I will explain the necessity of my covert operation. It may compromise my mission, but if I'm caught, I'm certainly not going to lie. I will do all I can to make sure that you are not punished, to assure them that your intentions were good."

"I hope it doesn't come to that."

Father Paton smiled. "So do I. You know, I'm curious to know exactly what you think about April. Do you believe she's touched of God? And if so, how do you reconcile that with her coma?"

"Well, believe me, I've done more'n my own share of wondering 'why me?' I hope there's meaning," Twyla added after a moment. "I'd like to believe that some things aren't just . . . bad luck. If there is a purpose in what April is going through, maybe there's hope for all of us. So, if I can help you validate that, it'll sort-of be like helping answer one of the big questions, wouldn't, it?"

"Yes it would."

"Okay. Sure. I'll get you in."

You and your blue eyes, Twyla thought.

Chapter 13

5:30 AM, the next morning:

A shadow had fallen over April from a figure which stood between her and the soft, cold glow of the ceiling's florescent lights. One of the bulbs had burned out, but there was still enough illumination in the room to see that, despite her still having the respiratory mask on, April's breast no longer rose and fell. The respirator stood eerily silent. The figure reached out, stroked April's hair, and thought:

Who's to say that April wouldn't want this? She's free. Departed at last, escorted by the angels who have attended her so faithfully during her suffering. Reunited with her mother . . . .

April's visitor at this early hour sighed and looked around the room at the relics sweating blood and oil. Quite a collection had been assembled here over the years. *"But of course,"* the visitor thought. *"They brought them to her."*

One had always stood out: the Saint Anthony that would still be behind the bedroom door that opened inward, the door that was concealing the icon from view right now. *Would it be so wrong to take it now, now that April no longer had need of its services?*

Then, somewhere in the wing, a floor board groaned . . .

Someone else was here. But *no one* was supposed to be in or around April's wing right now, not *this* morning.

The visitor immediately fled the room . . . but with or without being seen? It *had* been a bit too close. Vernon would need to know. Everything. And though things were far from ideal, there was no reason now, none at all, that everything should not proceed as planned.

No more divided loyalties.

Chapter 14

Twyla and Father Paton met in a convenience store parking lot down the road from the Gurley house. He left his vehicle there and climbed into the back seat of her car, lying down in the floorboard as Twyla drove them to the back gate of the Gurley mansion.

Twyla tapped into the gate's keypad the code to deactivate the alarm, then opened the gate door and walked through. She checked to be certain no one was around, very conscious of the security camera, unable to record though it was, as if it was a sniper's gun aimed her way. She quickly walked back to the car where Paton was still lying low. As she knocked on one of the rear passenger windows with one hand to signal him to come on, she checked her watch on the other wrist.

5:45 AM. *Ahead of schedule,* Twyla thought.

She left the gate door unlocked, in case Father Paton might need to beat a hasty retreat. Paton now followed her to the outside door that opened on the hallway that led to April's room. Twyla motioned for the priest to stay put, out of view, while she determined that April was, indeed, alone and then disconnected from the nurse's station the camera that monitored April's room. If need be, Twyla would motion to him to go back to her car, where he would resume his place down on the floorboard. And then – ? She still didn't think she could get up the nerve to try again.

Twyla opened the door enough to determine if the way was clear. She reached inside, felt for the hall light switch and flipped it on. She found the interior vacuous and silent. April's door was immediately on the right, and it was opened enough to see that no one but April was there. She quickly made her way to the nurse's station and disconnected the hard drive to the security camera so that she and the priest would not be recorded. She sighed, smiled, and quickly made her way down the hall and opened the outside door wide.

"Okay," she said. "We're in." She closed the door behind Paton and they walked into April's chamber of weeping and bleeding icons. Twyla was moving toward her patient to begin her routine ministrations. "Shut the door," she said, "and you can get to wor —

"— oh, dear Jesus!"

Twyla was staring with widening eyes at April's oxygen machine – for a heartbeat. In that moment she had realized that the normally still room had become *too* still – that the machine's constant, faint rhythmic hissing had ceased.

Then she was stabbing the stop/ restart button, but the respirator did not respond.

"Twyla?"

She heard Paton's voice as from a distance.

Twyla now saw that all that was left of the power cord to the respirator was a small bit hanging from the oxygen machine. From this stuck out the ends of frayed, gnarled wires where the insulation was stripped away during the cord's cutting.

She checked for April's pulse and found none, only skin that was cold to the touch.

"Help me, Jesus!" she cried as she began to pump the girl's chest.

Why hadn't the alarm gone off?

Now she heard Father Paton's voice again: "What's wrong?"

"Call 911!"

"Wait – what?"

"Call 911!"

"I can't . . . ."

46

"You don't have your cell? Take mine! It's in my smock's left pocket," Twyla said as she continued to pump April's chest. "Why are you still just standing there? Don't you understand? April's respirator was turned off when we got here! She doesn't have a pulse . . . I don't know how long she hasn't had oxygen . . . ."

Twyla looked again at the respirator, this time to where the back-up power source, a battery, *should* be.

Gone.

". . . The respirator's been sabotaged!" she screamed at Father Paton *"And why are you still just standing there?!"*

"I can't! I mean, they record 911 calls, don't they? Oh, man . . . *man!* It wasn't supposed to happen like this!" Father Paton whined, clasping his hands behind his head. Then his arms fell and he snatched up a prayer card that had already begun to weep oil – not one that he'd brought – and dashed with it for the door.

"Where are you *going?"* Twyla shouted after him as he disappeared. *None of this can be happening*, she thought as she continued trying to coax April's heart back to life.

"Help!" she screamed. "Mr. Gurley! Somebody help me!"

She could hear feet pounding down the hall in response to her cry as she pulled April's respirator mask off, tilted back her head, pinched her nose closed, and sealed her mouth with her own. She forced air into the stigmatic's mouth until her breast rose, then fell . . . .

Again!

Twyla now held her ear above her mouth, listening for even the trace of breath.

Then a nurse materialized beside her. Twyla started.

Where had she come from? Is she – an angel?

"I'll take over CPR," the nurse said.

Twyla pulled out her cell phone, flipped it open, and began tapping on its keypad. "Her respirator was off when I got here." She put the phone to her ear. "I don't know how long; there was no alarm –"

"911. What's your emergency?"

"I'm at the Gurley mansion. His daughter isn't breathing and we can't revive her. We're her caregivers. Yes – we've been trying CPR for about five minutes. Not working. Hurry! Come to the rear entrance; it's quicker to get where we are. Thank you."

"This don't make sense," the nurse said as soon as Twyla turned off her phone. "Even if there was a power outage, there should be a back-up battery –"

"Somebody got rid of the battery, too!"

"*What?* Who – ? And what do you mean 'too?'"

"The respirator's power cord to the wall's been cut!"

"*Cut?* Then the alarm should have –"

Twyla popped open the ventilator's alarm battery's protective plate. The alarm's power did not derive from either the house electricity or the back-up battery but from a separate source, so that if both the former and latter failed, help could still be summoned.

Twyla looked at the nurse. "Alarm battery's been taken, too."

She turned from Twyla, returned to breathing into April's mouth, withdrew, and listened for April's own breath to return . . . .

Nothing. She immediately began pumping the girl's chest again.

"Who . . . who would want this poor girl *dead?*" the nurse gasped out as she continued to administer CPR. "That can't be right . . . ."

The nurse was sweating now from her exertions to revive April, but when she finally looked up at Twyla again, she shook her head "no."

"Oh no . . . *no,*" Twyla's hand went to her mouth and she began to sob. "Maybe if they'll hurry up and get here . . . maybe . . . ."

She looked around the room, silently imploring the images and icons – the saints, the multiple Marys – all of whose eyes looked out with benign indifference upon the desperate scene in the room as though they were staring sedately into a fish aquarium.

Who would have wanted to kill April? Twyla wondered. *Who could have sat down and planned such a thing? And what had Father Paton meant, "it wasn't supposed to happen like this?" What? Was he involved somehow? He didn't want to be recorded by the police . . . but why? What did he have to be guilty about? Had he done something when she wasn't looking? Impossible! She was right there at April's side, and he was still across the room looking at some of the icons when she noticed the respirator was already off. There's no way,* she thought. *There's no way I contributed to this by bringing him here. It was obvious the whole thing took him off guard. The way he panicked....*

Now the ambulance was arriving. The nurse met the rescue squad at the back gate, led them inside to April's room, then joined Twyla off to the side. They embraced each other, their faces tear streaked. It was still dark enough that the ambulance's whirring light shone into the hall from outside, spinning dizzily from wall to wall, like a disoriented, frantic bird which had flown inside and which could do no more than reel about the room....

Chapter 15

Twyla sat down — hard — on the floor, shaking her head from side to side, though the reality had already overtaken her. The nurse sat down beside her.

"My name's Joyce, by the way," she said.

"Twyla," Twyla said, staring ahead into space.

"Who would've turned off April Gurley's life support? She never did anything to anybody," Joyce said and slowly shook her head.

"I can't imagine . . . ," Twyla said. "But whoever it was . . . . they meant to make sure there was no chance of reviving her: cutting the power cord, taking the batteries for the alarm and the back-up battery. . . . Who could have hated her that much?

"Her dad — does anyone know where he *is?*"

"Already gone to work, I guess?" Joyce offered. "Look, I got his cell phone number. I'll call him, assure him that I did all that I could. April was my company's medical responsibility, not yours. So I'll break the news to him." She sighed. "Sure not looking forward to it."

Break the news? I'm going to have to tell Shametrice. She never lost faith — she's going to be devastated.

"Hey," Twyla said. "You're with the Sutton Nursing Agency?"

"Yeah."

"I was told they didn't have anybody for this time."

"I was freed up, and they told me I could fill in an hour here, since April's regular nurse couldn't come in early."

50

"Yeah, that's why I was here. The nurse – do you know Janice?"

"No. She's the regular nurse?"

"Yeah. I'm normally here at 6:30. But Janice asked me if I would unofficially come in a half hour early to check April's vitals."

"But our boss didn't know about it? That's why we both ended up here now."

Twyla winced. She *thought* she had taken into consideration that the nursing agency might send a replacement without her knowing about it. She had checked before she let Father Paton in and found the coast clear. Why hadn't she taken into consideration a nurse coming in *after* they had arrived? Why did she assume that if someone from the agency wasn't there at five o'clock, she wouldn't be coming in at all? Because her crush on a priest and his blue eyes, her wanting to impress him, made her careless! She and Father Paton could have been caught.

"I had just set my things down at the nurse's station when I heard you calling," Joyce was saying.

"Joyce, we'll be under suspicion," Twyla blurted out.

"We would be anyway. Whoever discovers the body always is." Joyce shrugged. "Well, I got nothing to hide."

Twyla smiled slightly and forced herself, almost by degree, to nod her head in a manner that said "likewise."

Then she leaned back – hard – against the wall.

The police had arrived.

Chapter 16

The report of a possible homicide brought the authorities quickly, along with their forensic team. While the police took stock of the body and its surroundings for possible clues, and Joyce tended to a distraught Mr. Gurley in the den, a Detective Grell questioned Twyla in the hall outside April's room.

"Miss Chayne," Grell began. "Would you state your relationship with the deceased?"

"I've known her since we were kids. April and I were in the same grade. Not that we were ever friends. So I guess we never really had what you would actually call 'a relationship.' Before her accident, I mean. Since then, I've been one of her home health care technicians."

"Who do you work for, Miss Chayne?"

"Pittman Home Health Services."

"Please give me your account of how you found the deceased."

"I got here at 5:45."

"Is that your regular time?"

"Usually I get here at 6:30."

"So, why were you early today?"

"To check on April's vitals – her nursing agency was running short on help this morning. So I stepped in."

"What's the name of the agency? I'll want to confirm this."

"Oh – it wasn't official."

Detective Grell arched a brow at her.

"Oh? You took it on yourself?"

"No. The nurse who comes in at 7:00 – Janice Sasser – she asked me to check April's vital signs at 6:00. April's supposed to be checked on the hour, and there was nobody from the nursing agency to do it."

"But I saw a nurse here."

"She's from the nursing agency – the Sutton Nursing Agency. See, they found somebody to come in, but nobody told me."

Grell regarded her silently. Then: "And what did you do when you got here?"

"I went to check April, planning to wash her like I normally do, and then I immediately saw the respirator wasn't working."

"There was nothing out of the ordinary before then?"

I had this guy with me from the Vatican, who snatched a prayer card and took off like a coward instead of getting help.

"About April? No," Twyla said. "Not until I saw that the respirator was off. I mean, that was not more than a minute after I walked in the door."

"And when you saw the respirator was off, you naturally tried to turn it back on."

"Yeah, of course. When I couldn't, that's when I noticed the power cord to the ventilator had been sheared off, and that the back-up battery was missing. I immediately started CPR."

Twyla considered telling the detective of Father Paton's presence that morning. But her behavior would be suspect in light of what had happened, even though she was innocent of any wrong doing. Further, she was convinced Paton was guilty of nothing more than bad timing – and a yellow streak a mile wide. But how could she prove that? She didn't even know that she was going to ever see him again. So why bring him up? If the focus of the investigation were focused on him – and her – the real killer could slip away through the muddied waters.

"And when your efforts at resuscitation did not work?"

"I called for help and that's when Joyce came in and took over CPR while I called 911. But it was already too late."

"And that's all you know?"

"Yes, that's all . . . I guess. I was shocked. I still am . . . I mean, who would want to kill April?"

"Who wouldn't want her to come out of her coma?"

"Nobody," Twyla said. "I mean, the Gurley's yard fills up every day with people who want nothing more than for her to regain consciousness."

"Look, I don't know about motivation at this point, but we can start looking at who had opportunity: that includes those of you from outside the household who had access to this young woman while she was helpless and alone."

Twyla felt her ears and cheeks begin to burn and tingle.

"But I'm her home health care giver!"

"You are one of what I suspect is a relatively small group of people to whom she was vulnerable. And you deviated from your usual schedule this morning, which you expected would give you at least an hour alone with her. An hour in which you had no accountability for your actions."

Twyla flushed then realized: *April was murdered before I got here, so since the hard drive wasn't disconnected from the camera yet, the killer is recorded on it! Unless, of course, the killer disconnected the cable just as I did, and then reconnected it. Or did something to the camera. But there's still a chance the person responsible has been recorded in the act.*

"Why haven't you looked at the footage from the security camera in April's room? That should show the murderer in the act."

"I suspect there'll be no video," Grell said. "The cable to the hard drive at the nurse's station has been disconnected."

Twyla looked away, her cheeks stinging.

"We're trying to get fingerprints from it. *Your* fingerprints, –"

Twyla turned back. "You're trying to get *my* fingerprints from the cable?"

Grell looked at her sidelong. "N-o-o-o-o-o . . . I was saying, *your* fingerprints will be found on the respirator 's off/on button."

"Because I tried to turn it back on when I saw it was off! What did you expect me to do?"

"What you did was potentially obscure any other prints with your own. As well as those on the security keypad outside. And the doorknobs."

"What? Are you blaming me for *that*? How else was I supposed to get inside? How was I supposed to know what I would find —"

Twyla caught herself:

He's rattling me, to throw me off, hoping I'll make an incriminating slip.

Twyla sighed, making a point to look Grell in the eye while she spoke: "You just remember I am *not* the only one who could have turned that machine on and off," Twyla said. "Or knew the keypad code. Or ever opened a door in this place. And . . . . and could have disconnected that cable. You'll still check this morning's video right? Maybe something was caught before the killer disconnected the cable."

"We will be most thorough, Miss Chayne."

"And I'd appreciate it if you didn't mention me when you're questioning others."

Grell cocked his head. "And why is that?"

"Do you know what it'll do to my job if word gets out that I might not be trustworthy around the clients I care for?"

"Ma'am, I'm trying to solve a murder here. I don't have time to worry that when I'm questioning someone, I might inconvenience you."

"But —"

"I need to get back to work. Maybe I'll learn something that will clear you, hmm? Now, I think you should leave. The premises, I mean. Not town."

Her ears and cheeks stinging, Twyla headed for April's room. She was almost through the door when the detective caught her elbow and gently pulled her back.

"Uh-uh," he said. "That's a crime scene now. You can't go in there."

"But my bag with my car keys is in there."

"That's become part of the crime scene."

"You tell me to leave, but you're not going to let me have my keys? And I can't just not show up for my appointments."

"Okay," Detective Grell said. "If you give me permission to search your bag and everything appears in order, I'll give it back to you."

"Sure. I give you my permission. I've got nothing to hide." *Actually I do, but you don't need to know about my bad choice in men.*

"In the meantime, you stay right here," Grell said. Twyla nodded and watched through the doorway as he went over to her purse and emptied the contents out on a table.

Twyla found her own attention drawn to where April's body lay completely covered now.

Where were the angels? she wondered. *Why didn't Saint Anthony do his job?*

Grell had now finished inspecting the contents of her purse and was sliding the pile he'd made of them back inside.

"Your bag," Grell said as he handed it over the threshold to her. "Everything seems in order."

"He was supposed to protect her, you know."

Grell cocked his head. "Why haven't you mentioned this person before?"

"He's not real. I mean, he *was*. Saint Anthony. His statue's behind the door."

Grell pushed the door toward the doorway and looked behind it.

"No," he said. "There's no Saint Anthony statue there."

Chapter 17

"What? It's always there. Unless someone moved it?"

"The forensic team knows not to touch anything."

"No. I know that. But maybe it got moved around when the rescue squad came in? Someone just didn't put it back."

"Why would someone trying to save someone's life take time to move something that wasn't in the way?"

"Would you just please look around the room and see if it's still here?"

A search of the room revealed that it had not simply been misplaced. It was, indeed, gone. Did the icon, then, represent some kind of trophy for the killer? Twyla wondered. Or was the killer making another statement, a cruel one: as the restorer of health, Saint Anthony's services would no longer be required for April Gurley.

"He was supposed to guard her, and to restore her health —"

"Well," Grell said, "Saint Anthony is supposed to restore lots of things. He's the saint you call on to find missing objects . . . and now *he's* missing."

"That statue was always behind the door to ward off trouble."

"Nope. I don't think so," Grell said.

"Have you been in this room every week for the last two years like me? It was *there*."

"I'm not challenging you on that. I meant the part about his warding off trouble."

"Yeah, he does."

"You Catholic?"

"Well, no, but –"

"I am. Born and bred. And I *never* heard *that* about Saint Anthony. Now, was this a particularly costly statue?"

"No. Just plaster. There are more obviously expensive ones still setting here. I mean, it bled, but so do half the others in this room."

"Okay," Grell said. "There are lots of Saint Anthony icons out there. Did this one have any distinguishing marks?"

"Well, it bled. It probably still does. All of the icons that began bleeding around April continue to after they're taken from her room."

"There could be other bleeding Saint Anthonys out there. Was there anything else to distinguish it?"

"Yeah. The right ear was chipped. The plaster showed."

"Okay, good. Look, I'm one of a handful of Catholics on the force, so I want you to describe this statue completely to my men. His holding the Christ child and so forth. Include the colors of Saint Anthony's hair and clothes and all that. Hold on. I'll get one of my officers to write it down."

Twyla gave a description to a policeman, wishing she had a necklace like Myra's, with the little image of Saint Anthony. Then she could have just shown him.

The officer jotted down the details, and told her she could go now.

Her thoughts, as she made her way to the door, were about "Father" Paton. Why had he panicked like he did? It wasn't a gory scene, and presumably in his role as a priest he'd been around people who were dying or who'd just died. Why snatch up the prayer card, leaving behind the icons of his own that he had brought in for study? And what had he meant, "it wasn't supposed to happen like this?"

For the first time, she wondered if anyone had seen him fleeing the scene. If he *had* been seen, and the witness could establish the time, then the authorities could figure out that Twyla, from her own statements, would have been in the room at the same time Paton was running out of April's wing.

Her temples throbbed. She wanted to run from the house herself, but took a deep breath and told herself to stay calm, keep walking at a casual pace.

At least no one had come forward with that information so far, and she had purposely picked a time to bring Paton in when witnesses were unlikely. Of course, that scheme wasn't guaranteed, but maybe if her luck held –

"Twyla."

She turned to see Mr. Gurley coming from behind her. He took her elbow. "Could I have a word with you?"

Chapter 18

Twyla froze, expecting her luck had somehow run out. But she again forced herself to remain calm. *You do not want to act any more guiltier than you've already done with Detective Grell.*

And after all, there is no accusation in Mr. Gurley's tone. He looks distraught, like he'd aged ten years over those early morning hours.

"Please?" he asked.

"Sure, Mr. Gurley. I am so sorry about April. By the time I got here, there was nothing that could've been done to —"

"I know. I know, sug'," Mr. Gurley said softly. "Nobody's blaming you or Joyce. I'll have nothing but good things to say to your boss, that's for sure. You stuck by my girl. But could you . . . could I see you before you go? In private?"

"Of course," April said.

Vernon Gurley led her out of the wing that had housed April and through the large den with which the wing's hallway connected. Even under the circumstances, Twyla had to note the opulence: high ceiling with exposed wooden beams, large fireplace, a well-stocked bar, French windows that overlooked the golf course.

She suspected he would give it all up if he could have his daughter back.

They passed from the den to another hallway. This was the private wing. Twy had always wondered what it was like here, and she noted the lush, thick carpet on which they walked, the polished furniture that gleamed amber in the light, various framed paintings and sculptures – Twyla recognized one of the pieces from her old art appreciation textbook.

However, she was most impressed with the large, private gym she glimpsed as she passed through a set of double doors. Word was there was also an Olympic size pool somewhere under the mansion's extensive roof. *How many boxes of cereal did you have to sell to afford something like that?* she found herself wondering.

So taken was Twyla with the surroundings that she didn't realize until they were there that Mr. Gurley was leading her to his study. He smiled and beckoned her in, then followed her, shutting the door behind him.

Twyla was looking around the room, noting the largest flat screen TV she had ever seen that hung on the wall like one of Gurley's paintings. Then she noted the series of clocks on the opposite wall that showed what time it was in the six different zones of the continental United States, as well as Hawaii-Aleutian standard time. The remaining walls were lined with shelves that reached to the ceiling, holding books, video cassettes, and DVDs.

Vernon Gurley sat down behind his large, mahogany desk, also polished to a gleam and smelling of fresh lemon. A laptop computer was open on the desk, on top of a large desk calendar that was filled with scribbled appointment dates. Mr. Gurley snapped the laptop closed, and the sound struck Twyla like the sharp report of a judge's gavel. In that instant, she saw Vernon Gurley transform: the meek, mourning, beseeching father vanished.

And she was being called into account.

"Mr. Gurley?"

"You were here earlier than usual this morning, weren't you Twyla?"

"What?" she asked, taking a step back. His tone suggested he was announcing a fact more than asking a question. How did he know she was there early? Joyce, she realized, Joyce must have told him the story of that morning while she was tending to him.

"Don't squirm like that," Gurley said. "I know you were. What I need to know is, did you see anything out of the ordinary?"

Okay, Twyla thought. Now he *was* asking. He didn't know she wasn't alone. So she said:

"You mean, related to April's death? No. No sir. I told the police . . ."

"*Anything* unexpected? Anything you *wouldn't* have told the police?"

Twyla paused, considering what exactly it was that he was asking. After a few long moments, she still wasn't sure, so all she said was, "No sir. I told them everything."

Vernon Gurley studied her silently as Twyla tried to no longer squirm under his scrutiny. Finally, he said:

"I hope you're telling the truth, Twyla. I don't won't any misinformation out there that might preempt my daughter getting justice. I don't want a John and Patsy Ramsey situation here, where the innocent suffer and the criminal gets away."

What in the world does he think I saw, that I'm supposedly holding back? Him? But why would he think I had held back telling the police if he thought I had seen him? Why would he think I would protect him? Or was he trying to abort any suspected intention on my part of attempting to bribe him?

Twyla caught herself gnawing her lower lip, stopped, then looked Vernon Gurley in the eye just as she had with Detective Grell.

"Sir, I was here earlier, but I didn't see anyone who may have killed your daughter."

Gurley looked at her, silent. Finally, he said, "Okay, Twyla. As long as you and I understand each other. And that means you don't tell any one about our little meeting here today, too – because if you do anything that could divert suspicion my way, you're helping a killer walk free. Like I said, you've been good to stand by my daughter, and I hope you'll continue to do that by keeping quiet. I think you know it's in your own best interests, too. Right?"

Twyla felt her ears burning. Was he appealing to her sense of justice or threatening her or both?

"Sure, sir. I understand."

"Okay, you can go now. Let yourself out. I need some time alone."

Twyla turned and walked to the door, looking back to see Vernon Gurley had put his face on his desk, and his body was jerking with sobs.

After leaving the mansion, she actually made a point to drive by the convenience store's parking lot, to see if maybe Paton's car was still there, if maybe he was there –

No.

Of course, she hadn't really expected him to be. Not with her luck. She lowered her forehead against her steering wheel and sighed, reaching out with one hand and touching the fire extinguisher that rested on the seat beside her, just to feel the affirmation of *something* she could count on.

Why had she agreed to it? Why did he have to have such startling blue eyes and why had she fantasized about a *Thorn Birds* kind of vibe between them? Why did she have to meet him when she hadn't had a date in a year and was still heartbroken from Dwayne Woolard and was vulnerable to that sort of thing?

Chapter 19

The news of April's death broke over Tar Fork's local radio station while Twyla was working on her next client of the day. She'd apologized for being late, and hoped that no one would make a connection between her tardiness and what had happened at the Gurley home that morning. As it turned out, while there was much comment and speculation about April's death throughout her morning work, no one ever seemed to suspect that she should know any more than anyone else. And she wasn't about to volunteer any unique insights.

She returned home, entering the house through the door that opened from outside into her own "apartment": the guest room and bathroom that Twyla had taken over when she moved back in with her parents.

She had had to ask for it: her mother would have moved her back into her old childhood bedroom, a gesture Twyla saw as some misguided attempt at a return to innocence for her daughter, after her time "living in sin" with Dwayne Woolard. Not that her mother had been hard to convince, not at all. Just a bit reluctant. It wasn't like they weren't still under the same roof. The problem was her door. Her own door. To both her mother and Twyla it represented freedom: for Twyla, her adult autonomy to come and go as she pleased without having to explain her every move; for Twyla's mother, freedom for Twyla to mess up her life again.

Not that she'd ever bring a man back to her parents' house for the evening, even *if* she still did seek out such encounters. But her own door would provide her freedom to go to *his* house unquestioned – *if* she still did such things. Which she did not. But her mother didn't trust Twyla's resolve were she faced with temptation. Better not to give the devil an opportunity.

However, sex with Dwayne hadn't been satisfactory for their last year together, so her most recent memories of it weren't such that they made her eager to go back for more. She was sure that she would be able to hold out for love *and* marriage now.

Then why were you attracted to a priest? she asked herself. *Because he was safe? No possibility of sex there . . . or marriage, either.*

Of course, now she was wondering if he was a priest at all. Just her luck. If he *were* available, he had turned out to be a coward who flew to pieces under pressure and abandoned her.

"Do I know how to pick 'em or not?" she asked her Maine Coon cat, Izzy, who had rushed to the door to meet her, meowing up at her. Twyla reached down and rubbed the cat's head for a quick minute. "Okay, that's enough," she said. Izzy bounded up onto Twyla's perpetually unmade bed, and settled on the paper back book Twyla had left there.

"No, kitty, get off," Twyla said, tugging at the book beneath the cat until Izzy moved. It was the new catalogue for Tar Forks Community College. She'd been thinking seriously of going back to college and finishing that LPN degree she'd abandoned after a year and a half. She'd been tired of school by her senior year, and going on to college had been her parents' idea. She'd initially put it on hold for a year after graduation, opting to work the check-out at a local grocery. It had been that boring daily grind more than any intellectual drive that had finally gotten her into college.

Then Dwayne Woolard, the Gulf War vet, had come back into her life. She'd been working for a temp agency for a year or so, doing everything from administering soft drink tasting tests to Wahl-Mart customers to performing the more typical temp tasks such as secretarial duties. But Twyla was a lousy typist, and when she and Dwayne started talking about moving in together, she had needed more regular work to help make those mobile home payments. Thus she'd settled into steady employment as a home health aid. The schooling she already had more than qualified her for that position, and so she had abandoned college. For all time she'd thought.

Now she was thinking again.

In the last twenty four hours, though, two obstacles had appeared that could frustrate her self-improvement plans.

First of all, what if Mister Gurley decided she couldn't be trusted to keep her mouth shut about whatever it was he thought she was supposed to have seen? She'd been thinking about that all morning.

Did he suspect she'd seen something that would potentially incriminate him? Maybe something that would contradict his version of things?

Mr. Gurley had had to be called and notified of his daughter's death. But what if he already knew before he was called? Perhaps he'd checked in on April earlier himself and chose not to try to revive her. It may have been too late, even then, but he may have made a conscious decision to just let his daughter go.

Or pull the plug himself.

No one need ever know –

Unless he suspected Twyla had seen him in the wing that morning before anyone, besides the murderer, was supposed to know April was dead.

He'd made it clear she'd better not even think about blackmailing him. And she didn't like that tone of threat in his voice when he spoke to her. If he believed that Twyla might put suspicion on him, make him the biggest pariah in public opinion since the Ramseys, how far would he go to keep his good name?

And then there was the mysterious "Father Paton." If his presence in April's room that morning was ever revealed, she could be suspected of being a murderer herself or a murderer's accomplice. There would be no second chance at life.

And why would her life be so messed up? Because, once again, she'd thrown out good judgement running after some man. She could imagine her mother telling her just that; not verbally, of course, but with that disappointed look of hers that, paradoxically, would result from Twyla's having done exactly what her mother had expected of her.

There was a knock on the door that opened into the main house.

"Twyla, sug'?"

"Come on in, mama."

Her mother entered with a basket of freshly washed and pressed laundry – all Twyla's.

"Mama, I would have got to that." Twyla, it seemed, was always saying that to her mother about her laundry – always after her mother had gotten tired of seeing it pile up and decided to do it herself.

"That's okay, honey. I . . . heard the news. I didn't think you'd be much in the mood for chores. Are you okay?"

"Fine, mama." *For a murder suspect.*

Her mother set down the basket of laundry, quickly crossed the room, and hugged Twyla until Twyla had to wiggle free of her. "What if the killer were still there when you got to work, and you'd walked in on him? I couldn't stand that. We just got you back . . ."

Twyla gave her a quick kiss on the cheek. "I'm all right."

Tucking her head, her mother regarded Twyla from under hooded eyes. Her lips parted slightly as though she might speak, but she continued to only stare at her daughter.

"Mama?"

"I don't . . . I don't want to be the one to give you more bad news, but you should know –"

"What?"

"I guess there's no easy way to say it . . ."

"*What?*" Twyla demanded, feeling her temples beginning to throb.

"Your Uncle Tate is out of prison."

Twyla immediately sat down on the bed as though her mother had punched her in the stomach.

"You mean . . . he escaped?"

"No, no. He had some years taken off his sentence for good behavior."

Twyla looked up at her mother. "How do you get out of prison for 'good behavior'? If you were so good, you wouldn't be in jail to begin with!"

Twyla's mother sat down on the bed beside her daughter and embraced her again. "Oh, sug'. I know. It ain't right."

Twyla accepted her mother's comfort then slightly withdrew. "How did you find out? Did he come here?"

"No, sug', no. It was his sister who called to tell me. To gloat, I guess. But she did us a favor, really. I mean, I wouldn't want you to just bump into him at the mall with no warning."

"Well, he better just stay away. Or I'll get a restraining order, or mace him or . . . I'll turn my fire extinguisher on him!"

"Surely he won't try doing anything to you, hon'. He just got out of prison. He doesn't want to go back, I'm sure."

"Yeah. Well. Just more good news. My day is now complete," Twyla said, falling back on her bed.

Her mother rose. "Oh. You had a message from Myra. She wanted you to tell her about what went on at the Gurley house while you were there this morning."

"Yeah, well, I don't feel like it now. I'm just going to lay down here and study my Sunday School lesson."

"Okay. Supper –"

"I'll warm something up in the microwave."

"Okay. Try to talk to Daddy some before he turns in tonight."

Twyla's mother closed the door behind her. And Twyla tried to read her Sunday School lesson for that week: "Try the Spirits and See if They be of God" from the first epistle of John. But she knew when she started there was no need in even trying to concentrate. Her obsessive mind didn't make it easy to let go of any dogging thoughts about Tate. Eventually, she turned on her TV for some distraction.

The local news, of course, was about April Gurley.

The anchor announced that there was going to be a candlelight vigil for April that night at the Gurley mansion. Although Twyla did not feel like going out, she was afraid she'd look guilty to Detective Grell if she didn't attend. But self preservation wasn't her only motive. Twyla wondered how many of those who would be there had some hint of the person April had been before she was a saint. It seemed important that *someone* be at her vigil who could represent that too-brief period of her life in which April had been allowed to be a normal girl.

And that someone, Twyla decided, even though their school acquaintance had been slight, would be *her*.

Chapter 20

That night, Twyla followed the route to the Gurley mansion which took her through the water front area of Tar Forks. Originally a colonial town, dating back to the mid-1600s, Tar Forks had grown up where the Tar and the Pamlico Rivers flowed together into a single tributary feeding the Pamlico sound.

The brackish water brought inland the occasional spectacle of a school of dolphins, skipping like a handful of slick stones tossed over the river. Also, it wasn't unheard of for people to find sea-minted sand dollars up stream, deposited where they were not standard currency.

The small town, then, with its access to both fresh and salt waters, originally developed as a fishing village. And while most local businesses had coveted the water front area to more conveniently serve the fishermen, one business took pains to be at least a mile away from town. This was the local brothel, not much more than a cabin, located on an island visible from the waterfront, but outside the city limits and thus free from legal prosecution.

Which was not to say that Tar Forks had operated as some Wild West town. The Christian faith had always been dominant there. There were three or four church buildings which Twyla passed that evening dating back to colonial days and still serving congregations in the present. And there were plenty of churches of more contemporary establishments throughout the town as well. Tar Forks apparently possessed infinite potential among its finite population to support any new congregations that might spring up.

In fact, a fresh sowing of the field was what Twyla assumed was going on as she drove by a crowded tent revival on her way to the Gurley mansion that night. Its large awning was spread out over a traditional sawdust-scattered ground and rows of uncomfortable looking wooden benches. She noted the preacher held his closed Bible to the side of his mouth, like a megaphone, though he was using a contemporary sound system with a mobile mike.

Like Battle Creek, Michigan in the 19th century, Tar Forks, then, was a spot where various and sundry "isms" took root. And it was spiritual pursuits, ironically, which had brought the *Oro Boro Loops* breakfast cereal business to Tar Forks, establishing a new source of material prosperity for the locals, which soon rivaled the town's fishing business as its major source of income.

In the late 19th century, Absalom Jackage had migrated from the mid-West to establish a divinely inspired health resort based in the same Seventh Day Adventist faith as the one begun by John Harvey Kellogg in Battle Creek.

There was already a health resort established in Seven Springs, North Carolina, about fifty miles from Tar Forks. There, however, the emphasis was on the properties of the town's eponymous springs with their therapeutic and restorative properties that would allegedly make Ponce de Leon drool.

Jackage, by contrast, stressed a more spiritual based regime: stay away from alcohol and tobacco, toss the medicine ball regularly, and devoutly practice religion. He proposed temperance regarding meaty foods would suppress certain "animal propensities." "Purge Your Colon, Cleanse Your Soul," was the motto soon taken up by Jackage's disciples.

When Absalom Jackage needed to find a location for his proposed health complex, he turned his attention to the same island that had once facilitated the local prostitutes. Thirty years earlier, the cabin they had used had been burned down by a zealous local women's group. Time had effaced the island's taint of association with illicit sex, especially since what had gone on there, in light of the spiritual emphasis of the town, was no longer spoken of and there were few remaining who had actually frequented the business – or would acknowledge they had.

So, all things considered, it seemed fitting that the island, like everyone else in Tar Forks, be redeemed.

By the end of the 19th century, a beautiful, two-story art nouveau structure serving as a health resort stood on the island. There were plans for eventual expansion, but that never came. The island was not that large. Inland property would have to be purchased and the locals, mindful of the monetary success of the Battle Creek facility, were not going to let the real estate go cheaply.

Seeing how Kellogg had created a gold vein which his brother had then mined by popularizing cornflakes for mass consumption, Jackage was determined his health resort would obtain the land from profits earned by selling *his* formula for bowel purging fiber chips. Hence the beginning of the marketing of the cereal that would eventually become known as *Oro Boro Loops*. The factory that was still set halfway between the city limits of Tar Forks and the Beaufort County line was up and running by the end of the first decade of the twentieth century.

But during the twenties, Jackage made the mistake of going hardline on the Seventh Day Adventist's doctrine of keeping the Sabbath on Saturday, not Sunday. He lost much of his backing, both spiritual and financial, and finally had to sell predominate shares in his cereal business to one Zechariah Gurley, April Gurley's great-grandfather. Sugar was added to the cereal, and the channeling of funds toward a health resort was abandoned. Along in the change of formula, it was Zechariah who changed the cereal's name from *Grain Hoops* to *Oro Boro Loops*.

Absalom Jackage committed suicide in 1932, a victim of the Great Depression.

And his beautiful art noveau building on the island? It was abandoned and fell into disrepair. Then a group of touring carnival freaks, who annually passed through Tar Forks as they headed down the Atlantic coast to winter in Sarasota, Florida, had purchased the property (rumored to have been attained via some mysterious business transaction with the local Mystic Fez Lodge) and restored it. The freaks used it as a facility for an annual blow-out celebrating the end of the summer season.

With the arrival of Zechariah Gurley and his renovation of *Oro Boro Loops*, the Gurley family quickly became entwined with Tar Forks' history and society. Their estate, Twyla's destination that night, still boasted what had been the largest home in town for almost a century now. But its significance as the housing for April's ministry, both before and after her coma, had in recent years made the mansion more a monument to God than mammon.

Chapter 21

By 6:00 PM, a good sized crowd had already gathered on the Gurley lawn. In the front of the house, people were lighting candles at a makeshift shrine, piling up rosary beads and crosses and prayer cards on a long table on which a large, framed photo of April was placed. It was a portrait taken shortly before the coma.

Twyla had not been there long before April's father came out. His church's pastor, the Reverend Frank Uzzell, accompanied him. Twyla thought that more than grief stricken, Vernon Gurley looked genuinely haunted. Still, given her previous personal encounter with Mr. Gurley that morning, Twyla knew how quickly he could shift his emotional gears, so it all seemed pretty insincere to her.

Was he attempting to mask his guilt to the town? But guilty for what, exactly? Twyla wondered what his motive would have been, whether to choose to allow her to die or even pull the plug himself. Certainly, he wouldn't have done either simply to release his daughter from a condition he perceived as hopeless. Not when he could have gone through legal channels to have her taken off life support. For while April's followers would have protested, they had no power to block any rights Vernon Gurley had as family.

On the other hand – perhaps he worried about public opinion, about becoming a pariah in the community if he ordered April to be disconnected. If someone else – an anonymous someone else – could be held responsible for April's death, then no one could blame him. In fact, he would have all of Tar Forks' sympathy.

"That poor man," Twyla heard someone in the crowd say at Vernon's appearance. "It hasn't been any time since his wife passed."

The comment, overheard at random, struck Twyla like a directed rebuke. Certainly, Vernon Gurley would never end his daughter's life: he had lost his wife only a little over a year earlier, following her prolonged illness. His daughter was all of his family he had left, the only part of his *wife* that he had left. What she had taken as evidence of insincerity, his chameleon-like emotional states, could conceivably be those of a man suffering from shock.

"Thank y'all for coming," Vernon Gurley said, choking back emotion. "I know my little girl has meant so much to so many, and I just see so much love for her out here tonight. I can't make any sense out of any of this. I don't guess any one of us can. There are times when we just have to cling to hope in a higher power. April was a connection with that power for a lot of people. And even though she's gone now –" his voice choked again, and tears filled his eyes – "that power is still here. We have to believe that, even if we lack proof now. Just like we have to believe April's with her Lord. Thank y'all for coming out." He nodded toward the candles, the flowers, beads, and icons piled before April's picture. "This all means so much. Thank you."

With that, Mr. Gurley stumbled back; Reverend Uzzell, who had stood at his elbow during his speech, caught him, and, letting him lean on his shoulder, guided the grieving father back inside the house.

Looking away from the departing Vernon Gurley, Twyla suddenly saw a familiar face, though she had not seen it this grief stricken before, even with what her son had put her through in the past.

"Shametrice," Twyla said, reaching out for her, and she and the large African-American woman fell together, Shametrice's body jerking with sobs in their embrace.

"I'm so sorry, Shametrice," Twyla said, unsettled to see this normally strong woman shaken so. "About this – and Demarcus, too. This has been a bad, bad day hasn't it?"

"I just don't understand it," Shametrice said. "How could this happen? That's not the way it's supposed to work. You pray, and you have faith. I mean, I *tried* to have faith. I just wasn't strong enough."

"No, sug', don't blame yourself, now," Twyla said. "You just have to believe that those prayers count somehow. They don't just hit the ceiling –"

Shametrice pulled away from her. She cast her gaze toward the ground for a moment and then looked at Twyla. "You wonder though, how things can turn out so bad, and you know God doesn't fail, so you must have."

"This isn't just about April, is it?" Twyla asked after a moment. "You're thinking about Demarcus now, aren't you? You think you failed as a parent, but Shametrice, that's just not true. You gave him guidance, but Demarcus made his own choices."

"Listen, Twy," Shametrice said suddenly with a slight expelling of her breath that made it sound to Twyla like she had just committed herself to some irrevocable action, like jumping off a cliff. "I need to see you. Privately. Could we get together tomorrow, at my house?"

"Sure, hon'. You've certainly been there for me. I'll do what I can to help you through this problem with Demarcus."

"This isn't about Demarcus. This is another burden. And the good Lord knows there are so many that I've got to let something go, or I ain't going to be able to be any good to my boy. It's . . . this is something that's gonna come out. It's only a matter of time. And I need to talk to you first. I . . . I really need you to trust in our friendship, now."

Twyla cocked her head at Shametrice. She didn't like the desperate tone. It was unusual for Shametrice, and Twyla's alarm was only heightened by what her friend said next:

"Remember yesterday, when I told you I believe in second chances? About how we have to forgive? I hope you can forgive me, Twyla, that you'll try, even if it's hard at first."

"Honey, what have you done to me that needs forgiving?"

"I can't drop this on you now. Not here. You'll understand

tomorrow. When can you be there?"

"I have an hour for lunch at one. Will an hour be long enough?"

"It'll be a start. You'll see." Shametrice leaned and hugged Twyla tightly, and then without another word, she was moving through the crowd.

Twyla's eyes were tearing. *Whatever* this was about, it didn't sound a bit good.

Then as her vision cleared, she saw in the distance what she thought was another familiar face, though this one totally unexpected: the face of her old friend Lorna Doone Delongpre.

Twyla wiped her eyes with the back of her hand and looked again. But in that moment the striking blonde she'd seen, who'd stood apart at the outskirts of the crowd, had vanished.

Very unlikely that it had been Lorna, she thought. Nobody had seen her for years in Tar Forks except on a cover for *Low Rider* or *Hot Rod America*. She hadn't even come back home for her former boyfriend's funeral. Why would she be here for April's? Lorna had never even personally known April, who was already a recluse by the time Lorna came to town.

She thought about seeking the woman out, but after a few more moments thought she decided that, no, it couldn't have been Lorna: there was something about the woman's face that wasn't right for it to be her. So, Twyla decided it was time to call it a night. She had to walk down the street to get where she had had to park by the road because of the crowd. Other cars were driving away already, and Twyla had to wait for a van that had just pulled out before she could cross the street and get to her car. The van's headlights illuminated the customized plate and Twyla was able to read it clearly: Miguel's Mexican HQ.

"Huh?" Twyla blurted out loud.

Then the van, quickly gathering speed, was heading down the road. But if Twyla had any doubts, they were resolved by what she saw in the back window of the van: two decal images, on either side of the glass, of Our Lady Of Guadeloupe.

What was Myra's boyfriend – the Santeria wizard – doing at April's wake? What kind of connection could those two have had? The old fashioned, Bible-belt Christianity of the First Pentecostal Holiness church where April and her family were members would not allow for any common ground between their traditional Biblical beliefs and the occult.

Of course, April's family – who described themselves as non-denominational –and the ecumenical Shametrice Prayer *had* been open-minded enough to accept the Catholic interpretation of April's condition and even the Catholic trappings of prayer cards and saint icons right there in her room. Still, it was quite a leap from Catholicism to the occult.

Then Twyla remembered the Saint Anthony figure Myra had around her neck. Miguel's Santeria *did* share the same saints with Catholicism, at least superficially. She thought of how Detective Grell, who'd been Catholic all his life, had never heard about putting Saint Anthony's statue behind the door to guard against danger.

But Saint Anthony had significance in Santeria, so could it be a Santeria tradition that put his icon there?

Twyla didn't know, but after seeing Miguel's van, she had a sudden strong desire to find out. She could ask Myra, but she was nosey, and Twyla didn't want to raise her suspicions. That was all right, though, because she knew someone else who just might have the information she needed. She took her cell phone from her purse and dialed home.

"Mama?" she said when her mother picked up. "Isn't Reverend Sutton the Spanish outreach minister at church?"

"Yeah, hon. Why? You want him to get up with some immigrant family you're trying to get started attending church?"

"No. I just need to ask him something . . . Mexican. To help a friend. Would you look his number up in the church directory?"

She did, and soon Twyla was dialing Reverend Sutton. He picked up the receiver on the first ring.

"Hello?"

"Hi, Reverend Sutton. It's Twyla Chayne. From church."

"Yes. We did 'meals on wheels' last Thanksgiving, right? You had an interesting bumper sticker, I recall. What can I do for you?"

Mortified, Twyla still pressed on. "I had a question about Santeria.

You told the congregation about running across it in the Mexican community."

"That's right. What do you need to know?"

"Have you ever heard about them putting a Saint Anthony statue behind a door? He's a Catholic saint, but –"

"Yeah. I've seen it several times, as a matter of fact. For them, Saint Anthony represents Eleggua, the god of doorways. They say he's supposed to keep out trouble. I take it you've come across this in your home health care work?"

"I think so. Okay. That's what I needed to know. Thanks. See you Sunday."

So whose idea had it been, to put the icon in that spot? Twyla wondered as she turned off her phone. No one knew. Some one mailed it in anonymously as a well-wisher, stressing in a note the icon's power of restoring lost health and adding that the saint warded off danger if his statue was put behind the door. No one in the Gurley household and no one caring for April was Catholic, so none of them would have known that putting the icon behind the door *wasn't* a Catholic thing.

Could Miguel be the person responsible for getting it there?

Or taking it away?

Miguel's presence at the vigil that night didn't necessarily mean either one. But there was the possibility that *whoever* murdered April had removed the statue because he believed the icon's presence wouldn't allow his attempt on her life to succeed. The killer, then, could be someone who believed in, perhaps even practiced, Santeria.

And Myra's boyfriend was a potential link to that shadow world. Twyla assumed it would be a rather small cult in Beaufort County, and so there was a good chance Miguel was acquainted with the killer – though he might not necessarily know that.

Still, if Twyla could enter the Mexican migrant community as a friend of Myra's, she would have a better chance of gaining the trust needed to expose the possible Santeria connection to April's murder. More so than the authorities. And that revelation could remove her from the list of suspects.

It seemed she was going to have to reconsider Myra's offer to get together with her Mexican friends.

By the time she was back in her car, she'd made up her mind. Using her cell phone again, she called her friend's house, but Myra's mother said she wasn't home.

"Do you know if she was going to the vigil for April Gurley tonight?"

"No, she's working the nightshift at Wahl-Mart. If you want to talk to her, you better go there. We hardly ever see her at home anymore. Not since she started dating that boy."

So Twyla decided that she would pay Myra a visit at Wahl-Mart that evening before calling it a night.

Chapter 22

Twyla was barely past the check-out counters before she saw something that brought her to a complete halt. There was Father Paton, again dressed casually, buying something. He hadn't seen her yet, so she stepped backs into the foyer, where he would be exiting, and hid between two cola vending machine.

He seemed very pleased with his purchase: there was a grin on his face as he headed for the automatic doors.

After he passed her, Twyla quickly stepped out from behind, grabbed his arm and pulled him back. Jolted, Father Paton dropped his bag. When he saw Twyla, his eyes went wide.

"Oh, man," he said. "Twyla. I heard about April. I'm sorry . . . ."

"Maybe she wouldn't be dead if you had dialed 911 instead of running out of there like a coward."

"I can explain . . . "

"You're not even a priest, are you?" she asked.

Paton didn't say anything. Instead he stared hard into her eyes, rather desperately, she thought, like he was hoping she wasn't going to say something or see something –

She looked down at the dropped bag.

"No, no!" Paton said.

Twyla saw that his purchase had slid out of the bag. And she found herself staring into the airbrushed countenance of her old friend Lorna Doone Delongpre, in high heels and a bikini, draping herself seductively over a corvette on the cover of *Hot Rod America.*

Twyla's head looked up, mouth and eyes wide. "I knew it! You're no priest!"

Just my luck, she thought. *Now that he's available he's a letch as well as a coward.*

"What did you want in April's room for?" Twyla demanded.

"I wanted an icon."

"That is *so* weak!"

"No, really. That's all I wanted —"

"You could have asked. We move icons in and out of that room all the time. You didn't have to go to such lengths to swipe one."

"I had to physically get in! I had to be there."

"To kill her? Did you have something to do with April dying?"

"No, no. Will you hold it down? Let me get my magazine off the floor, and I'll explain, okay? I don't want you to go to the police about me. You haven't, have you?"

"No. Not yet, anyway. But you better start giving me a good reason that I shouldn't," Twyla said, hoping he wouldn't stop to think that such an action would incriminate her as well.

"I will, I will," he assured her as he gathered up the magazine, and slid it back into the blue Wahl-Mart bag. "Look, can we sit down and talk? In the Rednek Grill again?"

"Don't you try to run," Twyla said, shaking a finger at him. "Or I *will* go to the police."

Eyes cast down, the man who had called himself 'Father Paton' let Twyla take him back inside the store and to the Rednek Grill, where they'd met to a totally different vibe just yesterday.

Once they were seated at a table, Twyla said: "Okay, you start explaining why you had to sneak into April's room, and what that is all about. And you better tell me the truth. Starting with your name."

"Okay, sure. It's Lamar."

"Lamar? Lamar What?"

MURDER IN THE MIRACLE ROOM

"Lamar Larson."

"I want to see some ID. Some genuine identification this time. None of those bogus Vatican credentials you were passing around the other day."

"All right. Here." He pulled out his wallet from his back pocket and slid it across the table to Twyla. She snatched it up and began rifling through it.

"Hey, go easy with that," he said. "You just need to see my driver's license, right? It's right there in the front. See?"

Twyla stopped, glared at him from across the table, and then gently turned back through the cards. There, indeed, was an up-to-date driver's license with a photo of the man who sat across from her. And the name given on the license was Lamar Larson.

"You see?" He reached across the table to take the wallet back.

"Uh-uh," Twyla said, pulling it way from him, and holding it back. "Not until I get some answers that I like."

Lamar, whose hand had clamped down on empty air, withdrew, and leaned back in his chair. "Okay, sure. What do you want to know?"

"What do you think? Why did you impersonate a priest to get into April's room if you only wanted an icon? Like I said, people got them everyday. Could you just not wait, or what?"

Lamar sighed. "Okay. Where's the best place to start? The Mormons, I guess –"

"*Mormons?*"

"They have a baptism for the dead ritual –"

"What's that got to do with the price of eggs in China?" Twyla said, her jaw dropping. "What? You're Mormon now? You're undercover for the Church of Latter Day Saints? I want some straight answers, and I want them now!"

Lamar held up one palm to her. "Just stop, please, okay? And let me finish. I'm not 'with' anybody. Listen, I know this is going to seem like it's a million miles away from what you're asking me, but I gotta start somewhere. Okay?" He took a deep breath, paused, then continued: "So, did you hear what happened in the Mormon temple in Utah six months ago? During their baptism for the dead ritual? Do you know about that?"

Twyla shook her head "no."

"Okay. The Mormons have a vicarious baptism for people who have passed on without getting baptized during their earthly life. It's based on an obscure reference by Saint Paul in the New Testament. For Mormon young people to get dressed out in the robes and baptized like this is like confirmation in Catholicism. Anyway, it's a big deal at their main temple in Salt Lake City. And very, very esoteric. Anyone who's not a Mormon doesn't get in there.

"But six months ago, someone else did get in. We know this because suddenly this very secretive ceremony was being broadcast over the Internet without Mormon consent. An investigation revealed a tiny digital camera hid in a strategic niche. Who put it there and why is unknown. People assume it was to embarrass the Mormons, a prank, the work of a disgruntled former practitioner or a radical feminist group protesting the Mormon patriarchy. But the question remains unanswered: who is Utah's public enemy number one?

"Then, just this past week, Vatican World, a religious theme park in Italy was broken into. The manikins in the Hall of Popes —"

"— were arranged around a table with poker chips and playing cards. That one I know about," Twyla said. "But what has this summary of current events got to do with you getting into April's room — No. Wait-a-minute. You're saying *you're* the one who's been doing all this breaking and entering into these places and April's room was your latest? What, were you going to set up another digital camera while I wasn't looking so people on the Internet could see her getting bathed later on? That's your idea of a joke? That is *so* messed-up —"

"No, no," Lamar said, raising both hands, palms out toward her. "Nothing like that. None of that's what I'm trying to say *at all.*"

"So, what *are* you trying to say?"

"It's not me who's been breaking into those places. I never meant to do anything to humiliate April Gurley, I promise. Like I said, I just wanted to get in there and get an icon for someone."

"And like *I* said, you didn't have to sneak in to do that."

"But I had to, to prove something to . . . someone."

"Who were you trying to impress?"

"There's this girl –"

"A girl?"

"Well, a woman."

"And you thought a stunt like this would impress her?" Twyla asked. "To be able to say you got in covertly and got a weeping *prayer card* for her? Look, for future reference, most women would prefer flowers, okay?"

"But she's not most women."

"Beautiful, huh?" Twyla slid back in her chair, arms crossed.

"Yeah. I'll show you."

"What? You got her picture in here?" Twyla held up the wallet and gave it a little shake.

"No. Right here."

What happened next was, for Twyla, a real *Twilight Zone* moment, like the universe had secretly tagged a cosmic "Kick-me" sign on her back and had picked that moment to point it out to her.

For Lamar had pulled out the copy of *Hot Rod America* with Lorna Doone Delongpre in her bikini and high heels, and was holding it up for her to see.

"You got a prayer card for this girl on a magazine who doesn't even know your name, who you've only fantasized about –" Twyla began.

"No, you don't understand. She's a friend of mine," Lamar explained. "We met at the university where I worked and she was a grad student, and then we lost touch."

"Until you saw her on the cover of a hot rod magazine." So, Twyla thought, sizing up the situation immediately. *Lorna had a friendship with this guy, and then she moved on and cut him loose – like she did me and Tar Forks. This Lamar isn't accepting it though; he's fantasizing he can win her love by impressing her with some crazy stunt.*

Well, at least he knew well the object of his desire, judging by his choice of gift. Like she'd said, most women prefer flowers. But this, of course, was Lorna. She was eccentric in the things that turned her on.

Once, if her old boyfriend Boo could be believed, he had seduced her back to his place by offering to show her a weeping picture of the Virgin Mary.

"Yeah," Lamar was saying, "I saw her magazine covers when the first ones came out, about a year ago. Then, out of the blue, I got a call from her. It'd been over a year since she'd left the university. Other than the magazine covers, she was very vague about what she'd been up to in the interim. Anyway, she wanted to see me, and so I drove out here –"

Twyla lurched forward. "*Here*? To Tar Forks? Lorna's back here?"

"For months now. How did you know her name? You . . . know her? Sure. Tar Forks isn't large. You know her from high school, I bet."

"But, waitaminute," Twyla said. "You said you had to get into April's room to prove something to Lorna, not just to get her a gift. You had to prove what, exactly? That you could get into a secure religious sanctuary –" And then it clicked for Twyla:

"You wanted to prove you could get into a secure religious place just like *her*. Lorna's the one who's breaking into these places, the one who broke into Vatican World this week and the Mormon temple before that?"

Lamar squirmed in his chair, mouth working mutely. While he obviously didn't want to confirm what Twyla was saying, his expression said all she needed to know. Seeing from Twyla's face that he had given it away, he said:

"Yeah. That's what she told me. About the Mormon temple a while back, and about her plans to get into Vatican World this week. But I'll deny it if you tell anyone I told you."

"Who does she think she is these days? Lorna Croft, Relic Wrangler?" Twyla asked. "When she's not posing for hot rod magazine covers, I mean."

"The magazine stuff is over, she told me. This cover today should be the last one."

"And you've collected the whole set, huh?"

"Yeah," Lamar slightly tucked his head and glanced up at her, looking to Twyla like a twelve year old who'd just been caught by his mother perusing the latest *Sports Illustrated* swimsuit issue.

Okay, Twyla thought, *this guy's what? My age? He's got to know how much of a loser that makes him look like. Really, Lorna was out of his league even before she started the Lara Croft routine, and now that she is a sexy adventuress, he has to know she's totally unobtainable —*

— about as unobtainable as a priest, she thought and felt her ears burn.

And then she realized something else, and she eagerly turned the light away from self-examination and back on Lamar:

"You knew she was going to break into Vatican World. She told you beforehand, and you wanted to go adventuring with her, but she wouldn't let you, would she? She didn't think you could pull it off, and so you arranged this whole scheme to get into April's room to show you could be part of her world!"

"Don't start singing lyrics from the *Little Mermaid* at me, okay?" Lamar said, losing his contrition as he realized from her tone that she was dismissing his dreams as essentially hopeless, and him as a fool of the lovesick variety.

"I won't; you won't be hearing any singing from me," she said, suddenly ashamed of herself for mocking him even ever so slightly, and sorry to have hurt his pride. Dwayne Woolard had taught her a thing or two over the past year about wounded pride, and how it felt to love somebody who didn't return the feeling.

Though, of course, she hadn't got from their conversation that this Lamar had ever actually been romantically involved with Lorna. But he wanted to be, that was clear, even to the point of pulling the stunt he had. Lorna definitely made an impression. Even on her. Even after all this time. When Lamar had told her that Lorna had been back in town for months, and Twyla knew that she hadn't tried once to contact her, it had hurt. It made her friend's abandonment of twelve years ago painfully fresh.

"I want to see Lorna," she said.

Lamar winced at her request. "I don't know. I mean, don't you think there's a reason she hasn't got in touch with you?"

"That's what I'm hoping: a good reason. We were good friends, and then it was just over. Lorna owes me an explanation – for everything. And you owe me too, for having some faith in what you've said and not turning your tail in. So let's go."

"Right now?"

"Right now."

"I mean, it's kind of late."

"Right *now*."

Chapter 23

Twyla followed Lamar in her car to a mobile home park. *Was this where Lorna has ended up?* she wondered. *Right back in the low class environment she'd hoped to escape?* Lorna had seemed to live such a charmed life away from home, with so many guys –teachers and businessmen as well as guys her own age – deferring to her, that it had always been easy for Twyla to forget her friend had to go back at the end of each day to a fatherless home and insane mother.

Lorna had never let on to anyone how serious her mother's condition had become until things got so bad that Darla-Lu had to be institutionalized. How long had she silently endured alone her mother's increasing ravings that the demonic Lucifer Vesuvius murdered Lorna's father via radio wave transmission?

Twyla considered that maybe it was understandable if Lorna had thought of her days in Tar Forks as a bad time from which she had wanted to totally disassociate herself as soon as she could.

Lamar pulled up to the front of a small trailer on a dirt lot on which clumps of grass grew only sparsely. The car that was already there – presumably Lorna's – was a Dodge Omni, though what year it was Twyla couldn't say. It was a sensible, economical vehicle, and not the flashy type of sports car Lorna had openly admired as a teenager as "the kind I'd look good in."

Lamar pulled in behind the Omni and got out of his car, waiting for

Twyla, who, because there was no more room in the driveway, parked her car on the street in front of the trailer. When she had walked up to where he stood, he said, "Let me go in first and tell her you're coming –"

"No way, Jose," Twyla said, walking on past him. "I want to see her face, her initial *honest* reaction."

Lamar had to rush to overtake Twyla before she reached the porch. But just barely. He managed to push in between her and the door, intercepting her knock and rapping on it himself.

"Lorna? You home? It's Lamar."

"Door's unlocked," answered a voice from inside, muffled but still melodious.

Lamar opened the door partly, his body filling the space and blocking Twyla's view. "Hey, Lorna. I ran into an old friend of–"

Before he could finish, Twyla shoved by him and pushed the door open the rest of the way and saw Lorna, in the flesh, for the first time in twelve years.

Lorna Doone Delongpre sat on her couch, legs crossed under her, watching television and eating cereal from a bowl she held in her lap. Her mouth was full, and she was chewing when she saw Twyla, so she could only make a delicate grunt in immediate response, but her eyes went wide, lit with recognition.

Twyla had a few moments to scrutinize Lorna as she chewed on the mouthful of cereal. The lack of glamour stunned her: it wasn't just that she'd discovered an old friend she'd felt destined for the "lifestyle-of-the-rich-and-famous" living in a mobile home in the process of eating from a humble bowl of Oro Boro Loops. It was her *appearance* . . . .

This was *not* Miss Tar Forks, 1999, in her striking one piece bathing suit, or the waitress in tight shorts who had flirted a small fortune out of her appreciative male customers, or the bikini and high heels seductress on the covers of the automobile magazines. While Lorna probably still had the curves she'd flaunted for *Low Rider* and *Hot Rod America*, that perfect body was cocooned in a baggy jogging suit. And it was an unflattering maroon color at that.

Further, Lorna's long blond hair had been shorn to mere shoulder length, and dark roots were beginning to show at her crown. And she was wearing no make-up! This girl who used to not go to the breakfast table without "her face on" as Lorna herself put it. She realized now why she'd thought it couldn't have been Lorna she'd glimpsed at April's vigil earlier. Out in public without make-up and needing a fresh dye job? That was *not* the Lorna Twyla had known, and the plain countenance had thrown her.

Lorna put her fingertips to her mouth to cover her chewing. Finally, she'd swallowed enough that she could get out some semblance of the English language. "Twyla? Oh, gosh!" she managed between crunches of cereal. She sat the bowl on an end table, beside an exotic looking elephant sculpture.

By the time she'd crossed the floor, Twyla and Lamar were both inside. Lorna reached out and hugged Twyla. "Girl, it's so good to see you again!"

Twyla, whose arms hung at her side said, "Well, Lorna, it's not like I've been hiding all these months you've been back in town."

Lorna drew away from Twyla, her hands lingering tentatively on Twyla's upper arms. Seeing the hard look set in her old friend's eyes, Lorna let her hands drop. She looked at Lamar questioningly from over Twyla's shoulder, one eyebrow arched. "Oh," she said, then looked Twyla again in the eye. "Oh, sug'. Don't take that personal –"

"Like I wasn't supposed to take it personal you just disappeared the summer after graduation without even a goodbye?"

"No, Twyla, it wasn't personal. Back then, I was tryin' to get away from Boo. He was becomin' so possessive, he was scarin' me . . ."

"And you didn't think you could trust me? Your best friend?"

"I don't mean this in a bad way, but I could always tell when you were hidin' somethin'. And I figured Boo and Dwayne could, too. I couldn't risk it. This was my *life*, honey."

"And Boo's been dead for over a year, now, Lorna. What's your excuse been since then?" Twyla said, crossing her arms.

"It's just been best that I keep a low profile since I've been back."

"You mean to help you disappear after you've vandalized Vatican

World or embarrassed the Mormons over the information highway?" Twyla said. The realization of disadvantage on Lorna' face gave her a satisfying sense of payback. Lorna looked again at Lamar.

"I didn't tell her. Not intentionally, I mean. She just put some things together."

"Twyla," Lorna said looking levelly at her. "I know I don't have any right, but I'm askin' you to please have a seat and hear me out, okay? Please?"

Twyla gnawed her lower lip with her front teeth. She had no intention of telling on Lorna, but she had enjoyed the feeling of power she had for those few seconds.

"Okay," she said. "I wouldn't . . . I'm just hurt, Lorna." Her eyes began to tear and when Lorna tentatively reached out for Twyla's hands, she gave them to her, and let Lorna lead her over to the couch where they were both seated while Lamar took a chair across the room.

"I guess you're wondering how Twyla and I ended up together?" Lamar asked Lorna. It struck Twyla that Lorna was the one who was supposed to be doing the talking, and that Lamar was giving her taken off guard friend an opportunity to collect herself and think about what she was going to say before she spoke. But Twyla wanted a moment to get herself together before hearing Lorna's story, so she didn't interrupt when Lamar began answering his own question.

"Remember the home health care person I told you got me into April Gurley's room? That was Twyla. Not that she knew what I was up to at the time; but this evening in Wahl-Mart, she caught me buying a car magazine with one of your bikini covers, which meant *my* cover as a priest was blown. So, while I was explaining why I bought that magazine, we discovered we both knew you, and I let it out that you were here, and Twyla just had to see you. Right now. And here we are."

"You were April Gurley's care provider?" Lorna asked Twyla, a look of relief spreading over her face. "So, you've been around all the miraculous things that have happened around her since her accident? All those bleedin' and weepin' icons?"

"Yeah. Almost daily for the past year and a half."

Lorna's relaxed features drew a bit tighter. "What do you make of it, Twyla? Shrine or sideshow? Tell me the truth. It's important, 'cause of what I'm about to tell you."

"I've become a Christian – born again – since you last saw me," Twyla said. "Even joined my mama's church. So, yeah, I believe in miracles. I think something supernatural was going on with April. I don't understand what it was supposed to be all about, now that she's dead. Just like everyone, I was expecting her to come out of the coma and enlighten us."

"So, you believe in the Catholic explanation for the phenomena manifestin' around April, even though you aren't Catholic."

"Yes. Hey . . . are *you* Catholic now?" Twyla asked, a bit startled at the realization of the possibility. Did *that* explain the sackcloth Lorna was wearing, the ugly running suit and the lack of make-up? She'd undergone her own conversion since Twyla had last seen her?

"I'm sorta on the fringe," Lorna said, patting her hand. "But if we can agree on the Catholic interpretation of the stigmata and the weepin' icons, then you should be open-minded enough to take what I'm about to say seriously."

"*What?*"

"There *has* been a change in my life since high school. All the goals that I had when I left Tar Forks twelve years ago . . . don't matter any more."

"I saw you made it into the movies," Twyla said. "I read the article in the paper."

Lorna smiled and tucked her chin. "Well, it wasn't 'the movies,' really. It was a direct to video thing. I'm kinda embarrassed by it now."

"I still think it's great," Lamar chimed in. "And soon to be available on DVD: *Bodacious Barbarian Babe In Dinosaur Hell*."

Lorna smiled, shaking her head at him. "Lamar is the self-appointed president of my fan club. *I* wish that movie would just go away. "

"Why?" Lamar sounded wounded. "I mean, what's there to be embarrassed about. You look great in that ripped up safari outfit you're almost wearing, with that lacey brassiere. And then that cave girl get-up, just two little pieces of doe skin and you're squeezing out of that . . ."

"We get the picture, Lamar," Twyla interrupted him. Then she turned back to Lorna. "But when did *you* get so prim and modest? I mean, I waitressed with you. I've seen you in action, remember? You didn't have any problem working those tight little shorts for larger tips. And those hot rod and motorcycle covers I've been seeing . . ."

"That's over now," Lorna said. "I shot the last of those covers a year ago. And by then, it wasn't the same as the waitressin', or the Miss Tar Forks Beauty Pageant."

"It sure *looks* the same," Twyla said. "In fact, what you're almost wearing on those covers look *worse* than anything I ever saw you slinking around in at Pope's Sea Food or in any local beauty contest."

"The covers are more objectifyin'. You're right. But the motivation was different. I needed the money. But not for me. I thought posin' for them was the quickest route, and I didn't understand then that I had to wait."

"Wait? Wait for what?"

Lorna sighed. "Okay. Since you last saw me, I've been through a lot. Last year, I got involved in uncoverin' this conspiracy. I had a certain . . . truth revealed to me. I learned somethin' that I could not simply pretend I didn't know. One of my associates, I guess I could call him . . . I think he lost his mind because of it. He took his own life. In front of me."

Twyla's jaw dropped. "Lorna, that's terrible. I had no idea. Who was he?"

"If I told you who . . . you'd probably know. It was in the news. But I'm not goin' to say. My involvement has been kept secret by certain powers, both secular and . . . otherwise, I guess I can say. And some of those who are protectin' me would not be so kind if they knew I know everything that I do. I can't lose the element of surprise. Not while I am still not quite prepared."

"Lorna . . . girl . . . what are you talking about?" Twyla asked. "'Not prepared' . . . for *what?*"

Lorna smiled and laid her hand on Twyla's. "That's a secret. What I *can* tell you is that, while I was goin' through that strange, rough period, I had a vision. Of the Virgin Mary. *She* summoned me to this mission I'm on."

"What?!" Twyla started.

Lorna leaned in eagerly toward Twyla, slightly increasing her pressure on Twyla's hand. "Twyla, you said you accepted what happened around April. She had visions, too."

"She also had bleeding palms and statues and pictures that sweated oil. Where's your evidence?"

"I'll have it . . . when I can show the world. When my mission is accomplished. I'm sorry, Twyla. That's the best I can do."

"Well, that's not good enough. What's all this got to do with broadcasting the Mormon baptism of the dead over the Internet? Or putting all the Popes around a poker table?"

Lorna released Twyla's hand and leaned away. "I need to back up first. To explain about those hot rod and biker covers. You see, after I received the Marian revelation, I was at loose ends. I knew what I was called to do, but no further instructions seemed to be comin' on how I was supposed to accomplish my mission. I guess it was to try my faith or somethin'. But I just couldn't sit still, couldn't just go back to my life like it was before, like nothin' had happened. I realized that to do what I was called to do, I needed funds. And I wasn't goin' to get them by continuin' to pursue my doctorate degree. That might pay off big in the long run, but I felt I needed *lots* of money *fast*.

"I decided to become one of those supermodels, who haul in really big bucks. I know it sounds naïve, but you see, I thought I might have some help, a little celestial influence.

"But after several months of only gettin' offers for only the biker and car magazines," Lorna continued, "I started to think maybe I'd taken a wrong step. But I was stuck as to exactly *what* to do. Before I made any more decisions, I was determined to have a heart to heart with Mary. That's when I read in *The National Expose* about this guy back here in Tar Forks, Albert Metz, who started channelin' Mary a few years after I left town. I figured here was a way I could contact her for further instructions."

"So you came back to Tar Forks," Twyla said. "And you met with this Albert . . ."

"I met with *Mary*. Albert is just the medium, you know. And, yes, we get together regularly. I wish I'd done it sooner, but she told me that everything was on schedule. And then she told me –"

"Albert said this . . ." Twyla said.

"The Holy Mother, sug'," Lorna smiled. "Keep it straight now. *Mary* told me that I had to go through a series of preparations, of trials, before I was ready for the big event. And that's when I started with the, uh, . . ."

"Breaking and entering? Or is it relic wrangling?" Twyla asked. "A Lara Croft sort-of-thing? Or, wait, you've had a vision that told you to do this, so maybe you're Joan of Arc, too?"

Lorna smiled, seemingly pleased by both comparisons. "I have to develop my skills for my mission. Gettin' into the type of places I have is just practice. But needed practice. That's what Mary told me."

Lorna nodded at the elephant statue which set by her cereal bowl. Twyla noticed for the first time that, while the statue's head was an elephant's, it had a man's body with four arms.

"Look," Lorna said. "This is Ganesh. An Indian elephant god. You may have heard about the stir this idol and others like it caused throughout the Punjab back in the mid-nineties when they started drinkin' the milk their followers offered them. I pinched this one out of the first temple I broke into."

"The statues *drank milk*?" Twyla asked.

"It's well documented. But you don't have to take my word for it, not this time, Twyla," Lorna said with a smile. "Watch. I do this every morning with the milk I have left in the cereal bowl."

Lorna held the bowl up to the mouth below the glazed curled trunk of the tiny elephant god. Immediately, the milk was visibly absorbed until the bowl was empty.

Twyla's jaw went slack. She'd seen fluid coming *out* of statues, but nothing like this. Further, she'd never seen any kind of paranormal activity out of anything other than a *Christian* icon. But she'd heard the explanations skeptics had made about the leaking statues in April's room, and she quickly adapted them to this new phenomenon.

"The stone is porous," she said. "It's glazed except where the glaze has been scratched off at the mouth so that exposed stone absorbs the milk. I don't believe in Hinduism, but Lorna, if you took those people's idol from them, that was stealing."

"Twyla, there is a demon in that thing," Lorna said, her smile vanishing. "It was performin' miracles of deception. I couldn't leave it there to continue doin' that."

"So you bring it home and feed it milk every morning? Isn't that gettin' a little cozy with the devil?"

"To shame them, the ancient Romans paraded the enemy kings they'd conquered out in the streets. I've taken Ganesh from his seat of worship and turned him into a parlor trick. It's the same thing."

"Okay. All right, then. You humiliated the demon. But putting the Popes around a card table, having a friendly hand? Are you trying to embarrass the Catholics as well?"

"That Hindu temple was primitive, so gettin' in and out was relatively easy. It was perfect for my first pass, but my ultimate goal will be monitored by a state of the art security system. I had to see if I could break in and get out of somewhere a bit more 21st century, you see?"

"So, you break in, you break out, but making a joke of the Popes . . . ? Okay. I admit. I laughed when I heard about it, but that was still vandalism."

"I didn't break anything. It was just a harmless joke. Well, not *just* a joke. You see, when my big day comes, it's not goin' to be as simple as just gettin' in and gettin' out. I have to test how much I can get away with before I alert anyone. I need to know just how elaborate I can get, because pullin' off my ultimate task, it's gonna get complicated."

"And putting the Mormon baptism of the dead on the Internet?"

Lorna sighed. "What I have to reveal to the world . . . I can't physically remove it. That's just not realistic. So I'm goin' to have to broadcast it live over the Internet once I'm in there. Gettin' in to the temple in Utah, settin' up the camera and broadcastin' the baptism of the dead, it was just more practice."

"So you humiliate the Mormons . . ."

"People get baptized in public all the time. What do the Mormons have to be humiliated about?"

"Okay, Lorna, you're pulling all these elaborate stunts. But you quit your modeling job which wasn't paying much to start with. You're living in a trailer park. Where do you get funding for these capers?"

"I can't say whose auspices I'm under, Twyla. I thought you understood that."

"So, was your appearance at April's vigil another attempt at infiltration and then getting back out without being recognized?"

"No," Lorna said. "That was about bein' there for a friend."

Chapter 24

"April wasn't happy, you know. She was very lonely."

Lorna, Lamar, and Twyla now sat around Lorna's kitchen table, enjoying homemade lattes. Twyla noted that the coffee making machine, along with a personal computer, was the only extravagance in the mobile home.

"All that attention had made any kind of personal life impossible for her," Lorna continued. "And she knew it would be that way all her life. That was a heavy thing for a teenage girl. No one wants to be different anyway, and when you're a saint in everyone's eyes . . . you know, if you're this holy woman, then boys aren't goin' to be interested in you. Not in *that* way. I mean, you can understand how those bleedin' palms could just neutralize you romantically."

"I never knew that you knew April," Twyla said. "I mean, you never talked about it, and that's just the sort-of thing you *would* have talked about, being buddies with a stigmatic."

"I made a promise," Lorna said. "I told April no one would know."

"Why? You were popular. She would have been in with the in-crowd."

Lorna sighed after several long moments of silence. "I guess it can't hurt to say," she said finally. "Not now. Now that she's beyond it all."

Twyla noted Lorna's reticent attitude. Quite frankly, she was surprised that Lorna had ever kept her friendship with April secret. Back in her high school days, she couldn't talk enough about her brush with the local voodoo man, Doo-Buddy, and she'd only visited him one time to try and get a winning lottery number. It sounded like she and April had a much more substantial relationship.

Lorna sipped the froth of her coffee, drinking from a soup mug which she clasped in both her hands. Swallowing, she set the mug down on the table.

"It was her daddy who approached me about it. You know, I waited on him and those lodge brothers of his a lot. Mr. Gurley would always ask me how much I'd charge him to dance around his swimmin' pool in my bikini."

"He actually asked you that?" Twyla asked, her upper lip turning up. That certainly didn't jibe with the religious man she'd just seen speaking so spiritually about his dead daughter at her vigil. Or was that indeed just another mask, as she'd suspected? Of course, Lorna's waitressing days had been a long time ago, and what Vernon Gurley had gone through since then, losing his wife to cancer and his daughter to a coma, could have changed him.

"So . . . what was your price, by the way?" Lamar asked Lorna.

Lorna smiled and shoved his arm. "I didn't actually ever *do* it, goof ball. I'd just smile and wag my finger at him and say, 'Now, Mr. Gurley . . . shame on you.' And he and his lodge brothers would just break out laughing when I'd say it. Well, I didn't think he was serious. Not at the time. All those Mystic Fez Lodge guys flirted with the waitresses. And they were generous tippers —"

"Because you were generous with the amount of leg you showed," Twyla said.

Lorna patted Twyla's hand. "You looked good in those little shorts, too, girl. You've got great legs. Willowy, I always thought. Sleek, lean thighs."

"Yeah?" Lamar said, looking up from his mug, a foam mustache on his upper lip. Twyla hid a smile behind her own mug when she saw Lamar regarding her, plainly wishing for a personal appraisal.

"One evenin'," Lorna continued, "When I'd just delivered some fresh rolls to Mr. Gurley's table, he asked, 'Do you know my girl, April? She should be about your age.'

"I said, 'No, sir. She was already gettin' home schoolin' by the time I came to town. I didn't really have an opportunity to get to know her. She would be in my graduatin' class, though.'

"'That's what I thought,' he said. 'I'd like you to come over and meet her. I think she could learn some things from you. She doesn't have many friends. None of 'em seem able to get past her, you know, bleedin' all the time. Sort-of a conversation stopper, I guess. I don't know if her palms would make you sick or anything –'

"'No sir,' I said. 'Absolutely not.'

"'Well, they stay bandaged up all the time, anyway. But you can't talk about 'em with her. Not unless she brings it up. I would like you girls to get to know one another, though. Maybe even have one of them slumber party type deals someday. *If* you hit it off, I mean. Don't feel pressured. You can just drop by for an hour after school some afternoon. Let me know when it's convenient. Here –'

"He pulled out his wallet and gave me his card, and I told him I'd be in touch. He left a larger tip than usual that night. But if he was thinkin' I needed encouragement, he was wrong. A stigmatic had always represented somethin' of a fabulous creature to me, like a slender, shy unicorn from a medieval tapestry come to life. I called the next day to speak with April on the phone. Mr. Gurley answered.

"'Lorna,' he said. 'I was hopin' that might be you. April is right here. Hold on . . . . April . . . telephone!'

"After a moment she picked up, and I said, 'Hi April. This is Lorna Doone Delongpre. I guess your Daddy told you I'd be callin'.' So, you wanna get together?'

"'Sure. That'd be nice,' she said. "I remember. . . ," Lorna smiled. "I remember I asked, "'When's a good time for you?' And she said:

"'Anytime I'm not receiving the angel Gabriel from the heavenly courts.'

"'Are you expectin' him tomorrow?' I asked.

"'No. It's a school night,' she said.

"And so I had a date with the stigmatic girl."

Lorna took another sip of coffee and continued: "That was the first time I got to go inside the Gurley mansion, after all that time of just seein' how big it looked from the road. And I was bowled over . . . well, remember I was just a teenager, I hadn't seen much, and I was livin' in a trailer park then." She paused and smiled. "Still am. But back then, material things like the Gurley mansion impressed me more than they do now. These days I understand that things like that shouldn't be ends in themselves.

"Mr. Gurley met me at the gate himself. Then he showed me where I could park my car and I followed him inside.

"'April!' he yelled. 'Lorna's here!'

"And that's when I first saw April Gurley. She came to the top of the stairs, wearin' a housecoat and bedroom slippers. My attention was drawn to her bandaged hands in spite of myself, and when she saw me lookin', she quickly put them behind her back. I thought I'd messed up right out the door, but Mr. Gurley just squeezed my shoulder reassuringly.

"'There she is,' he said. 'Go on up Lorna. Maybe do each other's hair and make-up, order pizza, talk about boys. You know: all that girl stuff.'

"So I walked up the steps, wonderin' what kind of greetin' I could give her. I mean, shakin' her hand was out, so when I got there, what I did was give her a little hug. It was kinda inappropriate since we'd just met, and I felt kinda phony, but I wanted to do *somethin'* friendly.'

"'So you're April,' I said. 'I've heard about you.'

"'And I heard about you,' she said. 'Daddy's all the time talking about what a neat girl you are, and how he wishes we could be friends. I think . . . what he really wishes is that *you* were his daughter.'

"Well, I wanted to just shrivel up and blow out the nearest window when she told me that. 'No, April,' I said. 'I'm sure that ain't true. Probably what he means is he would like you to be more . . . more like what he thinks a teenage girl should be like.'

"'More normal,' you mean,' April said. 'But I ain't normal, and I'm not ever going to be. Not as long as I have this.' She held up her hands. 'The gifts and calling of God are without repentance.' Saint Paul said so.'

"'Right. In the Bible,' I said.

"'No. In my room last week. Sometimes he tags along with Gabriel,' she said.

"'Oh. Okay. Well, sug',' I said, ' nobody's askin' you to repent. I'm sure your daddy just wants you to be happier. He wants you to emerge out of this cocoon,' I said and tugged at her housecoat, 'a regular social butterfly.'

"'I'm supposed to be coming out,' she said. 'You know, debuting. He really wants it, but I mean, can you see me walking down that grand stairway at the country club with a strapless formal evening gown and my hands bandaged up with this bloodstain?'

"'Maybe you could dress 'em up a little,' I suggested. 'Some beads, or some charm bracelets might be cute . . .'"

"Oh, no. You actually *said* that?" Twyla asked.

"Well, evenin' gloves would have been too snug to fit over the bandages. Look, it was a dumb suggestion, I know. I knew it then. And so did April. But that was the icebreaker. We just both started gigglin'. I think it was the first time she ever had a sense of humor about her situation. 'Yeah,' she laughed. 'Why not a couple of diamond studded oven mittens? Wouldn't *that* become the fashion statement of the season?'

"And then I told her she wasn't the only girl who ever worried about bleedin' on a social occasion. We went in her room, and I shared some embarrassin' incidents I'd had with my period. Me, and my girlfriends. I thought it would make her feel more normal, you know.

"After that, we were gettin' together at least twice a week, and I'd go over and spend the night on some weekends. We did end up doin' make-up and talkin' about boys, just like Mr. Gurley had hoped we would. At first I was bustin' to ask her about her visitations, and what the angel Gabriel was like. But, believe it or not, I never did. It turned out, the time April was with me, that was the one time she didn't want her mind on heavenly things. I could tell it was the only time she felt like a regular gal.

So I didn't get one inside scoop on heaven, but I gave April the lowdown on makin' out with boys and what it was like to be kissed – when it was appropriate to use your tongue and things like that.

"So, finally I decided it was time to take her from theory into practice. I told Boo I wanted to bring April on a date with us.

"'I don't know about that, Lorna,' he said. 'Not with a saint. I just couldn't let loose, you know?'

"'I mean, a double date,' I said. 'Not her bein' a third wheel on one of ours.'

"'Who's she supposed to date? *Another* saint?' he asked.

"'Just a normal guy, silly,' I said. 'Can't you ask one of your friends?'

"'No way,' he said. 'I can't ask any of my friends to go out with her. That'd be like asking them to go on a date with a woman preacher. I already know they'd say 'no.'

"'Well, you *could* ask –'

"'Once I told them she's gonna have open wounds the whole evening, that'd be it. And I sure wouldn't *not* tell them, and just spring it on them when he got to the door.'

"Well, I laid down the law to Mr. Boo Wallace. If April wasn't goin' out that weekend, neither were we. And we wouldn't be goin' out any weekend until he could arrange a double date. Well, you know, a man'll do about anything to get his lovin' regular. But as it turned out, it wasn't Boo. It was *your* boyfriend who came through, Twyla."

Twyla started. "Dwayne Woolard went out with April and you guys?"

"No, no," Lorna was quick to correct her. "It wasn't ever suggested. No, you see, Dwayne told Boo he knew another stigmatic."

"What? Really?" Twyla asked. "How come I never met this person?"

"Well, they weren't buddies. He just had a noddin' acquaintance with the guy. I thought, 'what could be more perfect,' you know? One stigmatic datin' another. Kind of like when you see two really ugly people get together? That's so sweet.

"Not that I mean April's date was bad lookin'. He wore glasses, but I didn't think that would be a big deal – ."

"Well, right. It wasn't like April could be too picky," Twyla said.

"Well, the guy met us at Boo's place. And I didn't see any bandages on his hands."

"Uh-oh . . ."

"The boy's name was Billy Langston. He got in the backseat and he seemed nice enough. But I wanted to know a little more about him before we picked April up, so I could help facilitate breakin' the ice between 'em.

"So, as we were drivin' along, I said, 'So, Billy. How did you first hear about April?'"

"'Well, I'm new in town. Dwayne down the street told me there was somebody I might like to meet, so I said sure.'"

"And how long have you had the, you know . . . .' I felt awkward bringin' it up right out of the gate," Lorna explained. "So I couldn't actually say 'stigmata'; I just nodded at him."

"'Oh,' he said. 'Since I was seven.'"

"'Wow,' I said. 'That's young. April was twelve when 'it' happened you know, and it just changed everything for her.'"

"'Really?' he said. 'She shouldn't be so self-conscious. You can't let something like this affect your whole life. I mean, it's just one thing, you know? *Everybody* has *somethin'* about them, right?'"

"'You have such a positive attitude,' I said, and I was really impressed. 'You're just what April needs. You're goin' to be a shot in the arm for her, you know that? Now, tell me somethin' else. Does your, uh, condition, come with visions, like it does for April?'"

"'Visions?' he asked. 'Well, before I got glasses, I didn't know what I was seein'.'

"'Glasses?' I asked. 'What have your glasses got to do with it?'

"'Because of my 'stigmatism, you know.'

"I'd been turned around, looking over the back seat talkin' to him. I felt my face start to burn, and I turned back around quick and whispered to Boo: 'Did you hear that? He's *not* a stigmatic; he's got an *a*stigmatism. Your dumb friend Dwayne doesn't know there's a difference.'

"Oh, man . . . . Poor April," Twyla said. *Is there anybody's heart Dwayne*

Woolard hasn't *broken?* she thought.

"By that time we were pullin' up to April's house," Lorna continued. "And she was so eager, poor thing. I'd helped her pick out an outfit, and coached her on walkin' in heels, and we'd done her make-up. I told her not to look too eager, but she's excited, so she's right there at the door. Here she comes. And I hear Bill Langston in the back seat ask, 'Is that her? Hey, why are her hands bandaged up? Was she in an accident or what?'

"Well, I had to say somethin' and so I told Bill, 'Yeah, she burned her hands with a curlin' iron, gettin' ready. She's really self-conscious about it, too. So, Bill, you be sweet and don't bring it up, okay hon'?'

"He agreed, but unfortunately I didn't have time to explain things to April. And I decided maybe it wouldn't be a good idea *to* tell her. That she'd get really self-conscious. As it turned out, maybe I should have said somethin'. . . .

"I wish it could've been just like she wanted. And I thought for a while that we might make it through the night without any embarrassin' incidents. But by the time we were at the movies, her bleedin' was startin' to show through the bandages, and Bill said, 'Hey. You need to see a doctor or anything?'

"And April just said, 'No, why?' And why she was talkin' she just dipped right into her popcorn bag, got a handful, and then, without thinkin', held the bag out to Bill to offer him some.

"He turned pea-green, but he managed to answer her: 'Because of your accident... with the curling iron.'

"'What are you talking about – curling iron?' she asked.

"And then April realized he didn't know she was a stigmatic. And she figured out he probably wasn't one, either. She thought I'd lied to her and him, to get her a date. She was *so* embarrassed. And that ended the evenin' right then. We didn't even see the movie.

"So I had Boo drop me off with her at her house, while he took Bill home. He and April didn't even say 'goodnight' to each other. And I thought she wasn't goin' to have much to say to me, either. But finally, back in her room, I got her to open up:

"'Why did you lie to me, Lorna? You said he knew I was a stigmatic. You said *he* was a stigmatic.'

"'It was a mistake, honey. I promise you. Boo's friend told us about him, and he didn't know the difference between a stigmata and an astigmatism. I told him you burned your hands because he saw your bandages, and I had to say somethin'. I am *so* sorry.'

"I still remember how quiet she was after I said that, and her eyes were fillin' with tears. Finally, she said, 'Do you think he'll tell?'

"'Who? Boo?' I asked.

"'Bill. Do you think he'll tell his friends about our date? How . . . awful it was,' she said.

"'Oh, sug',' I said, reaching over and hugging her, and I was so relieved when she hugged me back. I knew we were okay then, you know? But that was about to change real fast.

"'Don't you worry none about Bill humiliatin' you,' I said. 'He was caught off guard and embarrassed just like you. But he wasn't a mean person. I don't think you have anything to worry about. If it makes you feel better, I'll look him up and explain your feelin's and I'm sure he'll understand.'

"She seemed relieved after I promised her that. I hung out with her a little longer, and then her dad came to the door and told me my ride had just pulled up. He said he'd walk me out, and I told April good-bye.

"We got a little way to where two hallways intersected. Mr. Gurley took one of my hands and said, 'Lorna, before you go, would you give me a minute?'"

"'I said, 'Sure, Mr. Gurley.'"

"'Please, make it Vernon,' he said as he led me out of the main hallway that led to the stairway and off to the side.

"'I just wanted to say,' he said, 'that I appreciate everything you're doing for April.'"

"'That's okay,' I said. 'She's a sweet girl. And she ain't all that different from everybody else, if people could just get to know her as a person.'"

"'I just wanted to say,' he said, 'that I won't forget all you've been doing.' And then he moved in and hugged me. And that was all right, you know; he was my friend's daddy, so it wasn't like I just knew him from flirtin' with me at the diner. So I put my arms around him. He gave me another squeeze. And then I felt his hands slide down my back and grab my butt.'"

"Oh, man," Twyla said. "Lorna . . . ."

"I guess I hesitated. I didn't really want to believe it of him. Even with him askin' about me dancing around his swimmin' pool like he had in the past. I mean, his wife and daughter were both in the house. What was he thinkin'? Well, I guess *that* was obvious. I pulled loose and told him I had to go, makin' a point to remind him that my boyfriend was outside, in case he was thinkin' about coppin' another feel.

"So, he didn't come after me or anything, and I was ready to get out of there and not come back. But I was thinkin' of April, too. I couldn't just stop seein' her. I was her only friend. Maybe Mr. Gurley had been drinkin' or somethin', you know? Or he'd been testin' boundaries. You know how a man'll do. And I'd reminded him that I had a boyfriend, so I figured it would probably be all right now.'

"When I came out to the top of the stairs, though, it became clear that there wasn't gonna be any future problems for me at the Gurley house."

"What do you mean?" Twyla asked.

Lorna sighed. "I mean, I felt eyes on the back of my neck, and I turned around, and there was April. She'd seen what happened with me and her daddy. It was all over her face. I'd betrayed her the second time in one night. I didn't know what to say. How could I defend myself and claim her daddy was the bad guy, not me? I couldn't, so I let her turn and run back down the hall to her room without sayin' anything.

"And then, the next day, I got a call from her mother sayin' that April wasn't interested in our gettin' together anymore. She said it was takin' time away from the Lord, and it hadn't been right for her to pursue worldly things.

"She also said April wanted my word that I wouldn't spread around what we'd done with make-up, and the boys we talked about, and our goin' out. I promised. I wasn't goin' to anyway; April had already got my word on that. That was the last communication I had with her. April and I never spoke again. I hope, you know, that she knows now that I never meant to hurt her. And that her dad wouldn't have done anything to hurt her; he didn't know she was lookin' when he grabbed me."

"It sounds like you're defending him, Lorna," Lamar said. "The guy was sexually harassing you, copping a feel like that. And – like you said – with his wife and daughter in the house! He didn't care about their feelings or he wouldn't have ever taken a chance on what he did!"

"You're right, Lamar," Lorna said and finished off her coffee. "But if you could have seen how he looked tonight at April's wake . . . . He's thinkin' about that now, about how he let his daughter down."

"Well, I can understand why you came out to the vigil tonight, and risked blowing your cover," Twyla said to Lorna. "And the fact that you never mentioned your relationship with April until now – you were discreet. You were . . . a friend."

Lorna smiled, reached across the table and squeezed Twyla's hand. "I was your friend, too, Twy. I still am. I know I haven't acted like it for a long time. And I wish I could make it up to you. But –"

"But your secret mission is going to be taking up your time, right?" Twyla said.

"It calls for sacrifice. I've accepted that. But I would dearly love an occasional coffee with you. When you can fit me in," Lorna ended on a hopeful note.

"It'll be more like when *you* can fit me in," Twyla said and patted Lorna's hand in response. "*Although* –" Twyla took a final swallow of her coffee and set her cup down on the table top, "you are not the only person on a mission."

Lorna arched an eyebrow. "Oh, really?"

"Really," Twyla smiled, rising. "So, Lorna. I'm staying at my mom and dad's. Our number is still in the book. Give me a call when you think you might wanna talk.

"'Father Paton'," she turned to Lamar. "Enjoy your magazine collection." *'cause it's obvious you are not ever going to get a chance at the real thing,* she thought as she left the trailer. And that thought she found touched by both satisfaction and pity.

But enough thinking about both Lorna and 'Father' Lamar. The mysteries that they'd presented were solved. Lamar's anyway, and Lorna's tolerably so. The major enigma of her life remained, but she was encouraged by her luck so far that evening in getting answers, so she drove back to Wahl-Mart to resume her search for Myra.

Unfortunately, by the time she got there, Myra had already gone home. And now it was too late to call her there. Tomorrow, maybe, they'd have lunch – but no, she'd already promised her lunch break to Shametrice. Hopefully that would clear up another mystery: what had Shametrice done to Twyla that she would need to forgive her for it? It could only be something her friend had imagined. And the poor dear had enough real problems to worry her. Demarcus . . . and April's death.

So she couldn't cancel out on Shametrice. She had to give her friend some relief first. Only then could she find out if there existed a link between Myra's boyfriend and April Gurley –

– and April's murderer.

Chapter 25

Twyla had not been to Shametrice's house in some time. She lived in the section of Tar Forks that decades after desegregation laws was still "the black section" of town. It had been Shametrice's childhood home, where she lived with her mother. She hadn't been gone from it five years before her marriage went into a state of permanent separation and she was back, this time with her young son Demarcus. When her mother died shortly thereafter, Shametrice inherited the house, and that was where she and Demarcus had remained.

The Prayer house (it was designated thusly by a plaque over the front door; the double entendre had appealed to Shametrice) set amidst a little meditation garden with a fountain featuring an image of Jesus as the good shepherd. A legend at the sculpture's base read: "He Leadeth Me Beside the Still Waters."

Shametrice's yard was a green island of grace in the middle of the asphalt, concrete, and barred windows that had become Tar Forks' version of an "inner city." Though the fence around her property could have been easily hurdled by anyone intent on vandalism, no one had ever tried. That was the kind of respect Apostlette Shametrice Prayer commanded.

But in the end, a more subtle evil had penetrated the Prayer homestead, one that insidiously left the property in top shape while defacing the soul of one of its inhabitants. When his father died in a car accident, Demarcus had finally acted out the anger he'd silently held inside throughout his obedient teenage years. The accident had been totally avoidable and the death needless, all due to his father's drinking and driving. Demarcus took this as a final betrayal, his father's nullifying any hopes that the young man still held for reconciliation.

Unable to strike back at a father who was beyond his hurting, Demarcus committed acts guaranteed to lacerate the heart of his very-much alive mother. It made no sense, of course, but since his father's death, Demarcus had become a creature of utter irrationality. Shametrice had often asked Twyla in confidence, "What's it going to take? What's it going to take to reach my boy?"

Twyla always listened sympathetically, but she had no idea, and though she wouldn't hurt Shametrice for the world, she couldn't help silently hoping as she pulled her car into Shametrice's driveway that Demarcus wouldn't be at home.

After putting her car in park, Twyla looked in her rearview mirror. Across the street was a convenience store, which, while it was open for business, had bars on the windows and door for when it was not. It was a stark reminder that not everything on this street was as safe as Shametrice and her house. Part of Twyla's typical obsessive compulsive behavior was checking and rechecking her car doors to see if they were locked. But in this neighborhood, such extra precautions were appropriate, and Twyla made certain her vehicle was locked up before proceeding to her friend's door.

She mounted the steps and rang the bell, hoping Shametrice would hurry. She peered inside the door's glass pane. And for the second time in two days she found herself regarding a space left empty by a missing Saint Anthony statue.

That icon had been a gift from Demarcus during a brief period of reconciliation with his mother. She had told him about the statue behind April's door and the reason for it, and Demarcus had brought one home afterward, telling her he wanted her to be safe when he wasn't around to protect her. The gesture had melted Shametrice's heart at the time, and,

Twyla figured that, like her, both Shametrice and Demarcus were ignorant that the action was a Santeria ritual, not a Catholic one.

Perhaps Shametrice had probably removed her statue after April's murder, feeling the silent, tiny saint in his guardian spot mocked her. Who could trust Saint Anthony for protection after his spectacular failure to safeguard April?

No one had come to the door. Twyla wondered if the bell was working. She knocked and waited. When Shametrice still failed to appear, she turned the knob and found the door unlocked.

She pushed the door inward and stepped partially inside.

"Shametrice? It's Twyla?"

No answer.

She paused, took a breath, then slowly walked inside. She proceeded carefully through the den area toward the next door, one that opened on the living room. It was only partially open, a tad bit more than a crack...

She moved closer, peeked through . . .

And in the next moment she was stumbling backward from what she saw, backing into an end table, and bumping it loudly and losing her balance. She was able to catch herself from falling and turned to run for the outside door, but it was too late. The living room door flew open, and the person she'd seen inside bolted for her, caught her –

And Twyla found herself in the rough, grappling hands of her Uncle Tate.

Chapter 26

Twyla screamed, but then Tate pressed his palm against her mouth and wrapped his other arm around her arms, drawing her in close and tight to him.

"Shhh, Twyla," he said. "Now, you just calm on down, all right? This is going to be difficult enough. No need to bring the law into it and me just out of prison . . ."

Twyla forced herself to calm down and was rewarded as Tate dropped his hand from her mouth, though he continued to hold her tight against him. Remembering the way he'd looked at her in prison, Twyla felt herself pale in his grasp. "What did you do to Shametrice?" she asked, her voice trembling.

As if in answer to that question, Twyla's friend appeared in the living room doorway, to all appearances unharmed.

"I'm okay, sug'," Shametrice said. "I was in the bathroom, and I guess Tate knew it wasn't a good idea for him to greet you at the door." Then: "Tate, let her go."

He released Twyla and stepped back, hands held up to indicate he was no threat as he moved to Shametrice's side. She did not appear at all frightened.

"I'm sorry," Tate was saying to Shametrice. "She was going for the door when she saw me, and, naturally, she expected the worst . . ."

"Sure, Tate. Just a misunderstanding. I'm sorry, Twy. This wasn't how I wanted this meeting to start off. I knew it would be difficult under the best circumstances. That's why I agreed with Tate to facilitate this reconciliation by having you meet in my home. With me here, and not him just approaching you on the street or going to your house."

Twyla's jaw was slack. It was too unreal, what she was seeing here, what she was hearing.

"Why are you facilitating *anything* for him? Since when do you even know each other?" she finally demanded of Shametrice, turning her stare on her friend to keep from looking at her uncle.

"Since he started attending my prison ministry. I've been counseling him for the last three months or so. Tate has changed, Twy. I've seen it, and he wants to make things right with you."

Still hardly believing what was happening, Twyla asked, "This is why you asked me over? Why you were saying what you did yesterday and last night about forgiveness?"

Shametrice nodded her head. "I knew that this would be hard, that I would risk offending you . . ."

"So why did you agree to it?" Twyla asked sharply. "Why were you willing to betray me like this?"

The hurt and anger in Twyla's voice seemed to slap Shametrice across the face, and she grimaced.

"Oh, sug'," Shametrice said. "Don't you see? I'm not trying to hurt you. I did this to help you. So you can part with that resentment that you've held in your heart for so long. You've got to let it go to enter the kingdom of Heaven."

"I'm really sorry, Twy," Tate spoke again at last. "I don't mean to defend things I've did, but if you'll just hear my side. . ."

"*Your* side? You already told me that, didn't you, Tate? When you were trying to blackmail me into doing a lap dance for you in prison? You were 'trying to hold on to your masculinity.' That's how you justified that —"

"I don't, Twyla," Tate said, raising one hand up, palm open toward her. "I don't attempt to justify that at all. And I know I can't ever make things right, especially about Grusilla. But I can try to help you —"

"*You* help *me?*"

"You came there to ask me something. About your aunt, remember? Shametrice explained what that was all about while I was still locked up. And now I want to give you some relief for a change."

"Then why didn't you just send me word by Shametrice? Why didn't you just put it in a letter?"

"'Cause I thought if we met face to face, you'd see my sincerity. You'd know I'm truly sorry."

"Crocodile tears is all I see," Twyla snapped.

"Sug'," Shametrice said, "can't we take this into the living room? So we can sit down, get more comfortable?"

"I'd be more comfortable sitting in a dentist's chair," Twyla said, glowering at Tate.

"Please . . ." Shametrice said.

Twyla took a deep breath. "Him first. And I don't sit beside him."

When they were seated, Twyla noticed that Shametrice had no problem being beside Tate on her couch. And, even more astonishingly, Tate, who had never been one to shy away from the word "nigger" or publicly mourning the South's losing the Civil War in mixed racial company, was sitting, contentedly, beside Shametrice.

"A lot of changes took place while I was locked up," Tate said.

Apparently so, Twyla thought, regarding the unlikely pair sharing the couch.

"I mean, whenever I walk down the street in Tar Forks these days, all I see is Mexicans with a bottle of water in one hand and a cell phone in the other."

Then again . . . .

Shametrice slightly inclined her head toward Tate. "Go ahead, Tate. Tell Twyla what you're here to say. Don't try her patience."

"Yeah. Twy, what happened with your aunt . . . I'm not trying to justify anything, but I didn't mean for her to die. I hit her, yeah. And I'm not proud that I'd done it before. But she went down that time, her head struck the corner of the wall, and it killed her.

"I didn't mean for her to die. I know that's no excuse; I'm not here to make excuses. But I didn't do it cold-blooded or anything like that."

"So you set her on fire to cover that? Why didn't you just tell the truth?" Twyla asked.

"I had a . . . how do they put it on *Matlock*? 'A history of domestic violence.' That didn't put me in the best possible light. It was all my fault; I know it; I know I never had a right to raise my hand to Groo. That's how I feel now. But I was desperate then. My history would get me some kind of a murder charge, and even if I got a lesser sentence, when I got out, I'd be the murderer in everybody's eyes.

"But Groo *had* been fascinated with spontaneous combustion. That much was true. And I was desperate. I'd read one of Groo's *National Exposes* on the john and it had this article on the famous 'cinder woman.' The writer gave a natural explanation for what was really happening. This lady, fell asleep in her flammable pajamas while smoking a cigarette. She was a big woman, like Groo, and the flame fed off her body fat. They called it 'the candle effect' in the *Expose*. Anyway, the only thing left of the cinder woman was a foot. Everything else was gone. If that would work on Groo, I figured that'd take care of the head wound that killed her."

"And you say you weren't 'cold-blooded'?" Twyla spat out at him, sliding up to the edge of her seat as though ready to leap across the room and attack her aunt's killer. But Tate didn't move to defend himself.

"Not in the killing. But after she was dead, there was nothing I could do to change things for Groo. It was awful what I did. But I've changed, Twy. And that's why I'm telling you this, though I know it'd just make you hate me more. You don't have to worry about going up in smoke yourself. Spontaneous combustion doesn't run in your family."

For a long moment, Twyla could not speak. She was trembling, eyes burning at Tate.

"Sug' . . . ," Shametrice began, reaching out to touch her friend's arm.

Twyla jerked away and rose to her feet. "Can you even *begin*," she started, glowering down at her uncle, "to comprehend the hell I've lived with literally for years because you didn't tell this to me when I asked you?"

"But I'm telling you now . . ." Tate began.

"Too little too late, Tate!" she snapped, turned on her heel and headed for the front door.

"Twyla, wait sug'!" Shametrice called out from behind her. Twyla did not stop and Shametrice had to overtake her before she stepped outside. Shametrice caught and gently but firmly grasped her young friend's upper arm. Twyla stopped and turned to face the woman she'd considered a trusted friend.

"Twy, you have to forgive him, honey," Shametrice said to her. "You just have to."

"Oh, no, Shametrice. What he's done is unforgivable! Can't you see how hard it would be for you if you were in my place? And why are you taking his side, anyway? Why should you care about making Tate feel better?"

Shametrice started to speak but halted. Her mouth opened slightly and for a moment the tip of her tongue appeared, as though gingerly trying a sore place on her lower lip.

"See, you can't give me a good reason," Twyla said in the face of her friend's silence.

"I could tell you . . . ," Shametrice began, "that Tate is that one lost sheep the good shepherd must leave the other ninety and nine to find. But it's not all altruistic on my part. This is a hard time, Twyla. A hard, hard time. And I need to see God's grace manifested now. To see it incarnate. I've lost . . . . I find these days that I can't operate my gift of discernment. I can't just go on faith; I need sight."

"Shametrice," Twyla began, then bit her lower lip and cast her gaze to the floor for a moment. She was forcing herself to get past her own anger for just a moment and consider all of what Shametrice was going through before she spoke again.

When Twyla looked up at her friend, she softened her tone, though her expression was firm. "I'm in a rough place right now, too, Shametrice. What you're asking of me would feel near impossible in the best circumstances. And I just . . . . I can't. I'm sorry to let you down, but . . . . I just can't."

And then she was out the door. This time Shametrice did not try to stop her.

Safely out of Shametrice's neighborhood, back at the Tar Forks' waterfront, Twyla pulled her car into a parking place, switched off the ignition, and with a heavy sigh, laid her head back against her seat's headrest. She had to get herself together before her next appointment. And she had to get back on track to finding out who killed April. She reminded herself that she was still a suspect, and if she were to go to jail now for a murder she didn't commit with Tate walking free even though he *had* taken a life —

"Okay," she said to herself, raising her head from against her seat's head rest. She drummed her fingers on the steering wheel. "Maybe this was a good thing. I knew Tate was out, and it was probably a matter of time, and now that 'awkward moment' is out of the way. And if he is what he says now, he should leave me alone. . ."

She glanced over at the fire extinguisher in the passenger's seat. She was so used to having it there, it was like another arm or something. But she didn't need it. She'd never needed it. At least she didn't have to obsess about that anymore . . . . Although, as she understood it, if she ever managed to accept spontaneous combustion was no longer a threat to her, her obsession would probably transfer to something else. At least she had worked out a system for handling spontaneous combustion that she was familiar with. A new something, why, she'd be back at square one . . .

Another gift from Tate. The man just kept on giving, didn't he? A regular Santa Claus, that guy.

Okay, she reminded herself. Being bitter wasn't going to help her at all. She'd probably be too focused on the mystery of April's death right now to obsess on anything else for a while.

So, she would get going at that. Myra should be at work now. Twyla still wanted an opportunity to talk casually to Myra's boyfriend Miguel, and get on the subject of the Saint Anthony icon in April's room. Just his reaction at unexpectedly having that statue brought up might tell her loads.

So that was the plan. Twyla just had to ring up her next appointment and reschedule, which she didn't like doing. But this was urgent, after all.

This was about life and death.

Upset, she hadn't noticed the car that had been behind her almost since she'd left Shametrice's. And now she was so intent, she didn't pay attention when it pulled from the side of the road, where it had stopped when she had, and continued to follow her.

Chapter 27

Twyla found Myra in the electronic section of Wahl-Mart. Myra looked up from pricing some DVDs, saw her friend, and smiled broadly.

"Hi, girl! You out here wanting to do lunch? 'cause my break just ended . . ."

"This ain't about lunch," Twyla said. "Did your mom tell you I called last night? I was at the vigil for April."

"Did you find her . . . April . . . when you got to work yesterday? Or had somebody already called the rescue squad?" Myra asked.

"Yeah, I 'discovered the body', I guess you could say – even though she was in the same spot she'd been in for two years."

"Girl, that's terrible," Myra said. "That must have been horrible for you. You gotta give me all the details."

"Well, I don't have a lot to add to what you probably already know. Other than what the authorities want kept secret, so it won't compromise their investigation."

"You mean stuff only the murderer would know, right? Like they say on *Matlock*?"

Twyla only smiled in response.

"You know you're just making me want to know even more, don't you?" Myra asked. "C'mon, this is Myra, your old 'lunch at the Rednek Grill' buddy."

"Can't do it. Sorry," Twyla said, "but there's something I *can* do. If your offer still holds, that is."

"Offer . . . ?"

"You know: Miguel's Mexican HQ, the trip to see Our Lady of Guadalupe out at Jack's Neck with your friends?"

Myra cocked her head slightly. "Huh? Why'd you change your mind? I mean, what happened to that guy you were having lunch with here yesterday?"

Twyla smiled. "That wasn't really a date, Myra. Besides, I can tell you right now that *that's* not going anywhere."

"But you never acted liked you wanted to get together with Miguel or his friends before. What made you change your mind?"

"I think it would be real interesting," Twyla said, thinking, *okay, if I put it that way, it's not a lie.*

"Well, sure. That'd be fine. That would be great, in fact. We'll drop by and pick you up about six thirty tomorrow, okay?

"Well . . . sure. Okay," Twyla said, forcing a smile. "That'll be good."

Chapter 28

This could be bad, Twyla thought the next day, standing on the steps that led to the door to her room. *Please, mama, don't see Miguel's van drive up and me get in —*

"Sug', you all ready for your date?"

Twyla's mother had walked around the corner of the house, watering her flowers. But Twyla knew she was really spying. "You really look pretty," her mother said.

"Thank you, mama. But this isn't a date. It's just a get together with Myra and some of her friends. Like I said."

"I watch *Oprah*, sug'. I know getting together in groups is how you young people go about courtin' today."

"Okay, Mama: I'm thirty, not a teenager. And I know the difference in a date and just hanging out . . ."

She was interrupted by a car horn sounding notes from a trumpet played mariachi band style. Miguel's van had just rolled up.

Twyla's mother's jaw dropped as the side of the van slid open, disgorging a cloud of blue cigarette smoke and blasting out raucous music fit for some dive south of the border. The smoke cleared enough to reveal three silent, young Mexican men inside, apparently awaiting Twyla to join them in what her mother had to think was a mobile den of vice.

"Hey, Miss Chayne! *Queue pasa?*" Myra shouted from the passenger's window, waving at Twyla's mother.

"Well, that's my ride," Twyla said, already trotting off across the yard toward the van, wanting to get in and drive off and end this embarrassing moment. For *now*. Already she knew visions of Twyla and Myra as painted floozies, fallen women in Spanish Harlem, were dancing before her mother's eyes. Now she'd have to endure her mother's pained expressions and worried remonstrances when she got home. She'd *really* wanted to meet them some place else, but she was afraid she'd insult Myra – and Miguel – if it became obvious that she wasn't comfortable with Miguel and his friends picking her up at her house.

And she had to get on Miguel's good side, even if that meant riding around in his "HQ" with some of his friends. *And* presenting herself as a romantic possibility to them. She was under suspicion for April's murder, and anything she could find out about who was really responsible could only help her out as well as help to see that justice was done for April.

Her plan, then, was to gently ply Miguel for information with Lorna-style southern belle charm. Assuming the role of Lorna, however, wasn't something with which she was comfortable.

"*Hola*, Twyla," Myra said cheerily to her friend, looking over the back of her seat. The side door to the van slid shut, and Twyla looked around at the Mexican men regarding her eagerly as she felt the van begin to move.

"Hi," she said pleasantly, raising and dropping her hand quickly.

"From left to right," Myra said, still looking over the back of her seat, "that's Rodriqo, Esteban, and Jesus."

Twyla nodded pleasantly at each young man as she was introduced, "*Hola*, Rodriqo, Hi, Esteban, Hey . . . Zeus."

"And this is Miguel," Myra said, looking at the man behind the steering wheel. "Now, Twy, you just remember that *this* one's taken," she added, fondling Miguel's shoulder.

Miguel looked up from the road momentarily, regarding Twyla in the rear view mirror. "*Hola*," he said with a smile, and Twyla got her first good look at Myra's beau. He had a thin, lean face, dark hair, and a pleasant smile . . . though she didn't see the resemblance to Antonio Banderas Myra always mentioned when talking about him.

Keenly aware of three pairs of eyes trained on her back, Twyla turned around to face her admirers. They just stared without saying anything, though after a moment, Esteban said "drink" and held out a can of beer to her from an open cooler.

"No, thanks," she said, shaking her head "no" in an exaggerated manner. The offered beer was withdrawn and dunked back in the cooler.

Twyla's admirers continued to watch her silently, smiling. She was *really* beginning to feel uncomfortable now – Esteban had licked his lips a couple times while looking her up and down. She felt, for once, the negative side of getting the kind of masculine admiration Lorna had always drawn. She found a new respect for Lorna's graceful handling of awkward situations when Mr. Gurley or any other undesired man had come on to her.

But Twyla wasn't Lorna. She didn't have her experience or her grace, so with an abrupt "excuse me" she turned away from the guys with her in the back to talk with Myra and Miguel. *He* was her reason for being here, after all. She just hadn't wanted to zero in on him too soon, to be too obvious.

Miguel was holding forth – in good English – on some topic that seemed very important to him. And Myra. She was watching him attentively, like she was afraid she might miss one golden syllable from her love's mouth. Twyla found something a bit unnerving in Myra's demeanor. She had a look that was beginning to blur the line between the adoration of the lovesick and the adoration of a cultist. She remembered how Myra had excitedly rambled off about Santeria and her Saint Anthony necklace. Twyla felt she was witnessing Myra being programmed as Miguel let loose a spiel on his theory of the paranormal happenings in Beaufort County, North Carolina:

" . . . what most people don't realize is this weeping Lady of Guadeloupe is not an isolated event. Just last week, the man Jamie works for – whadoyacall'im? – Booger Grubbs? Yeah, Booger Grubbs lost two emu over night. Jamie found the birds: precise puncture wounds, no blood left in their carcasses. So he was watching the next night for the creature responsible, and he heard a rustle in the bushes, which this hissing came from. The sound made him physically ill and he started to pass out. It could be only one thing –"

Myra's eyes were wide as a child's hearing a bedtime story.

"*El chupacabra!*" Miguel said.

"At Booger Grubbs', there's a guy who channels the Virgin Mary, too," Myra said.

"Yes . . . her presence is known to us," Miguel said. "There have also been sightings of *La Llorona*, the *bruja*, weeping for her children – we may even pass her along the road tonight! These various . . . epiphenomena . . . originate from a singular source. Salvador Freixado said that. It is . . . Jungian, yes? 'Archetypal,' I think is the term."

"Wow, Miguel," Twyla said. "You're doing real good with your English. I mean, I know people who've been speaking it all their lives and they don't know some of those ten dollar words you were just throwing around."

He looked back at her in the rearview mirror again and smiled. "I try to read a book a week. A book in English," he clarified. "Plus, I take classes at the community college."

Twyla had looked Miguel over good by now, the angle of the rearview mirror giving her a clear shot of his torso from her spot in the back. *Nice pecs and a hard flat stomach*, she observed. *The tight T-shirt he's wearing shows 'em both off. I know Myra likes that.* The shirt featured the picture of a silver masked man, a famous Mexican wrestler and movie star. She knew this, because Myra once had shown her a replica of that silver mask that she was planning to surprise Miguel with for his birthday. What was the wrestler's name? Samson, maybe?

Miguel also wore some interesting colored sea shells in a necklace. She guessed it had some significance in Santeria. If it did, she wondered if inquiring about it would be inappropriate, maybe too direct. So, even though she was unclear on the wrestler's name, she decided to ask about the T-shirt anyway. Besides, the way he was holding forth with Myra, he would probably enjoy educating her as well. And if Twyla acted like she was hanging on his every word – he might relax around her so that she could get an opening to bring up the Saint Anthony statue from April's room.

"Miguel, is that Samson, the Silver Masked Man on your shirt?" Twyla asked.

Miguel kept his eyes aimed ahead at the road, but he smiled in response.

"You know El Santo? They called him 'Samson' in the American dubbed movies over here. But that's not a translation. 'El Santo' means 'the Saint.' And, like one of the saints, Santo has become an icon. My religion, Santeria, is the way of the saints. So, you see, when I put on my Santo shirt it has more significance than someone would think who only sees a Mexican wrestler. It's . . . syncretism? You know . . . how the Catholic saints became associated with the Santeria gods to start with."

Okay, Twyla thought, there's my opening –

"Miguel," she said, "Myra told me you got her this little Saint Anthony she's wearing. That was really sweet."

"I know I think so," Myra said and squeezed one of her guy's biceps. Miguel acknowledged Twyla's compliment with a smile and a nod, momentarily looked at her again in his rearview mirror, then returned his gaze back to the road ahead.

"So who does Saint Anthony represent in Santeria?" Twyla asked innocently as she could. "Myra said El Leggo something . . ."

"Eleggua," Miguel corrected her. "He who opens the door between worlds . . . and all doors in *this* world; they also are his domain."

"I knew a girl who had an icon of Saint Anthony just like Myra's – but this was a statue in her room. You probably heard of her: April Gurley, the stigmatic girl who passed the other day."

Miguel's eyes, still looking at the road ahead, but visible in the rearview mirror to Twyla, slightly narrowed.

"Wonder where you could get something like that?" Twyla asked innocently. "I mean, they can't be that common around here. Beaufort County is pretty much Protestant country."

"Anyone can get a Saint Anthony icon who wants one . . . from any dealer off the Internet," Miguel said. His tone sounded a little defensive, Twyla thought.

"So, how did you know April Gurley?" he asked.

"Oh, sug'," Myra said, squeezing Miguel's knee. "I *told* you: Twyla works in health care services. April Gurley was one of her clients."

"Yeah," Twyla said. "My job, while she was in her coma was to wash her. Groom her. Keep her presentable."

"You were at her vigil, so I'm sure April wasn't just a job to you," Miguel said. "You must have cared for her. Unless your appearance was just a professional courtesy?"

Twyla felt her face began to burn, and she hoped Miguel didn't notice her blushing. "I was fond of her, Miguel," Twyla said, recovering. "I mean, we were the same age, and I knew how sweet she'd been . . . kind to people. It was a privilege to care for her."

She paused, then asked, "How . . . did you know that? That I was at the vigil?"

"I told him you were there," Myra announced.

But has he told you he was, too? Twyla wondered. However, she knew better than to ask Myra that, even privately. She didn't want Miguel to find out that she had taken notice of him. It might confirm that she was indeed pumping him for information about the Saint Anthony statue just now, feeling out a connection between him and April. Of course, he had been very quick to make such a connection appear unlikely –

So, are you hiding something, Miguel? she wondered. *And, if so, why?*

Chapter 29

At the old Overton's department store converted into the *capilla* that housed the reproduction of Our Lady of Guadeloupe, Miguel took Twyla aside, much to the annoyance of Esteban who had cornered her for the last ten minutes, verbally barraging her in a mix of Spanish and English that was not so much broken as fragmented to Humpty Dumpty status – post-wall. Twyla's discomfort and disorientation had not been helped by his constantly dropping his gaze to her breasts.

"Thank you, for rescuing me," Twyla said to Miguel, immediately realizing that putting it that way was insulting his friend.

Fortunately, Miguel only smiled in response. "Esteban can be . . . 'pushy' I think is the figure of speech . . . with the ladies."

"Oh, well," Twyla said. "I'm just interested in being friends, anyway."

Miguel continued to smile. "Yes. You've obviously never dated a Mexican before. Which is one reason I think I should talk with you . . ."

Twyla arched an eyebrow. "Why does that make you think you should talk to me? And talk about what?"

"You cared for April Gurley – personally as well as professionally. Do you still want to help her, even though she's gone?"

"Very much so."

"Then come with me to my van. Right now."

Twyla stepped back from him. "What about Myra? Where is she, anyway?" she asked, craning her neck to look over Miguel's shoulder for her friend.

"Gone to the ladies room. She talked like she might be there for a while. Too many pork rinds for supper."

"Yeah, right. I mean, I'd feel better if she came with us."

"Well, you see, there is information that I have . . . in confidence. And Myra isn't discreet."

"Wait . . . 'confidence?' Whose confidence?"

Miguel said nothing in response; he only continued looking levelly at her.

"You mean . . . April's?"

He nodded.

Twyla's heart quickened. April had taken Miguel into her confidence? When did that happen? Could Miguel be who April had been sneaking out to meet secretly?

"How well did you know her?" Twyla asked.

"Not here," he said, voice low.

So, Twyla thought, *do I trust him? He knew April*, and *he believes in Eleggua. So, he* could *either be the person who sent her the Saint Anthony statue —*

— or the one who removed it.

Do I want to be alone with this guy?

"Miguel, I don't know," Twyla said. "Why do you have to tell me of all people? We just met."

"And before I met you, I knew no one whom I thought could use this information. You live in a nice, *white* neighborhood. And," he nodded back toward a still steaming Esteban, "you don't date Mexicans."

"Okay, then. I need to ask you something."

"Yes?"

"I mentioned earlier the Saint Anthony statue in April's room . . ."

"Yes?" Miguel asked, his eyes slightly narrowing.

"Well, you know, April's Saint Anthony was supposed to restore her health. That's what whoever sent the statue said in their letter. But they also insisted the statue be put behind the door for April's protection from harm. Now, I'm not Catholic, so I didn't know any different, but I was talking to this Catholic guy who knew about Saint Anthony, and he'd never heard about putting his icon behind a door. Someone else told me it was a Santeria thing."

"Yes," Miguel said slowly. He appeared to be thinking over whether to say any more or not. Then he continued. "Saint Anthony in that spot represents Eleggua, the lord of doorways. No one gets through without his permission."

"So . . . why did he permit April's killer to get in?" Twyla asked, hoping that she had cornered Miguel into having to acknowledge that the statue, and Eleggua's protection with it, must have been removed first. If *he* was the one who took it, she was hoping his reaction to being forced to acknowledge the statue's removal, even indirectly, would cause him to give himself away.

But Miguel was either too wily or too innocent to do that. Instead, he said, "Eleggua obviously allowed it . . . to fulfill some greater purpose. He is also the dealer of justice."

"What happened to April *wasn't* justice, though," Twyla said.

"Eleggua himself will decide what is just; what is truth; and what is a lie. Do not assume his perspective is your own. Things are not always as they seem. To the uninformed eye, 'Skim milk masquerades as cream.' Gilbert and Sullivan said that."

"*Who?*"

"Never mind. The important thing for you to know is that I can give you information. If you will only hear me out."

"But, you see, before I can do that, there's something else you and me have to consider."

"And that is – ?"

Almost in a panic now, afraid of losing the opportunity if she kept stalling, Twyla blurted out, "The possibility that whoever murdered April removed the Saint Anthony statue – and his protection – *first* so that he *could* get to her."

"But only a follower of Santeria would believe in the significance of the statue's placement," Miguel said, then realizing: "Oh . . . you are saying a disciple of Santeria might have killed April? Then, the statue *was* missing from behind the door when you found her?"

Twyla cast her gaze to the floor.

"Yes, it is, I can see that I'm right. You knew from Myra, from her Saint Anthony that I gave her, that there was a Santeria significance to that statue. And then you saw me at the vigil, didn't you? But we'd never met. Though Myra could have shown you a picture – no. You saw my van with 'Miguel's Mexican H.Q.' on it. You thought I could have taken the statue. That *I* could be the killer. That's why you came here tonight – with us," Miguel said.

Twyla raised her head and looked him in the eye. "That was one possibility. Look, I couldn't just ignore that, could I? Just because you're Myra's boyfriend?"

"Twyla, listen to me: you are looking in the wrong place for the source of April's troubles. I sent the Saint Anthony statue to protect her, because I feared for her safety. April . . . she was my friend."

Though she had suspected as much, hearing Miguel actually say it was a bit startling. "But how?" she asked. "How did that happen?"

"I will tell you . . . in my van."

"Miguel, I won't go with you without Myra."

"I understand your reluctance because of your suspicions . . . yes. Yes, it would be good if Myra were with us."

"And we don't leave the parking lot," Twyla said.

"We will not leave the parking lot, I promise."

"And I hold the van's keys. *Both* sets."

Miguel smiled. "I'll get Myra."

Chapter 30

When Myra returned from the restroom, Miguel called her aside, then said some things in Spanish to Jesus, Esteban, and Rodriquo. From time to time, the three men looked in Twyla's direction while he spoke, obviously unhappy that Miguel was making off with all the women.

Miguel opened the van's sliding door and he and Myra climbed inside. Twyla, however, stood outside until Miguel handed her the keys. Both sets. Then she stepped inside, and Miguel slid the door closed.

"Sug', why are you giving Twyla the car keys?" Myra asked.

"A gesture of goodwill."

"So, why do you need to make a gesture?"

"I am suspect in Twyla's eyes. For the murder of April Gurley."

Myra's jaw went slack. She looked back and forth from Miguel to Twyla for a few seconds, then her gaze riveted on Twyla.

"Why would you . . . ?" Myra asked. "Because he's 'a Mexican,' so he must be trouble? Twyla, I get that from Mama and Daddy, and I don't need it from a friend. If you *are* my friend . . . . I mean, that's why you wanted to get together? You were never interested in getting to know my friends, huh? Did my Mom put you up to this, to make Miguel look bad to me?"

"Myra," Twyla began. "It's nothing like that at all. I didn't mean to hurt you."

"It's a betrayal, Twyla," Myra insisted. "And it *does* hurt."

Twyla sighed. In Myra's tone, she heard her own bitterness and disappointment when confronting Lorna the other night. She really didn't know what to say. Why had Miguel felt the need to verbalize her suspicion?

Then Miguel spoke up. "Myra," he said, "there are things you do not know about April Gurley and me. Things I did not tell you because I was afraid you couldn't handle them . . . discreetly."

"I couldn't handle it? You mean, you were . . . together?" Myra asked, and clapped her mouth

Twyla hated seeing the pain in her friend's expression, but she couldn't help but think about those secret trips that April had taken.

"No, no," Miguel said, patting her hand reassuringly. "We never met . . . physically. Over the Internet."

"April frequented chat rooms?" Twyla asked. She immediately could see that as a possibility. April would have had anonymity that way; she could've slipped out of the mansion, in a matter of speaking, without worrying about drawing attention. And she was certainly lonely enough to reach out for some kind of human contact; Lorna had made that clear the other night.

"Not just any chat room," Miguel said. "April and I both joined an Internet support group: People Who Encounter Non-Corporal and Disembodied Entities. It was built around the same principle of any type of support group: the only people who truly understand your experience are those who share it. It's very difficult if not impossible to find empathy otherwise."

"But, Miguel baby," Myra whined. "I thought you and me *connected* . . ."

Miguel clasped her hand. "This was before you, my love. Both April and I needed a special friend. We began to branch off into private chat rooms apart from the rest of our group. That was when she started to open up and I began to learn things, deep feelings she was not free to share with anyone . . ."

"Even her mother and father?" Twyla asked.

"*Especially* her mother and father. These were things that, initially, could only be shared in mutual anonymity."

"Such as – ?" Twyla asked.

"*Such as* . . . she resented her stigmata. She questioned how such a thing could be of God. And she wanted to be rid of it. I don't think she could have ever acknowledged that to anyone who knew her; she'd been burying her questions and resentment for some time and she was miserable on the inside.

"Then she started investigating the history of her condition, and she learned that the stigmata is recorded nowhere in the New Testament. It is not among the miracles of the apostles. In fact, it was never reported until after the first century church was long gone. The first undisputed case did not occur until 1224 A.D. with Saint Francis of Assisi.

"That fact stirred her curiosity . . . and her suspicions." Miguel smiled. "I suspect her parents would not have gotten April the Internet if they knew how she was going to use it to educate herself right out of her sainthood."

"What? She got into Internet porn?" Myra asked.

"No, no," Miguel said. "She began to research secular explanations for her condition. She learned about something called *psychogenic purpora* – lesions resulting from emotional trauma. This spontaneous bleeding was documented as internal as well as external, and could come from areas atypical of traditional stigmata, such as the nose. *Psychogenic purpora* could also be linked with hallucinations –"

"Which would account for her visions of Gabriel," Twyla said.

"That was what April thought. Finally, she got up the courage to approach her mother about what she'd discovered. At first resistant to the idea, her mother's religious beliefs gave way to maternal concern. She was seeing for the first time how unhappy her daughter was . . . and had been for a long time. Of course, the family was not Catholic; I'm sure that made it easier to discard the Catholic explanation for her condition. So, April secretly began seeing a psychiatrist. To get rid of the stigmata."

"Get rid of it? How?" Twyla asked.

"April had learned of a case, a young black girl, who was a stigmatic, who was cured by hypnosis. She hoped that would work for her. But something was holding her back, something her doctor told her she would have to open up about before hypnosis could be effective."

"Then, she never did," Twyla said.

"Why do you say that?" Miguel asked.

"Because she was still bleeding from her hands in her coma – up to the day she died," Twyla said. "But wait; you said she went to her mother about the psychiatrist . . . what about her father?"

"April was most concerned that *he* not know."

"But, from what I've heard – from somebody who knew both Mr. Gurley and April – he wanted her to have a more normal life than her saintly status would allow. I would think he would be all for her losing her stigmata. Unless he was embarrassed by his child needing mental help."

"April was uncomfortable around her father," Miguel said. "She had been for some time, before our Internet conversations or her therapy began. But she wouldn't say why."

Because she'd caught him feeling up one of her friends, Twyla thought.

"In fact, during one of our chat room sessions, she even went so far as to say she felt threatened by him."

"'*Threatened?*' She put it that way?"

"Yes. Those are her words."

"Well, did she say why?"

"Other than it had something to do with her visits to the psychiatrist, no. I wasn't completely comfortable with her telling me everything – and to tell you the truth, I'm not comfortable now, speculating out loud," Miguel said.

"I mean, the fact we were anonymous during our initial Internet correspondence helped her open up at first," Miguel continued. "But by the time April told me about feeling threatened by her father, we'd exchanged our real names. It was getting kind of too real, you know? And I thought, too, 'What's the point?' Me, this Mexican immigrant, what could I do? Take on a rich, powerful white man like Vernon Gurley? I don't even have a green card. I couldn't afford to come under legal scrutiny."

"But you believe what April and her psychiatrist talked about *then* might have something to do with April's death, *now*. You don't have any idea who her doctor was?"

"No. But . . . she did tell me that she was keeping a record of their sessions on her computer diary —"

Twyla cut him off. "April kept a diary?"

"She had locked it away in her laptop's hard drive. Perhaps it records if she and her doctor discovered why she should feel threatened by her father."

He's really dancing around actually saying it because of Myra, Twyla thought. *But after what Lorna told me last night about Mr. Gurley groping her . . . . Maybe April broke off her friendship with Lorna, not out of anger, but to keep Lorna from being subjected to attention from Vernon Gurley that April was already receiving.* She winced.

"At any rate, as far as I know," Miguel said, "no one else knows about that diary, except for me, and no one could access it without the password anyway."

Twyla leaned forward, "And she gave you the password?"

Miguel sighed. "No. She wanted to, but I did not want that burden. I urged her to give it to someone else. She said there was no one else she could trust. Maybe she eventually found someone, I don't know. But, like I said, *I* couldn't go public. Not me. But you . . . you live in a nice, white neighborhood. You're a local woman. You have a respectable job. You could . . ."

"Not without the password," Twyla said. "If it's just my word against Vernon Gurley's, I wouldn't fare much better than you would, Miguel."

"We could . . . get the password," Miguel said, solemnly.

"What?" Twyla said. "You said you didn't know if she ever gave it to anyone else."

"I don't know anyone she gave it to, no. But I know someone who can . . . recover it for us, by his own means."

"You mean like a computer hacker?" Twyla asked. "But we'd have to get the computer first . . ."

"He should be able to help us with that as well."

"Well, when can we talk with this guy?"

"Tonight. Possibly within the hour. If you wish."

"I wish," Twyla said.

Miguel smiled and held out his hand for the return of his keys.

Twyla hesitated, then nodded at Myra. "Myra's coming to?"

"Try and keep me out now," Myra said, squeezing Miguel's arm.

"And what about your friends, Esteban and the other guys?" Twyla asked.

"I'll speak with them. They have friends and family here. It should be easy for them to arrange another ride home," Miguel said.

"And who exactly is this person we're going to see?" Twyla asked, reaching into her pocket, producing the keys, and handing them to Miguel.

"Saint Anthony," Miguel said with a smile. "The finder of lost things."

Chapter 31

Miguel went back inside the *capilla* to tell his friends that they'd have to change their plan for transportation. He was gone for only a few minutes, then returned to the van, cranked it up, and pulled out of the parking lot and onto the road.

"Now that those guys are gone . . . ," Miguel said, flicking on the van's CD player. Immediately Jim Morrison musically observed how strange people could be.

"So, they were okay with our ditching them?" Twyla asked.

"Not really," Miguel said. "They were disappointed that they wouldn't be seeing more of *you*, Twyla. I had to promise them another get together with Myra *and* her friend."

"Oh. Really?" Twyla said, smiling, wanting to appear agreeable so that she wouldn't offend Myra, but knowing that she would never again be hitching a ride in Miguel's Mexican HQ if it meant subjecting herself to being the object of desire for his friends.

Miguel turned his van now into the parking lot of Jack's Neck's only convenience store, the *Pick-Up Shop*.

"Does he work here?" Twyla asked. "This guy we're meeting?"

"No, no," Miguel said. "There are things here he likes."

"You mean you gotta bribe him to help us?"

"He will need persuading, yes. But don't worry. He usually ends up cooperating. *If* you approach him correctly. Are you two coming inside?" Miguel asked, hand hovering by the key in the ignition.

"I could use a soda," Myra said.

"Yeah, me, too, I guess," Twyla said.

"Very well, then," Miguel said with a smile, pulling the key from the ignition switch, opening the door, and stepping out onto the parking lot. Twyla and Myra followed.

Inside the store, the two women headed for the refrigerated sodas, Twyla picking a caffeine free diet soda, while Myra took a sugar enriched bottle of *Judder* – and a snack cake. When they caught up with Miguel, he was holding a box of dark-chocolate covered cherries.

"Does he have a sweet tooth?" Twyla asked, indicating the candies with a nod.

"Don't worry – he'll share," Miguel said with a smile. "I'll probably end up finishing these off, myself. Or give them to Myra."

Would Myra mind getting second hand candy from her boyfriend? Twyla wondered. She glanced over at her chubby friend who'd just finished shoving the snack cake she'd purchased into her mouth, and was sucking frosting off her fingers. *Probably not*, she decided.

At the check-out counter, there was a display box of $1.50 cigars. "Ah," Miguel said, "he'll want three of these."

What is it with this computer hack we're going to see? Twyla wondered. *You gotta bribe him with sweets* and *smokes? I know these geeks can be eccentric, but still –"*

Their purchases complete, the trio climbed back into the van and headed for their meeting, this time to the strains of Jim Morrison's insisting his fire be lit.

A mile down the street from the convenience store, Miguel took a left turn and Twyla saw that they were entering Jack's Neck's equivalent of Spanish Harlem. In front of a row of run-down houses, a thin man, barely more than a boy, was sprawled shirtless on the sidewalk, a bottle of *Jack Daniels* overturned beside him. A convenience store building, abandoned by the franchise to the encroaching Latin populace, had been converted into a homegrown grocery store carrying "authentic Mexican foods"— *Tienda Mexicana*. Miguel's Mexican DVD, or, as it was rendered on the sign, *Los Videos Latino de Miguel*, was at the corner across from the grocer.

In between was a community billboard, advertising *Minchew's Bail Bonding* ("*Se Habla Española*") and displaying posters for several Mexican bands and musical groups that drew their audience from the local migrant population.

Miguel pulled into his store's parking lot, switched off the van, unbuckled, and, opening his door, started to get out. Myra was also opening her door. Twyla hesitated.

"Wait," she said. "I don't understand. Why are we stopping by your store? Are you going to bribe this guy with some free rentals or something? Or does he work for you?"

"No," Miguel said, turning around to address her. "But we *will* meet him here. Ah, I almost forgot . . . ," he turned back around and ejected the disc from the CD player, ". . . The Doors are a particular favorite."

"So, you're gonna call him?"

"Yes," Miguel said, closing the door to the driver's side with a smile. "Exactly."

Miguel opened his store's door, ushered the ladies in, and flicked on the light. Twyla found herself looking at rows of video and DVD boxes, posters, and promotional cardboard stand-ups, with logos and blurbs all in Spanish. Myra walked over to the shelves, a section marked *Novellas de Television*.

"Darn," she said. "That Erik Estrada soap is always out."

Miguel excused himself, opened a door, and stepped into the back of the store. Twyla could tell that there was someone else there. Was this their contact? She quietly stepped toward the back, wanting to get some idea of what she was in for.

And then she turned a corner, and her eyes started at what she saw. It was the last two people she would have expected, and certainly not together: El Santo and Lorna Doone Delongpre.

Chapter 32

She immediately realized that she was not looking at Lorna or Santo, not in person, but a life size cardboard cut out of them. Lorna was wearing an outfit resembling a French cut one-piece bathing suit with most of the middle missing, showing off a fair amount of her ample bosom. *Though,* Twyla thought, *that two dimensional cut-out is the flattest Lorna's chest has been since she was eleven.*

The logo at the bottom of the stand-up read *El Santo y La Voluptua Ensemble Contra des Mujenas Vampiras.*

She hasn't ever talked about her movie career beyond Bodacious Barbarian Babe In Dinosaur Hell, Twyla thought. *I wonder if Lamar knows about this?*

Recovering from the surprise, she continued to make her way toward the back, where Miguel was still talking. Suddenly, a young white man with piercings in his nose, brow, and ears, stepped through the door, almost bumping into her. In his hands, he carried a jar with a large hairy spider inside it. He looked at Twyla, smiled, then held up the jar.

"She took this out of me," he said. "She reached inside my wrist and no more carpal tunnel syndrome. You're in good hands now."

He blissfully walked on by her and out the video store's front entrance. "She?" Twyla asked the empty space where the man had stood, then looked through the doorway.

A middle aged woman with a premature shock of gray running

through her hair, dressed in a smock over her street clothes, stood at the base of a shrine, tiered to resemble a Mayan pyramid. Her hands were covered in fresh blood, apparently that of the young man who had passed her, though she had seen no bandage nor open bleeding wound on either of his wrists when he had held up the jar to show her the spider.

"Twyla, come on in," Miguel said. He had stepped up beside the woman. "This is Jenny Barefoot."

Twyla stepped into the room but hesitantly. She was able to see the shrine better now. Among the icons of saints were jars filled with rotting roses dropping petals, giving a sickening sweet scent to the room. At the pinnacle was a large crucifix, the Christ on it bleeding. Side by side, on an equal level with the Christus, was a statue of a man dressed as an ancient Aztec. It, too, was bleeding.

"Jenny," Miguel said, "this is Twyla Chayne."

"Nice to meet you," Jenny said. "I don't mean to be rude, but I have just finished an operation. I must show my respects to Cuauhtémoc." Twyla watched the bloody hands of Jenny Barefoot reach out and touch the base of the Aztec man – three times, she noted.

"Jenny was in the same Internet support club for People Who Encounter Non-Corporal and Disembodied Entities as April and I. She performs psychic surgery with her bare hands on people in need." Miguel nodded respectfully toward the statue of the Aztec. "Her spirit guide was tortured to death by the Conquistadors."

"Is this who we're here to meet?" Twyla asked, hoping the answer was "no." Because she knew something about so-called psychic surgeons like Jenny Barefoot. The ones she'd read about in the tabloids were people in the Philippines, and they didn't have any spirit guides, Aztec or otherwise. But they pulled tumors and things out of people with their bare hands. Or that was what they claimed, anyway. Twyla had watched a cable expose on the "phenomenon" that revealed it as sleight-of-hand trickery.

I mean, Twyla thought, *you can almost buy a tumor that's pulled out of someone, something that looked like it might grow inside you, but taking out a* spider *from somebody's wrist? Saying* that's *the cause of carpal tunnel syndrome?*

"No," Miguel was saying. "Jenny's here because I let her use the back of my shop for her surgeries. She – and Cuauhtémoc – will be leaving in few minutes. Then our contact will join us here."

Oh, April, Twyla thought. *What kind of shams were you associating with, honey? Were these the only people you could go to, to talk about your problems?*

Miguel had barely stopped speaking when there was a banging on the front door.

"Is that who we're waiting for?" Twyla asked.

Miguel's eyes narrowed and he cocked his head slightly. "No," he said. "That's the front door. He wouldn't come that way. That's just someone who can't read the 'Closed' sign wanting to get in the store. He checked his watch. "We closed thirty minutes ago, so it looks like whoever it is is going to have to go to *Redbox* instead. Or they can use the drop-off box if that's what they need to do. C'mon –"

The pounding began anew, harder now. Miguel yelled back something in Spanish. Whether the person there heard or not, they were not letting up. Miguel rolled his eyes. "Excuse me, ladies," he said and stepped out of the back room to answer the door.

Twyla turned around and looked at Myra, who shrugged her shoulders. Then Twyla noticed that Jenny Barefoot – and Cuauhtémoc – had disappeared while Twyla's back was turned. The bleeding statue of the Aztec warrior *and* the crucifix with the bleeding body of Christ were both missing from the apex of the tiered shelves with their jars of wilting roses.

She could hear a voice that wasn't Miguel's – he must have opened the door and let the guy in. So maybe it was their contact at the front door after all.

Twyla stepped out of the back room to see, and almost immediately ducked out of sight.

Because there was Shametrice's son, Demarcus, talking angrily to Miguel, and he'd flashed his scowl her way when she'd stepped out of the back.

"Who the hell's that? Who's back there?" she heard Demarcus demand of Miguel.

Knowing Demarcus's record, this could be a robbery, Twyla thought. But he was supposed to be in jail again. Shametrice must have been able to post bail. Was Demarcus that inconsiderate of his mother, or just so crazy, that he'd immediately commit another crime?

Or was Demarcus their contact?

Twyla hoped not. That boy was trouble. But Miguel *had* said that their contact could get the laptop out of the Gurley house. That could involve breaking and entering. But could Demarcus dredge up the password to April's computer? She didn't know where he would have learned to hack in the crack houses Shametrice said he lived in.

At least he hadn't recognized her. Twyla knew him from pictures Shametrice carried in her pocketbook – innocent childhood pictures, and several of a teenage Demarcus smiling shyly. That was an image hard to reconcile with the furious face that had looked her way momentarily before Miguel had turned, seen her, and stepped in Demarcus's line of vision. Miguel obviously didn't want Demarcus to be aware of the girls back there.

But Demarcus *had* seen her. If it was robbery, would he be content with the cash register or safe, or would he come for her and Myra, too? She wondered if he would stop with robbing them. Was Demarcus capable of rape or murder?

Twyla saw that Myra was obviously doing a "loves me; loves me not" plucking the petals of one of the wilting roses from the tiers. She looked so childlike, Twyla thought, so innocent. Quite the painful contrast with the potential violence that was brewing just a few yards away. Again, she felt protective of her friend, more intensely than she had the day before at Wahl-Mart when she'd cautioned Myra about Miguel. And she also felt a bit guilty for giving Myra the impression that she thought her relationship with Miguel was okay by pretending she wanted to meet him and his friends.

Twyla strained to listen, to catch some hint of exactly what was going on out there. What was Demarcus saying?

". . . no good now . . . not with her . . ."

Who? Twyla wondered. *He saw me in the back. Am I who he means?*

Maybe this is a robbery, but somehow he knows my face, knows I know his mother, and I could identify him.

She chanced another peek, and saw that Miguel and Demarcus had now gone into a little office cubicle from where Miguel managed his business. The door was shut, but there was a window, and Twyla could see an open sack on Miguel's desk, and Demarcus looking at him no longer angrily but expectantly.

Good, Twyla thought. *I hate for Miguel to get robbed, but if that'll satisfy Demarcus, it coulda been a whole lot worse.*

"What's keepin' Miguel?" Myra asked.

"Must've had to take care of a disgruntled customer, sug'," Twyla said.

The answer satisfied Myra, who turned her attention back to the roses on the tiers.

"Where'd she go, by the way?" Twyla asked.

"Jenny?" Myra said. "I didn't see her leave. You hardly ever do; or see when she arrives. Nobody knows where she goes when she's done, either. I don't know how anybody would ever get in touch with her if she wasn't on the Internet. Except for Cuauhtémoc, of course. They're a team, you know."

A regular Mork and Mindy, Twyla thought.

After a few more minutes, Miguel reappeared smiling apologetically, but alone. He was carrying the sack that Twyla thought Demarcus had brought. And it wasn't empty.

"What was that about, baby?" Myra asked, nodding toward the bag. "You got some returns from somebody there?"

"That was other business," Miguel said, looking at Twyla, whom he knew had actually seen Demarcus.

"'kay. Excuse me. I really want to see what you got, but –," Myra stepped into the employees' restroom. "Pork rinds," she explained as she shut the door behind her.

"But it wasn't an overdue video, was it, Miguel?" Twyla asked when they were alone. "I know that guy. I mean, I work with his mother. Were you in trouble just now?"

"No. Demarcus was returning some Santeria mystical objects."

"Wait . . . Demarcus is into Santeria?"

"Not really. He'd heard of some criminals in Florida who'd used Santeria to make themselves invisible to the authorities, so he showed up on my doorstep demanding some mystical protection of his own. I gave him some icons and charms to position around his home and for a while he was practically invincible. But his mother . . . when she found out what those objects were for, that they weren't Christian but occult, she made him take them out of the house. Refunds are not normally my policy, but, as you probably saw Demarcus wasn't going to take 'no' for an answer."

"You were smart not to make him any madder than he was. I know about him. That boy's trouble."

"Yes, well, I was very willing to accommodate him when I saw what he was returning. Look what he brought us —"

Miguel pulled out a statue of Saint Anthony from the bag.

Chapter 33

For an instant, Twyla couldn't help but wonder if she was looking at *that* Saint Anthony, the one from April's room. But, of course, it wasn't. This was the Saint Anthony that she'd noticed missing from behind Shametrice's front door the other day.

"What do you mean, this statue is for 'us'?" Twyla asked.

"I told you you would meet the restorer of lost things tonight."

"And *this* is him?"

Miguel chuckled. "No. That's not what I meant. I didn't even know Demarcus would be returning this icon tonight when I invited you over," he said, carrying the Saint Anthony statue to where it would be behind the back door when it was opened. *Just like in April's room*, Twyla thought.

"But everything interconnects," Miguel was saying. "And I don't think Demarcus's showing up with this is mere coincidence, either. More like 'synchronicity.'"

"'Synchronicity?' Didn't Sting say that?" Twyla asked.

"Karl Jung and Wolfgang Pauli. This icon is a good omen, that he will be receptive to us this night, that he is favorably disposed our way. The arrival at this moment of the Saint Anthony is his gracious way of acknowledging *you*, Twyla. After all, that's how you know him."

Twyla looked back at the Saint Anthony statue where Miguel had placed it, behind the door. "Eleggua," she said. "Saint Anthony in that spot means Eleggua –"

"You'll probably need to offer him something directly, you know, to show you appreciate the attention. I usually give the cigars. Here –" Miguel tore the plastic from the box of chocolate covered cherries and handed them to her.

She did not take them. "Huh? Wait a minute. What are you saying? Eleggua is our 'contact?' You said –"

"I said we were going to meet Saint Anthony, the finder of lost things. We are."

"No," Twyla said. "You tricked me into coming over here. I'm not participating in some Santeria ritual with you. What – do you think you can convert me, like you did Myra?"

Miguel withdrew the box of candy and smiled. "No, Twyla. You misunderstand."

By this time Myra was coming out of the restroom. "What's goin' on out here?" she asked.

"He wants to get me in on a ritual, Myra. That's what this is all about."

"He's tryin' to *help* you Twy, for April," Myra said with a frown, taking her place at Miguel's side and hooking his arm with hers. "That's all."

"Don't make me the bad guy here, Myra. He set this up. Can't you see that? He made me think we were meeting somebody, a person –"

"We *are*," Miguel said.

"You let me think it was a computer hacker! And how much did you know Myra? Back at the store when we were picking out things to offer Eleggua?"

Myra's face turned red, and she tucked her head slightly. "Miguel told me I wasn't ever supposed to tell anyone about the rituals. Anyone that wasn't one of us."

"Well, wasn't it obvious to you that he intended to make me 'one of you' tonight? Myra, I'm a Christian. You know I wouldn't want to do this witchcraft. And now you've let him get me here, stranded I guess. Well, you two do whatever you want to. I won't be any part of it. I'm out of

149

here."

Right, she thought. *I can't exactly walk back to Tar Forks on my own. Maybe they'll let me sit in the van until they're done.* She started toward the door.

"Wait, Twyla," Miguel said. She stopped, hoping he was going to hand her the keys to the van.

"You can't go," Miguel was saying. "The ritual requires a minimum of three people. Like I got three cigars at the store? Three is Eleggua's number. The ritual won't work unless its three or a multiple of three –"

"Then I guess you're out of luck," Twyla said, putting her hand to the door knob.

"Have you forgotten what we're here for?" Miguel asked.

Twyla stopped, though she didn't turn around.

"The password to April's diary is lost. Eleggua, Saint Anthony, finds lost things. He opens doors, and we need him to give us the key we need to open her computer file, How else are we going to see that her killer is punished? That justice is done by April? Eleggua is the minister of justice."

"C'mon, Twy," Myra said. "I know you're a Christian. So am I. I still believe in Jesus. But Santeria does good stuff, too. I mean, if Eleggua helps us see that justice is done, he can't be bad, can he?"

Twyla turned around to face them. Myra's question suddenly made her suspicious of just what Miguel was trying to accomplish here tonight. She remembered she'd thought it odd how Miguel had the sudden change of heart back at the *capilla,* when he'd decided it might be a good idea after all for Myra to join them in the van. Maybe Miguel had seen a way that he could profit from letting Myra in on his secrets?

You already know the password to April's computer journal, don't you Miguel? she thought. *April did tell you. And you would have told me back in your van, and this ritual wouldn't be happening, if you hadn't brought Myra into it. All of this is an act of yours to confirm for Myra that Santeria is true, that it is a benign alternative to Christianity. Just like Myra had said, wouldn't Eleggua's helping to bring April's killer to justice be a good thing?*

That would widen the gulf between Myra and her church-going parents, whose

MURDER IN THE MIRACLE ROOM

disapproval of Miguel probably has to do with his occult practices. He admitted he has no green card. He needs Myra to marry him or he could lose the business – the life – he's made for himself in America.

So now, if I play along and ask "Eleggua" the password, I'll be helping Miguel deceive Myra. But it's not likely that Miguel will give the password any other way now. And having that password could make the difference in determining if April's father was the primary suspect for his daughter's murder.

So what do I do?

Then she remembered the scam Jenny Barefoot was running in Miguel's store's backroom. *You're in on that, too, aren't you, Miguel? I bet you're no more a wizard than your friend Jenny is.*

And if you're a fake, it's not really witchcraft, is it? And maybe I can get the password you know and still discredit you and your Santeria to Myra.

"Twy?"

"Okay, Myra, you're right," Twyla said. "I can't let my narrow mindedness get in the way of helping April get justice."

"Excellent," Miguel said. Myra smiled. Then Miguel placed the three cigars he'd bought in his breast pocket. "By the way, you mentioned Sting and The Police when I mentioned synchronicity. But remember the band of choice tonight – *his* choice – is The Doors." Miguel produced the CD he'd played in the van, walked over to a portable stereo on a shelf nearby, popped in the disc, and pressed "Play."

Jim Morrison immediately repeatedly exhorted breaking through to the other side to a driving beat at the stereo's maximum volume.

"'We must clear the borders of perception.' Aldous Huxley said that. Now, excuse me," Miguel shouted over the din, "I go to call Eleggua."

Miguel walked out of the door that opened onto the backyard. The night was warm and for a moment, before the door closed behind Miguel, Twyla recognized a barn yard smell.

"Why couldn't he just do what he's going to do in here?" Twyla asked Myra loudly.

"You probably don't want to see –"

"I see a lot of stuff in home health care –"

151

"He's going to tear off a chicken's head, coat his face in blood, pluck feathers, and stick them in the blood. On his face."

"Oh. Okay. You're right. I don't want to see that. I mean, you like it on your plate, but you don't want to see how it got there, right?" Twyla swallowed hard. "Although . . . I guess Colonel Sanders didn't actually rip off any chickens' heads by hand, huh? P.E.T.A. would be all over that. Does Miguel ever worry about them? P.E.T.A.?"

She was rambling, she knew, but she was nervous. Even though she believed Miguel was faking his actual conjuring, she doubted he was faking the decapitation going on out there.

"*Subisse el santo a su caballa* is what they call it," Myra said, beaming at her success in getting that phrase out of her mouth. "It takes some getting used to at first."

"Well, I don't plan to get used to it. This is it for me and Santeria. You make sure Miguel understands that."

The door began to open. Twyla beat a quick retreat to the other side of the room. She wasn't going to be standing close by if Miguel was still dripping chicken blood – or chicken *anything* for that matter.

The back door now open, a shadowy Miguel stepped inside. Behind him, in the night, illuminated by a street light, feathers swirled in the air in slow motion, like flakes shaken inside a snow globe. The effect was tranquil, in contrast to the violence that had sent the feathers floating. Some of the gory aftermath of his endeavors coated Miguel's face now: blood and feathers, just as Myra had said.

There was also blood dripping from his hands where she saw a half-plucked headless chicken. He dropped the carcass at the base of the Saint Anthony statue. It landed with a wet sound, splattering the icon.

"Okay, you made the sacrifice. Did Eleggua give you the password?" Twyla asked, stomach lurching slightly.

"Twy, that's not Miguel. Not now," Myra said. "His body has been mounted – like a horse – to convey Eleggua, so Eleggua can talk to us."

"You're saying Miguel's possessed now?"

"It's not like that, like you're thinking, like *The Exorcist*. I mean, yeah, when the *orisha* enters Miguel's body, he might get thrown around some, but it doesn't hurt when it's one of them. He'll feel like he's just had a good nap when he comes to."

Both girls looked at Miguel who still had not spoken. Despite his disheveled appearance, he stood so regally poised that he seemed to Twyla to have actually grown taller. He beckoned toward the CD player which was still playing Doors music.

"Silence the *bembe*," he commanded, a baritone in his voice that wasn't there before. Immediately Myra clicked it off.

Keeping his eyes on Twyla, Miguel took one of the three cigars from his breast pocket, lit it up, puffed on it, and blew out a plume of blue smoke from the corner of his mouth.

"You see, Twyla," Myra, who had walked over to where her friend stood, said. "Miguel doesn't smoke. But Eleggua does; did you see how he just lit that cigar up and went at it? And Miguel's not even sick or anything."

"Silence!" Miguel said, cutting off Twyla's response. "Myra, do not cast your pearls before swine."

"*Excuse me?*" Twyla said.

"I tire of your ingratitude. You do not even honor me as Saint Anthony when you should for what I've already restored to you. Why should I help you now?"

"What?" Twyla asked. "What do you mean? I haven't lost anything –"

"But you *have* found something that was lost. Just recently."

"I don't know what you're talking abou– ." Twyla stopped. He was still looking her in the eyes.

Lorna, Twyla thought. *I found a lost friend.*

She felt her cheeks burn and knew that Miguel knew that he had hit a nerve.

"Okay," she said, trying to recover. "If you know so much, what did I find?"

"Do not presume to try me," Miguel said, royal displeasure in his voice. "I consider your questions and answer them as I think fit. I do not perform at your command."

But you are performing, Miguel. All this is just smoke and mirrors.

153

"Twyla," Myra was saying, "don't you think you should apologize to Eleggua? I mean, we *are* trying to help April, right?"

Twyla sighed. "Okay. I'm sorry."

Without speaking, Miguel held the palm of one hand out to her.

"What?" Twyla asked.

"The *candy*, Twy," Myra said.

"Oh," Twyla said, hastily opening the box and producing a chocolate covered cherry which she put in Miguel's hand. He didn't withdraw it though, and his glare returned.

"Three, Twy," Myra reminded her. "You only give him gifts in three or its multiples."

Feeling much put upon, Twyla took out two more pieces of candy and put them in Miguel's palm. This time he accepted, withdrawing his hand, though he regarded Twyla with the expression of someone contemptuous of a fool.

Two of the candies he put in his pants pocket, then removed his cigar so that he could bite into the third chocolate covered cherry. He chewed it slowly, with relish, then held up a severed piece of the candy still in his hand, the scarlet fruit bright against the dark chocolate.

"These are my colors," he said. "Three is my number. My gifts to you are also threefold. Listen: the word that is lost sang real."

"Sang real *what*?" Twyla asked. "'Real' good? Who was doing any singing, anyway? April?"

"You are not listening. And you're asking the wrong question. 'Those who wish to succeed must ask the right preliminary questions.' Aristotle said that."

"So, what – you're channeling Aristotle, now?" Twyla asked.

Miguel frowned. "No. I was quoting, actually."

"Okay, so what about *this* question, Aristotle, or Karl Jung or whoever else you got in there: how are we supposed to get April's laptop? Miguel said you could help us get in the mansion."

"My gifts are threefold," Miguel repeated. "You have the key that you need."

"I have a key that *Mr. Gurley* gave to me. But he could've changed the locks, and the entry number to the security system's key pad could have been changed –"

"I have set before thee an open door, and no man can shut it. The door before you is opened, and you will certainly pass through. And yet one more door will I open for you."

"No, that's okay."

"There are many doors, and Eleggua opens them all," he said. "Do you want justice? I am the god of justice."

"Well, sure."

Twyla noticed there was a faraway look in Miguel's eyes while he was saying this last bit. It had not been there before. When had his eyes glazed over? After he quoted Aristotle?

"Then remember *I* will decide what is and is not just. There are many perspectives. Sometimes a door opens to somewhere else, a place that holds what we did not suspect. And then we see what has always been there, and we cannot help but see it afterward, even after the door is shut again. Even when we wish we could stop seeing."

He took another drag on the cigar, and expelled again the magically blue smoke. Then Miguel jerked three times, as though a sneeze shook him, except there was no actual sneeze. His eyes focused again. Suddenly aware of *something* in his mouth, he let the cigar loll over his lower lip for a moment, then let it drop.

"Anybody got a breath mint?" he asked.

Chapter 34

The next morning, Twyla found herself staring at the phone in her room. Occasionally, she would pick up the receiver, her finger would circle the air above the dial, and then she would put the receiver back in the cradle, and stare at it again.

Okay, she thought. Here's the thing. *Do I want to pursue this when I have no real idea what to do next? For all his mumbo-jumbo posturing, I'm not sure that Miguel actually gave me any password. Or did I miss something?*

Because Miguel had seemed really certain that he – make that "Eleggua" – *had* given it to her. Of course, the catch was, that since he was supposed to be possessed at the time, he could have no memory of what "Eleggua" had said. Anyway, that was the way he had explained possession to Myra, and now he had to stick to those rules.

Otherwise, he would be open to any accusation she might make that he already knew the password, and that it was Miguel, not Eleggua, talking last night.

In the van, on their way back to Twyla's home, she had complained to Miguel of the cryptic nature of the message. But Miguel insisted, "Eleggua has told you all that you need to know to access April's diary. He has given you the key. You must put it in the lock and turn it yourself."

Ah, yes . . . that elusive lock. There was going to be no point in figuring out the key if she couldn't get a hold of April's laptop. She could, of course, simply tell the authorities what Miguel had told her about April's fear of her father, hoping that they would consequently confiscate the computer. But they wouldn't be willing to affront the powerful Mr. Gurley without knowing the source of her information. In which case Miguel would come under the scrutiny that could result in the deportation he'd sought to avoid by not coming forward himself. And as much as Twyla thought that would be a good thing in the long run, she didn't want to be responsible for giving that emotional blow to Myra.

And, of course, if it came out that she got the password through a Santeria possession ritual, she would be dismissed as a flake. All she would accomplish would be to alert Vernon Gurley to the existence of April's diary and give him the opportunity to make it disappear.

No, she was going to have to get to that laptop without April's father knowing.

And her best chance to do that was to contact Shametrice.

Twyla was still stinging from her friend's betrayal. In truth, the fact that it was Shametrice she'd have to go to for help was as much a cause for her hesitation to pursue this lead as anything.

But this was about justice for April. And clearing her own name . . .

She dialed Shametrice's number, still half way hoping she was out, maybe at the Fall Festival going on at the Tar Fork's waterfront today. Though, of course, it was doubtful Shametrice felt much like celebrating anything.

"Hello?"

It was Shametrice's voice, but there was a weariness in her tone that was atypical. Twyla felt an involuntary rush of pity for her old friend. Even when things had gone bad with Demarcus in the past, Shametrice had remained positive because of her faith. But when Shametrice added April's death to Demarcus getting in trouble yet again – and now Twyla's own falling out with her – well, it was no wonder if circumstances were taking their toll on her.

"Hi, Shametrice, sug'," Twyla said.

"Twy? Oh, honey, it's so good to hear from you."

"How are you holding up, sug'?"

"Well, I was able to post bail for Demarcus. I thank God for my congregation's mercy and compassion. But he hasn't even said 'thank you Mama' or anything that might indicate he's sorry. If he was truly repentant, you know, I could get through this, 'cause I'd have some hope things would get better."

Twyla, of course, thought of the angry Demarcus she'd seen the night before. No doubt Shametrice didn't even know where her son had been last night. And Twyla certainly wasn't going to tell her.

"Sug'," Twyla said. "You just hang in there, okay? Look, I'm sorry I stormed out of your house the other day. I mean, I'm not apologizing for being angry, I think I had every right, but I know you weren't trying to hurt me. . ."

"Honey, that was the last thing I meant to do. I knew Tate would try and contact you eventually, and I wanted to be there for you as well as him when that happened. I was just trying to make a bad situation not so bad. I'm sorry."

"It's all right. I forgive you. So, don't let that worry you anymore, okay? I'm gonna get back over there before too long, I promise. So . . . look . . . with all that's on you, I didn't know if you've had time to close down April's website or not. Are you working on it at the mansion or at home?"

"Not at home. I can't have something expensive like that laptop around the house for Demarcus to steal and sell for drug money. I couldn't afford to replace it. No, the laptop's still in the Gurley mansion. But, see, I can shut the website down using one of the computers down at the public library. No need for unnecessary risks."

"Yeah, well, look: it looks like there's something back at the Gurley mansion that I need to get. Is the security code still the same?"

"No. No, it's not. Mr. Gurley told me he was going to change the security code as soon as he could. There was no need anymore for anyone else to know how to get in the mansion, now that April was gone. You'll have to talk to him."

"Oh. Okay. Well, then . . . you take care, sug'. I'm praying for you."

"Thank you, hon. God bless you."

Twyla hung up, not quite knowing to feel relieved or frustrated. If the only way she was going to get to that laptop was to sneak into the Gurley mansion and take it – well, then it wasn't going to happen. Not if all she had to go on was Miguel's clue. It was just too sketchy a thing, and she'd be taking some major risks –

The phone rang, the vibration of the receiver still under hand startling her.

She picked it up.

"Hello?"

"May I speak with Twyla Chayne?" A man's voice, familiar but not one she could place.

"Who's calling?" she asked.

"Detective Grell. Tar Forks P.D. I'm investigating the murder of April Gurley. I questioned you at the crime scene."

Twyla couldn't speak.

"Miss Chayne?"

"Yeah, detective," she said, winding the phone's cord tightly around the fingers of her other hand. "I remember. Sure. What, uh, can I do for you?"

"You can come down to the police department."

"For?"

"For more questioning, Miss Chayne. This is still an on-going investigation. And you're still one of the suspects."

" 'One of?' So you have others."

"I can't discuss that with you, Miss Chayne."

"Waitaminute . . . you're still looking at suspects . . . . Then, the surveillance video at the nurse's station . . . that didn't show the killer?"

"I can't tell you that, Miss Chayne –"

"You've already told me by telling me I'm still a suspect! If you had footage of the killer in action, that wouldn't be the case. How can the killer not be on the video?"

"Miss Chayne, I'm asking you to come down to police department for further questioning. Will you come on your own? Or should I send someone over for you?"

"N-no. That won't be necessary. When?"

"Right now. Will that be a problem?"

"No. No problem. I'm, uh, on my way."

Gnawing her lower lip and disengaging the hand she'd entwined in the phone's cord, Twyla returned the receiver to its cradle.

"Not good," she said to herself, wondering if they had been able to lift a fingerprint from the power cord to the hard drive recording what the camera in April's room saw. Any other fingerprints in the wing, she had figured, were neutral in terms of casting suspicion and probably more than her own were on the door knobs. But if they had evidence that she had handled the cable to that hard drive which they'd found disconnected . . . .

"Not good at all," she said again.

So, she thought as she made her way to her car, *do I come forward with accusations against Mr. Gurley, even with nothing to back it up but Miguel's word that April had feared her father?*

No, she decided. *That would look desperate, like I was just trying to throw off suspicion. But, if they don't lock me up, I'm going to really have to reconsider getting April's laptop out of the Gurley mansion.*

As she neared her car, she noticed something wasn't right: the door on the driver's side was partially open. That she would have left it that way was very unlikely. Due to her obsessive compulsive behavior, she was prone to circle the car at least twice after getting out, checking each door by repeatedly tugging on their handles "You're gonna pull 'em off, Twy," her mother had told her more than once.

So, she was certain she'd left them locked. Had her mother or dad been in her car while she was out last night? Unlikely. They both had their own automobiles, and there was no reason either of them would be looking for something in her car.

Pulling the door the rest of the way open and bending inside, she immediately noted the carrying case she kept her CDs in was not where she usually left it. A quick search inside confirmed that her CDs were not just misplaced. They had been taken.

Slamming the door shut, Twyla swore mentally and then immediately repented. *I oughta be praying instead of cussin'*, she thought. *Lord, help me. You know I'm innocent.*

At least she would be taking the car to the police; that ought to expedite getting on the trail of whoever had robbed her.

You know . . . a real criminal.

She cranked up the car, pulled out of the driveway, and began a trip she would never complete.

Chapter 35

Twyla chose to drive along Highway 54 to circumnavigate the downtown traffic of the Fall Festival going on at the waterfront. The festival crowd would mean no available parking close to the police station. She'd probably have to walk several blocks. In the Indian Summer heat. Great. Just great.

Then her car cut off with her a good two miles from town. Tempted to swear out loud this time, Twyla managed to coast the automobile to the side of the road before it completely lost momentum.

A few attempts at starting the car produced not-so-much as a spark from the ignition. She had her cell phone, of course, but who would she call for help? Not her mama or daddy, of course; she didn't want them to find out she was being questioned a second time. And her mom could always pick up when she was trying to hide something. Lorna had pegged it right the other night: when Twy was a kid, she always gave herself away. That was probably why Detective Grell was calling her in now. He could tell she was hiding something the first time he questioned her.

Thank you, Lamar, she thought. *Thanks so much for deceiving me and making my life so much more interesting. I wonder if it's dawned on you yet that you've got a snow ball's chance in Gehenna with Lorna.*

Of course, she could just call the police. That's where she was heading, after all. But then she thought of the police station, right on the waterfront, and the Fall Festival going on. The whole town would be there, and somebody she knew would be certain to see her ride in with a police escort. She knew how she always thought the worst when she saw someone getting a police ride during Fall Fest: you assumed they were public drunks who'd been acting disorderly. And if her respectability were trashed, all it would take would be one call to her boss – and what could she say in her own defense? "Oh, I wasn't really drunk. I'd just been called in for further questioning concerning the death of one of my clients."

She couldn't reach any of her friends by her cell. Nor was she calling one of her church family to drop her off at the police station. *No, that would* definitely *get back to Mama –*

The town towing service, then.

"The truck is out and there are four other calls ahead of yours," she was told.

Of course. Fall Fest. Mozingo Towing*'s Biggest Day. Illegal parking everywhere. And* somebody *had to get the wrecked cars of those drunk drivers the police had hauled in.*

Then she became aware of a car pulling to the side of the road, just ahead of her. The driver's door opened, and she immediately shrank in her seat.

Uncle Tate.

The air conditioner had gone out with the car. She'd had to roll her window down. Now she quickly rolled it back up.

Smiling, Tate bent down to look through the window.

"Hey, girl . . . havin' car trouble?"

Twyla didn't say anything. She just shook her head emphatically "no."

Still smiling, Tate said, "Oh? You're just sitting in there sweating cause you're trying to drop a few pounds?"

"Go away, Tate," Twyla said, the glass muting her voice but not her revulsion.

Tate made a rolling gesture with his hand. "I think I could help. You know I'm a mechanic."

"I said, go away. I don't want any help from you."

"C'mon, Twy, this is silly. Let me help you. I know you gotta be burning up in there. Roll down your window."

Twyla held up her cell phone. "I'll call the police," she said.

"And tell 'em what? You're being harassed by someone trying to help you get your car started? Look, at least pop the hood so I can look at your problem. I might only need to connect something back."

"Or you could disconnect something and make me have a wreck."

Tate cast his gaze to the ground. After a moment he looked up.

"Twy, Shametrice believes in me. Why can't you?"

"If you really want to help, get somebody else to come out here to help me. And then you don't come back with them."

"Twy, I understand you don't have any use for me, but you're still my niece, and I'm a changed man. The Bible says to do good expectin' nothin' in return, and that's what I'm prepared to do. But if you'd rather roast than trust me, then you're just being bull-headed.

"What if someone else doesn't come by? It's too late in the year for beach traffic and everybody in town is down on the waterfront. Are you gonna get out and walk in this heat?" Tate asked.

Her jaw set, Twyla's stare at Tate was sizzling . . . but so was the heat.

She popped the hood.

With that, Tate went around to the front of the car and began feeling for the release mechanism under the front of the hood.

"All right, Tate. You've succeeded in the first stage of your campaign to help the little old lady across the street whether she wants to go or not."

At least the raised hood blocked him from her view.

And then she saw another car suddenly appear in her rearview mirror.

Her elation immediately began to lose air, however, as she realized two things. First, she'd have to get out of the car to flag the car down and thus expose herself to Tate. Second, anyone driving by, even if they were inclined to help, would see Tate under the hood and assume she didn't need any more assistance.

In another moment the car was rapidly moving on by her, its occupants doubtless late-comers to the Fall Fest and relieved they wouldn't further be delayed by having to stop and help someone out. By this point, Tate was walking back around the car, back to her window.

He knocked on the glass. "Try to start 'er up now," he said.

Twyla hesitated. Perspiration was dripping from the tip of her nose, and she was having to constantly blink sweat from her eyes. There was going to be no way to look cool and collected at the police headquarters now, and if she either didn't roll the window down or start the car's air conditioning, it would only get worse.

She did what Tate told her.

And immediately the car cranked up, the air conditioning vents gasping out welcomed cool air in a hazy vapor.

Back in front of the car, Tate was looking over whatever he'd done, and then he was bringing the hood down. Looking at her through the windshield he waved good-bye and turned to go back to his car.

Twyla sat there, gnawing her lower lip. Then she honked the horn as he was about to open his own vehicle's door. He looked toward her and she beckoned him back. He approached the car carefully, perhaps expecting her to run him down. Well, that's what she felt like . . .

Instead, she beckoned him around to the driver's side again.

"What do I owe you?" she asked him through the glass.

"Not a thing. Like I said: I do good without expectin' anything in return. Except – naw, forget it. I'll see you around, Twy."

"What?" she asked as he turned to go. He stopped and turned back to her.

"What'd ya say?"

Twyla crack the window an inch. "I said," she said, talking through the crack, "what could I do for you in return?"

Tate stepped forward, head slightly tucked.

"You could roll that window all the way down and say 'thank you.' I'm not askin' for a hand-shakin' or nothin'. It's just . . . if I could know you might be able to forgive me just a little."

Twyla turned and looked down at the floorboard, sighing heavily and working up her resolution. Then, feeling as though her hand was a separate entity from herself, she was rolling down the window and looking back at him.

"Tate . . ." she began, not quite able to get out the words. Instead she focused on his grease stained hands. "You need a handkerchief or something?" she asked. "I guess I owe you that much, at least."

"No. Got my own. Now," he said as he reached into his back pocket. "Did you want to tell me something?"

Still struggling to say "thank you," Twyla forced herself to look him in the eye, but could only maintain contact for a moment. Then her vision dropped down to his hands. Was that a plastic bag he was taking his handkerchief out of? Maybe Tate had developed some obsessive compulsive behavior on his own.

"What's up with the bag?" she asked, trying to joke. "Afraid of breathing germs? You gonna start wearing a surgical mask in public like Michael Jackson now?"

What was that smell?

Then Tate was lunging forward. It all seemed to be moving so slowly, she knew what was coming, but she couldn't react fast enough to stop it.

Tate's one hand shot in through the opened window and grabbed her from the back of the head. Immediately he was pushing her face into the handkerchief. She tried to fight. Not to breathe.

Don't breathe girl . . .

But he wouldn't let up and she couldn't squirm free. She had to breathe; it just wasn't an option not to.

And so she drew in deep and lost consciousness.

Chapter 36

Twyla slowly opened her eyes on the steel toe of a work boot by her head.

"Wake up Dorothy," her uncle's voice croaked down at her. " 'cause this sure as hell ain't Kansas! I'm afraid there're none of them friendly singing midgets to greet you, just your ol' Uncle Tate! I done licked the lollipop guild, and now it's your turn."

Tate was here? They'd let him out of prison?

Her eyes focused on the boot.

No ankle stocks.

Then he's escaped. He's free? And standing over me?

"Hey, sleepyhead. Ready for all your worst dreams to come true?"

"Wassup, Tate?" Twyla slurred, rising partially on her elbow from a cement floor and trying to focus. "Where are we?"

"Deep inside the *Oro Boro Loops* factory, sug'."

Twyla now realized she was perspiring; she craned her neck to look back over her shoulder and found herself staring at the large, open mouth of what looked like an oven, an opening big enough to walk into.

"That's one big-ass incinerator, huh? Can you guess why I brought you here?"

She could. The realization jolted her with adrenaline, bringing her up from the floor. Tate grabbed her by the shoulder – it purpled under the clamp of his fingers – and shoved her back down on the floor. She cried out in pain, and he kicked her hard in the side with one of his steel tipped shoes. Twyla opened her mouth to cry out again, but robbed of her breath, she could only gape mutely.

"You're goin' up in smoke, Twy!" Tate announced gleefully. "Just like you been fearin' all these years. Just like with my old lady. Well, not exactly . . . I mean, she was *already* dead when I lit her up. But I intend to see that you're alive for some of the fun anyway. See, if I were to just toss you in the oven and shut the door, you'd probably suffocate pretty quick-like from the heat. Now, what it is is, I've got this here dolly –"

Twyla noticed it for the first time, a five foot long metal plane raised by wheels about a foot off the ground.

" – and I'm gonna slowly roll you in the furnace on it –

For emphasis, he stepped on one end of the dolly, made it rise up like a skate board on its two back wheels, then let it drop with a slam onto the floor. Twyla winced.

"–starting with your feet and proceedin' on up. I understand you're supposed to be some kind of big Christian now. Well, before I'm through, you'll be happy to cuss God just to make it stop, even for just a second.

"Now, pull off your shoes and socks and then your pants. I want that heat right on your flesh."

"Tate, please . . ."

"Do it now!"

Tate looked ready to go off any second, and Twyla knew it wouldn't help her chances to get away from him if she were beaten to a pulp. It wasn't easy to control her own panic – she couldn't allow herself to think of what he was proposing to do to her, or she knew she'd lose all rational thought – but she began working on a shoe and a sock. She didn't want to rush – with each moment that went by she was becoming more able to focus. Her fingers were thick and clumsy with the after-effects of the chloroform, so it wasn't hard to play that up and move slowly.

"Tate," she began, "why the whole conversion story? Why bring Shametrice into this? Did showing a change of heart get you out of prison earlier?"

"Nah. That had nothin' to do with it. I only started going to chapel and talkin' to Shametrice *after* I already knew I'd be getting out. I'd been plannin' to get back at you and your family for some time. Of course, I knew I'd be suspect if somethin' happened to you with me free. That's why I needed a character witness from someone respectable, like your black mammy."

"She can't be your alibi for this afternoon. She won't lie," Twyla said. "And, look, even if there's no guards here, there've got to be security cameras, and you must of set off an alarm when you broke in . . ."

"Who said I broke in?"

Twyla stopped in the process of peeling off a sock. Her eyes widened.

"And I've put all the security cameras all on 'pause.'"

"You mean . . . what?" Twyla asked. "How could you do that? Do you have some kind-of 'in' here? Are you a janitor or something? I can't believe Vernon Gurley would hire someone with your record . . ."

"I *ain't no* 'janitor.' And Vernon Gurley's known what he's doing. Every. Step. Of. The. Way."

Twyla's jaw locked; *every* bone in her body seemed to lock down. Tate smiled at her disconcertment for awhile, then kicked at her again. "Keep strippin'."

"Vernon Gurley . . . wants me dead?" Twyla managed to get out as she quickly finished pulling off the sock and started on the next shoe. "Why? Because . . . he thinks I saw something that morning? I didn't! I didn't see him kill his daughter !"

"Actually," Tate said with a crooked grin, "that's why he got me out of jail. Not to be no janitor. To turn off April's life support. Couldn't bring himself to do it, but he figured if I could kill my wife and burn up the body to get rid of the evidence . . . well, I obviously couldn't have that big a problem takin' out a stranger. And it won't like she was what you'd call 'livin' anyway."

"Bastard!" Twyla had spit it out before she could help herself, and in the same moment she was erupting from the floor for him, slapping about his head. "April never did nothin' to you . . . she was helpless . . ."

Laughing, Tate endured Twyla's feeble attack for a while, simply blocking her hands before she could actually land a blow. Then he backhanded her across the face and sent her back to the floor. Twyla lay there, looking up at him, sobbing.

All glee suddenly drained from his face now, Tate looked down on her, frowning.

"Finish undressin'," he ordered.

Twyla took off her last shoe and sock and rose to her feet. She went to unfasten her pants, but, as she remembered how he'd looked at her from behind the glass when she'd come to see him in prison, her fingers refused to work her button-fly.

"So . . . wait," she began, still stalling. "You were in April's room that morning. And I got there early – Gurley thinks I saw *you*? He's afraid I would identify you and then you'd talk to the authorities, and bring him into it?"

"You really didn't see anything, did you?" Tate asked after a moment, smiling. "Ol' Vern was convinced you were hiding somethin'. Well, I can't exactly let you go now. And anyway, you brought this all on yourself, Twy. You could have left a long time before that mornin'. But you just wouldn't go, wouldja? You insisted on carryin' your own fire extinguisher around with you –

– he jerked a thumb back over his shoulder, indicating an extinguisher that hung on the wall behind him –

" – when the one by April's room went past its expiration date."

"You know about that?"

"Know about it? It was my idea! After talkin' with Shametrice in prison, I knew what your obsession was all about. So I passed that info on to my new best bud, Vern.

"See, I've been enjoyin' the good life over there in the Gurley family's private quarters, working out in the gym, using the Olympic size pool, watching high definition TV. I had to be kept close, see, until the moment presented itself for me to perform my services. It was gonna be tricky, with the nurses around the clock with April. He figured it'd be real conspicuous if he gave everyone the night off and April 'just happened' to get turned off.

"Then that nurse asked on her own to get off early, and the other'n that came after her said she couldn't be in 'til her normal time. So that was the openin' ol' Vern had been waitin' for."

"You . . . really did it? You actually killed . . ."

"Honey, you just don't know how easy it *was* to make that million dollars. And then I shoulda been out of here, sunnin' on the beach in Honolulu. But you stuck your nose in that mornin', and so I got an extended gig, to take care of you.

"Not that I exactly minded. I was headed back to Tar Forks to do somethin' to your family after Hawaii – after everything had calmed down about April. 'course I get paid for you, too, so I didn't mind steppin' things up.

"I've been watchin' you, followin' you, waitin', and with the festival goin' on, and everybody at the plant havin' the day off, Vern and I saw this was the perfect opportunity to do away with you. Though, he just meant for me to kill you quickly and painlessly and then burn up your body down here. But I wasn't goin' to let you off that easy."

"You broke into my car . . ."

"Had to get in to pop your hood, do a little sabotage that would make your car break down along the road. So I followed you when you pulled out this mornin' and waited. Oh, and I took the CDs cause I saw I wasn't goin' to be able to get in your car without doing some noticeable damage. To throw you off track as to my true goal. Smart, eh?"

Twyla tried to ignore the heat from the furnace prickling her back and looked him in the eye. "Yeah, well . . . you don't know everything, Tate."

"Meanin' what?"

"Meanin' the police called me in for questioning in April's murder. That's where I was headed. They'll be looking for me. Probably already started."

Tate smiled. "That's great! Couldn't of planned it better. See, they'll find your car deserted by the road, and signs of another pullin' over and leavin' – with you, obviously. It's gonna look like you cut out of town instead of goin' in for questionin'. And, of course, no one will ever hear from you again. You're gonna break Ma and Pa Chayne's hearts. They'll go to their graves hopin' for a call from their heartless daughter."

"Shut up!" Twyla snapped at him. Her eyes were clinched tight against the unbidden image of her parents, haggard and aged before their time over her. Tears spilled and trembled over her cheeks.

"Get off your pants!" Tate snapped back. "I'm not tellin' you again!"

Shaking, Twyla unbuttoned her pants, slid them down to her ankles.

The heat from the furnace radiated more intensely now on the backs of her exposed legs.

Tate let out a puff of breath as Twyla worked her feet free of the pants piled about her ankles and stepped out of them. "I musta been harder up than I realized in prison, tellin' you to come over in a short skirt. I've been with a different woman every night since I been out. Classy bitches with some meat on 'em. You're nothin' but trailer trash with a pair of skinny legs, Twy."

"They're willowy," Twyla said in a small voice.

"Twigs for kindling's what they are." Tate put his foot against the dolly again, and shoved it squeaking across the floor toward her. "Now, lay down on it."

Tate produced some flexible wire that he meant to strap her down with, material that wouldn't burn like rope, and would add its own blistering torment to her skin as it heated up.

But Twyla was concentrating on something else. She'd seen – just possibly – a chance for deliverance.

And if it worked, she would owe it all to Tate.

Chapter 37

He had been used of God.

Not that that made him any less guilty, any less a pig. But she realized now *why* . . . *why* she had had to develop her peculiar obsessive compulsive behavior.

It was for this moment.

Of course, she wasn't safe yet. She had to get by him first.

Lord Jesus, help me now.

"I said *lay down!*" Tate barked.

She knew then, what she had to do. She could visualize it happening.

She made the motions of obeying him, but actually she was positioning the dolly length-wise between them. Then she stood up straight, and quietly but firmly announced,

"No. I won't."

Tate cocked an ear toward her. "Excuse me?"

"Come over and make me. I don't think you have the balls."

Tate flinched as though she'd smacked him. His jaw churned as a mumbling noise grated from deep in his throat. He had been totally unprepared for her to defy him, standing there half-naked and helpless.

He stepped toward her.

And Twyla shoved the dolly – hard – into one of his shins.

Tate bellowed, jerking up the bruised leg and hopping back on the other foot.

"Bitch!" he shouted, bent over, his eyes hot on her, but unable to reach her because of the pain radiating up his leg. One hand continually held it, while the other alternated between also holding his throbbing leg and reaching out and clawing at her. Meanwhile Twyla was maneuvering around him, keeping the dolly between them, while drawing near to that fire extinguisher on the wall.

Reaching it, she shoved the dolly back at him again. Tate hopped away before it struck him again. Then he was testing his hurt leg, tentatively putting it forward. Ready to come for her.

Let him, Twyla thought as in one quick, fluid motion she removed the fire extinguisher from the wall and enabled it, all with a clarity of mind – focusing regardless of the worst-possible circumstances – that she had honed and developed all those years she'd believed she could burst into flame at any time.

She whirled around just as Tate was closing in on her, and fired the extinguisher in his eyes, and his cursing, opened mouth.

Tate bellowed in pain, grasping at his burning eyes and choking on the chemicals filling his mouth. He simply couldn't breathe. Twyla had known, of course, that he wouldn't be able to: the chemicals were designed to snuff out oxygen to put out flames.

Tate fell back, gasping in welcomed air. But that moment of disadvantage the spraying dealt him was all that Twyla had needed. She lunged in, cylinder of the fire extinguisher raised, and smashed it into one of his temples.

He staggered.

She struck him in the head again, and this time he lost his balance, arms circling the air widely. He fell onto the dolly that had rolled behind him, where it had come to rest after she had shoved it . . .

Putting Tate spread prone and in line with the opened door of the furnace.

Twyla shoved the dolly hard, and by the time Tate had any idea of what was going on, he was rolling. In a moment his head was inside the furnace, followed immediately by his upper body.

Tate screamed. Still half-blinded, in pain, his hands scurried frantically about over the hot, metal inside walls of the furnace, touching on the burning refuse, blistering his palms and forearms as he sought relief.

At the same time, his hair and shirt went ablaze.

Bellowing, he finally worked his upper body out of the furnace, blistered hands first grappling at his hair – a nest of writhing, stinging glow worms – then beating at the flames engulfing his torso.

"Twyl-uh-uh-uh!" Tate screamed. "Pummeeeouttt! Pummeeouttt!" He jumped to his feet and began running faster and faster around the basement in a misguided effort to assuage his agony.

She stood there with the fire extinguisher, the hose drooping in her hand, watching his mad darting about.

"Would you have done the same for April?" she shouted at him. "If she'd even been able to beg you? Like *I* begged you?"

"Didnnnadewit!"

"What?"

"Ididdd not do it!"

"You liar! That is such a lie! Do you think I'm stupid?"

She wanted him dead. It wasn't Christian. But it didn't seem smart to give him any relief, give him the opportunity to hurt her again, now that she had hurt him, and he was *really* mad.

She remembered what her late grandfather, a retired minister, had told her once, long ago when she was a child, long before her wild years, when she regularly earned a tinfoil-gold star by her name in children's church every Sunday. She'd asked him about a moral conundrum, in what to him, at the time, must have seemed like a scenario unlikely to ever happen, merely a child's wild imaginings. She'd asked him,

"Grandpa, if someone was trying to kill me, and I had a chance, would it be wrong for me to steal their car and get away?"

"Honey," he, the sweetest man she'd ever known (but also a veteran of the Pacific Theater during the Second World War) had told her, "if someone was trying to kill you, it wouldn't be wrong for you to take their car and run over them with it."

"Thank you, grandpa," she said softly, dropping the extinguisher to the cement. "I love you."

Tate, meanwhile, squirmed on the floor, a convulsing heap of ashes and blisters. The smell of his burning flesh finally registered on Twyla and she gagged.

Choking back bile, she looked around. There was a telephone on the wall. She went to it, dialed 911.

"And Detective Grell," she said after she'd given her location. "Send Detective Grell. He should be looking for me."

She looked at Tate. And he looked at her.

A smile cracked his blackened, burned face.

"I . . . I know sumpin' . . . . sumpin' ew . . . . dunno. Figgered it out," he gasped out.

"Shut up."

"See, I saw s-s-sumpin' duh-duh-duh dat mornin'. Make you rich . . . no, make *me* rich. Jusss . . . make *you* hurt. I wanna hurt you, Twy," he hissed. "With my last dyin' breath . . . . Jus' come closer so Unca Tate can whisper in yer ear . . ."

"Shut up! I'm not coming near you so you can hurt me! Do you think I'm crazy? I hope you die, Tate! It's what you deserve!"

". . . no sumpin' ew dough no . . ."

Then Tate shook violently one more time, and there were no more words, only the rhythmic hissing of his breath from between blackened lips.

Chapter 38

Tate died from his burns two days later in the hospital. He never regained consciousness. Twyla decided that he had no big secret he was trying to reveal to her as he lay in agony, that it was just a ploy to get her close to him. Because even impaired, even with third degree burns, he was still vicious enough to hurt her, even if it were – literally – the last thing he ever did.

As for Twy, she was still under suspicion for April's murder, of course, though her ordeal had bought her a few days before she'd have to go in for questioning. The authorities were considering April's murder and Twyla's abduction and attempted murder as two unrelated cases. After all, Tate's animosity for the Chayne family was already well established. Twyla's testimony against him was certainly motive enough for him to seek revenge. And no one knew or even suspected a connection between Vernon Gurley and Tate.

No one, that was, but her and Vernon Gurley.

That kind of knowledge, for her at least, was dangerous.

She didn't say anything to Detective Grell indicating that her current misadventure had anything to do with April's murder. She had thought about it while she was waiting for the authorities to arrive. But Vernon Gurley had been able to get a convicted murderer with several years still on his sentence out of prison. He obviously had powerful connections in the legal system. What might he do to her or her family and get away with if she accused him?

Almost immediately, she received a letter from Vernon Gurley, expressing his deep regrets that she had nearly lost her life at his factory. He included a check for $50, 000 which he hoped would help soothe the trauma to which she'd been subjected.

Vernon Gurley to all appearances was trying to forestall a lawsuit of some kind. But Twyla suspected he was worried about what Tate may have told her. In that case, accepting his check would be tantamount to taking hush money for his role in the murder of his daughter.

So Twyla sent his check back with a letter saying she did not hold him, or *Orro Boro Loops* Inc. responsible for her late uncle's actions.

More welcome was a beautiful card she received from Lorna. At the time, Lorna was out of the country on another one of her relic wrangling missions, this time to nab from its holy place a menstruating idol of Kali in New Delhi. She was armed only with her wits and a box of Kotex. She promised to come and visit as soon as she got back to Tar Forks. Twyla hoped it would be soon.

Because I've gotta get April's laptop without Mister Gurley knowing anything. And I don't know nothing about breaking and entering –

But Lorna does.

She's got in and out of places with a lot more security than the Gurley mansion, I'm sure. And maybe the security cameras are still down. But will she do it?

Well, she said in her card to let me know if she could do anything, Twyla thought. *And, besides, she was friends with April. She'll be shocked to hear Mr. Gurley may have paid to have his daughter killed, but he did make a move on Lorna, after all. She can't really believe he's that good of a guy.*

But a couple of days went by and there was still no word from Lorna. Twyla would soon be questioned again. She couldn't wait for Lorna to get in touch with her – if she were already back, the adventuress might sleep a day or more when she got back to town before she contacted Twyla. And Twyla just couldn't wait.

She hadn't thought to get Lorna's phone number the other night, so Twyla headed unannounced to her old friend's trailer. Parking in the street in front of Lorna's home, she saw Lorna's car wasn't there, but a vehicle Twyla recognized was.

Twyla knocked on Lorna's door. It opened almost immediately. And Twyla found herself again face-to-face with Lamar.

Twyla was wearing a short skirt – the result of Lorna's praise of her thighs the other night. Lamar's eye level immediately dropped momentarily to meet her skirt's rising hemline. She noted, with a happy sense of triumph, the resulting smile on his face couldn't have been broader if he were greeting Lorna in a short dress.

Take that, *Tate,* she thought.

"Twyla, wow!" he said, his glance bouncing back and forth from her eyes to her legs. "I mean, I'm glad to see you . . . after all you've been through, I mean."

"Good to see you too, *Father* Lamar." She couldn't resist chiding him for his obvious fleshly desires.

"Lorna's not here. But I know she's back in town. You're more than welcome to wait with us for her."

"'Us'?" Twyla asked, eyes narrowing slightly.

"Yeah," Lamar said. "She called me and asked for a ride out here. Hold on a minute. I used Lorna's spare key to get in; let me put it back while I'm thinking of it."

"'She'?" Twyla asked, an unwelcome sense of fresh competition creeping over her. She watched from the porch as Lamar quickly trotted down the steps with the key. He pulled up a particular brick from the walkway, one that wasn't a brick at all, but actually a hollow fake.

"'*She*'?" Twyla asked again from the porch, not waiting for Lamar to finish placing the key in its place and putting the *faux* brick back in the walkway.

"Yeah," Lamar said, as he made his way back up the steps. But he didn't proceed directly inside; he paused in the doorway, looked Twyla in the eye, and said, "I guess I need to prepare you –"

Prepare me for *what?* Twyla wondered. It was hard to imagine a more formidable rival than Lorna, and she really doubted that Lamar was friends with another girl *that* spectacular –

"– she's not what you would expect –"

"Who?" Twyla insisted.

"The Virgin Mary," Lamar said.

"*Who?*"

She saw in his expression that he was serious, then charged into the trailer's living room.

"Twyla, wait," Lamar said after her.

But by then Twyla was already inside. And the room was empty.

Oh great, she thought. *Lamar's having visions now, too? Just my luck – now that he's not a priest and he's interested, he's going crazy.*

Then she heard water running down the hall, heard a faucet squeal as the water was cut off. The bathroom door opened, and down the hall walked a middle-aged African-American man. He didn't say anything. He just immediately looked Twyla up and down, then pinned her with a squinted-eye stare.

"Twyla," Lamar said, coming up behind her. "Meet the vessel of Mary, mother of Jesus."

"Wait," Twyla said. "This is the guy from Booger Grubbs ostrich and emu farm, right? Albert –"

"Albert Metz channels Mary occasionally," Lamar said. "That's Albert's body, yes, but the consciousness it currently conveys is not his own. He – I mean, she – has a message for Lorna. Said it was urgent. So, I was glad to give her a ride up from Booger Grubbs' place. Albert can't drive, what with his Tourettes syndrome, and Mary can't, since you know, her time was a bit too early for Henry Ford. So, I was glad to help out. You don't have any idea where Lorna might be, do you?"

"No," Twyla said, eyes still on Albert who silently continued to regard her, his lips puckered in disapproval. "I haven't seen her since the other night. I need to talk to her, too."

Okay, Twyla thought. *Why does he keep looking at me like that?* Despite the fact that she didn't officially accept that Albert Metz was channeling the Virgin Mary, his demeanor was making Twyla feel very underdressed – again. *First "Father Lamar" and the belly shirt and now a miniskirt and the Virgin Mar* – she caught herself thinking. *But Lamar wasn't a priest and that's* not *Mary*.

"Well, looks like we're all in the same boat," Lamar said. "All waiting for Lorna. A couple of her old friends . . . and the Virgin Mary. I guess the whole universe *does* revolve around her, huh? Have a seat, Twyla. If you have time."

"Okay," Twyla said. She sat down on the couch with her knees held primly together, tugging down at her little skirt that, short already, was now riding up her thighs. Lamar, seated across the room from her, seemed interested in just how far it was going to go. Twyla was at once pleased and embarrassed with Albert Metz over there affecting this matronly distaste at her underdressed presence. She grabbed a cushion from the couch and put it in her lap in an attempt to cover her bare thighs.

Sorry, Lamar, she thought as she rested her arms on the cushion to anchor it.

"So, what have you been up to?" he asked. "Other than getting kidnapped, that is."

"Well, I've been looking into April Gurley's murder on my own. And I might have gotten a clue. I don't know . . ."

Lamar leaned forward. "Wow," he said. "Have you gone to the authorities?"

"I can't really, not yet," she said. "That's why I came to see Lorna. That's why I need her . . . expertise, I guess you'd say."

From his place across the room, Albert *har-rumphed* loudly. Both Lamar and Twyla looked his way. His expression suggested that someone had silently broken wind and the unfragrant *faux pas* had just registered on him.

"Could we talk in the kitchen?" Twyla asked Lamar. "Just you and me?"

"Sure," Lamar said, rising. "Excuse us," he nodded toward Albert, who silently tossed his head in mute acknowledgement.

"I don't think he likes me," Twyla said to Lamar once they were seated at the kitchen table.

"I wouldn't take it personally," Lamar said. "Mary's just very protective of Lorna. You know, she's got a lot invested in her and the mission she's called her to. I guess she doesn't want her to have many outside distractions from the task at hand. Now, what have you found out about April?"

Twyla told him all about her outing with Miguel and Myra, and what Miguel claimed.

"Going out on your own like that, infiltrating the shadow world of Santeria . . . well, that was Lorna*esque*," Lamar said.

That was high praise – the best possible praise, in fact – coming from Lamar, and inwardly Twyla beamed, though she was careful that her countenance was coolly dismissive of her accomplishment.

"No big deal," she said. "All I did really was use a little southern belle charm, and, you know, show 'em a little leg." That last bit wasn't accurate, as Twyla had actually worn jeans during her get-together with Myra and her friends. Still, it worked as a figure of speech, and she embellished it by crossing her legs when she said it, giving Lamar the choice view of thigh that Albert Metz's presence in the next room had denied him earlier.

"And how do you think Lorna does it?" Lamar asked, smiling. "Sex appeal is the number one tool in her arsenal. Though she doesn't use it for selfish ends, anymore."

"Totally altruistic, huh?" Twyla asked with a smile. "Well, it's her other skills I need now. I need her to override the Gurley home security system, so I can get to April's laptop."

"But you know you can't take it," Lamar said. "Unless the police have a warrant for it, any evidence on her computer, if it's taken illegally, couldn't be used in court."

"I thought about that," Twyla said. "So I'm going to copy April's diary to a flash drive, read it, and see if she mentions who her psychiatrist was. She never told Miguel. Anyway, her doctor might know something from their sessions – I know there's 'client confidentiality,' like they say on *Matlock* – but maybe . . . . Look, he's got to know April was murdered. If she told him anything that would indicate her father was the killer, he may be sitting on the fence about whether to make that known, 'confidentiality' aside. Maybe if he reads the diary, that'll push him over.

"If it's information coming from a professional, the police probably will be more likely to pursue a lead that there's something incriminating on April's computer more so than if it's just me bringing an unsubstantiated charge against Mr. Gurley. Then they could get a proper search warrant for the laptop itself.

"But I'm not making one step toward the Gurley mansion until I'm sure I have the password to get into April's diary," she said.

"And Miguel insisted he'd given it to you – speaking as Eleggua. But you don't believe it was Eleggua talking."

"It's a scam, I told you, just like that psychic surgeon he's got working out of his backroom. You don't believe it was actually a Santeria deity dropping a clue, do you?"

"Well," Lamar said, "I mean, we *do* have the Virgin Mary in the next room."

"Surely you don't take him seriously?"

"Well, the thing is, he's got Tourettes syndrome. But have you heard him yell anything inappropriate or even jerk or twitch funny since he's been here? Been here as Mary, I mean?"

"Well, no –"

"Me neither. And he wasn't doing it on the way over, either. He never has any symptoms of Tourettes when he's claiming to be Mary."

"But that doesn't mean he's really channeling Mary's spirit. I've heard of cases of multiple personality people having ticks and stuttering in one personality and not their others. That could be what's happening with Albert."

"That *would* be another way to account for it."

"Anyway, getting back to whether or not it was Eleggua or Miguel speaking, I don't want the authorities to know I was supposedly getting information from a spirit, you know?"

"Yeah, you're right, of course."

Twyla noted Lamar didn't have any trouble acknowledging she was correct – even though she was a woman and didn't have his education. Dwayne Woolard would never concede anything, and she *did* have more education than he did.

"What was it again that Miguel said?" Lamar asked.

"He said, 'The word that was lost sang real. Could that be another way of saying it 'rang true?'"

Immediately, Lamar slapped his forehead. "No. It's something else, I'd bet."

"What?" Twyla asked.

"Okay, first of all, he was speaking, so there was no punctuation, but did you notice if he paused after 'lost'? Like you'd put a comma there. And what comes after the colon is not two words but one: Sangreal. That's an old word for the Holy Grail. See, if you divide it between the 'n' and the 'g', 'Greal' is an old way to spell 'grail' and the 'san,' is from the Latin 'sanctus' which means 'holy.' 'Holy Grail.'"

"I can see 'greal' and 'grail,'" Twyla said. "And 'san' – like in *san*ctification, the Second Definite Work of Grace? Or like *Santeria*? 'The way of the *saints*.'"

"'The holy ones', yeah," Lamar said. "You're into your church, right? 'Saint' in your Bible is translated from the Greek word 'haigos' and that means 'holy one.'"

"Do you study the Bible?" Twyla asked, smiling at this unexpected bit of Biblical explication on Lamar's part.

"Well, I had a Bible as literature course in college. And one in Arthurian Romance. That's where I learned about 'Sangreal.'"

"But why would that be April's password? Why would she pick that?" Twyla asked.

"Because there's a play on words there that might have appealed to a stigmatic. If you divide the word after the 'g' instead of before it, 'Sang' could be short for 'sanguis' which is Latin for 'blood.' And 'real' means 'royalty,' but in English there's a pun in that 'real' can also mean 'true,' like you said. So if you divided 'sangreal' at the 'g' and 'r' you get 'sang real' which could mean 'true blood,' the genuine blood of Christ."

"And April's stigmata was supposed to truly represent Jesus's genuine blood," Twyla said. "She thought of her own bleeding as genuine, too: 'sang real.' But it wasn't," she added after a moment. "She came to realize that, so she may have changed his password, huh? *Since* she chatted with Miguel over the Internet?"

"Maybe not. I mean, she could have meant it ironically, and besides, it was a cool password that her father wasn't likely to figure out. If it ain't broke, don't fix it, you know."

"So, 'sangreal' could be it."

"Yeah," Lamar said. "I don't know if it was upper or lower case, or divided or one word, but you should be able to find that out relatively easy."

"Right. Well, Lamar, thanks a lot. I mean it. You may have made the difference in whether April gets justice or not."

"I hope so," he said. "I mean, I can't make it right, running off like I did when she needed me, but . . . . And leaving you in the lurch, too."

Twyla touched his hand. "You don't have to feel bad about that. About deserting April when it looked like she was in trouble, I mean. You wouldn't have made any difference that morning. She was already dead when we got there."

"I noticed you didn't say I didn't have to feel bad about deserting you," Lamar said.

Twyla smiled. "You can let that go, too."

"I should make it up to you."

"You just did – figuring out April's password."

"Well, that was for April. I would like to . . . could I take you out to dinner? And I don't mean *The Rednek Grill* at Wahl-Mart this time."

Twyla looked him in the eye. "Because you think you owe me?"

"Because I'd like to go out with you," he said, meeting her gaze. They were both silent for a moment and then Twyla tucked her head, smiling.

"All right, then," she said. "That would be nice."

"Great," Lamar said. "Let's work out the details while we're waiting for Lorna."

"Okay. I get off work –"

Suddenly, she sensed a presence. She looked up, thinking that Lorna had walked in.

But it was Albert Metz in the room with them, breathing heavily. "Do you know what is happening?" he insisted more than asked, his eyes radiating desperation. "Everything is in jeopardy, now. You're going to give her to them."

Chapter 39

"Who? Give who to who?" Twyla asked.

Albert looked at Lamar. "Already she has grasped the hand of the dark one."

"Who?" Twyla asked. "Me?"

"Sometimes a door opens," Albert said, "and you see what was always there, what you didn't see before."

"Have you been talking to Miguel?" Twyla asked. Albert was saying essentially the same thing Miguel did during the Santeria ritual, when he had gotten the far off look in his eyes.

"Listen to me," Albert said. "A door opened. I saw a gathering; their faces were hidden. They take counsel in darkness. That is their way, those who move behind the world. 'Who will go for us?' one asks. Then the trickster whispers . . . to . . . fit her? They want to know – does it fit her? A statue is moved from its place and put where it should not be; innocence is lost. Do you understand?"

Twyla, brows knit, looked at Lamar. He shrugged. Then Twyla made her own connection:

"You mean the statue from April's room?" she asked. "How do you know about that?"

Albert's eyes went wide. His lips stammered. He fixed his gaze on Twyla, and quickly slapped his thumb and forefinger in an "L" shape against his forehead.

"Are you – you're calling me a loser?" Twyla asked. *What kind of loser do you have to be to get called that from the Blessed Mother of all people?* she thought.

Albert emphatically shook his head "no" and then quickly used the same hand to make a "V."

"What? 'Victory'? Is that what you're trying to say? 'Victory' for who?" Twyla asked.

Albert was trembling by this point, gnawing his tongue with his head down. Lamar reached out, held him firmly by the shoulders. "Are you having a seizure? No? What are you trying to say?"

Albert's head jerked back up. Wide-eyed, he shouted, "I'M NOT WEARING ANY UNDERWEAR!"

"*What?*" Twyla asked.

"It's you now, isn't it, Albert?" Lamar asked. "Mary's gone, isn't she?"

"Y-yeah. All gone. Where am I – I – I'M A PENITENT MAN AND I WANNA BE NAKED!"

"You're at Lorna's house. Mary called, through you, and asked me to bring you over here. From Booger Grubbs' place."

"Middle o' the day," Albert said. "TAP-TAP-IOCA! 'supposed to be at work now."

"Oh. Not to worry. Mary clocked out for you before we left."

"G-good. Don't want –" Here the gesticulating Albert repeatedly jerked his head down harshly as though trying to cast the words out of his mouth. "– don' wanna get paid ef ain't doin' the work."

"You *are* conscientious, all right. I guess that's one of the reasons Mary picked you."

"She d-does it for my b-benefit. I have th-these bad thoughts and she comes in an' takes all that away for awhile. B-but s-she can't stay. I come b-back. Don't unnerstand why. Nuthin's perfect in this life, I guess."

"Okay, Albert. I'll get you back to work," Lamar said. "But listen – you came here today . . . you brought Mary here today to give Lorna an important message. But evidently your possession went on too long. She was losing her hold and Lorna still hasn't shown. Mary tried to give us the message, but we couldn't understand. Do you know what all that was about?"

"N-no. NO UNDERWEAR!"

"Okay," Lamar said, lightly patting Albert's shoulder. "Twyla, I'm going to take him back to work. You're welcome to come along. Or keep waiting for Lorna. I'm sure that would be all right."

"Well, then I'll wait for her a little longer," Twyla said. "I want to catch her before she's off on some other big adventure."

"Right. Well, I'll be back as soon as I can. We can talk about dinner tomorrow? I mean, we'll talk *today* about eating dinner *tomorrow* when I get back, okay?"

Twyla smiled. "Sure. I'll look forward to it."

"C'mon, Albert," Lamar said.

Twyla watched as the pair headed out across Lorna's yard to Lamar's car. Albert screamed "I WANNA BE NAKED" at the top of his lungs at a young mother wheeling a baby carriage through the trailer park and sent her and her child rolling along quickly in the opposite direction. A teething ring bounced out of the carriage. The mother didn't try to reclaim it.

"That ain't right," Twyla said softly, shaking her head. Then she returned to the living room to wait for Lorna.

Looking around the room, Twyla noticed for the first time that the cereal-sucking Ganesh idol was no longer on Lorna's end table, or anywhere in the living room for that matter. Frankly, she was glad; the thing gave her the creeps. Her rationalization of the Virgin Mary's possession of Albert Metz aside, she *did* believe in the supernatural. The thought that a demon was in that thing and thus in the trailer with her – alone – was unsettling.

She was relieved to hear a car pull up outside, especially when a look out the window revealed it was indeed Lorna. Lorna seemed a bit taken back at the presence of Twyla's car, and seeing her reaction made Twyla feel that, her earlier invitation to get together sometime aside, Lorna didn't welcome her presence here.

Chapter 40

Twyla opened the door for her, an apology already half-formed in her mind, but it withered quickly away on the back of her tongue when she actually came face-to-face with Lorna.

Her eyes were swollen slightly from crying. She wasn't upset that Twyla was there, just a bit chagrined . . . and sad.

"Hi Twy," she said, her voice small. "You'll have to excuse me about . . . *this* . . . ." she sniffed.

"Oh, no, Lorna. *No* . . . Why are you apologizing to me? This is your home. I'm the one who showed up here unannounced. What's wrong, honey?"

"Been out to Falkland. To the nursing home. You know . . ."

"Oh. Oh, sug'. Your mama?"

" She don't even know me, Twy."

Twyla reached out and took Lorna into her arms, gently encouraging her to let it all out. Twyla could hardly remember Lorna crying during the three years she'd known her – except in her senior year of high school, when she'd had to commit her mother to a mental institution. Twyla had tried to console her then, feeling very awkward as a teenager in the face of such grief. She was more seasoned now, and so she was able to act as a soothing cushion for Lorna's pain.

Without yielding her embrace, Twyla led Lorna to the couch, to sit down, and finish out her cry on her shoulder. After awhile, she volunteered to get some tissue, but Lorna had a handkerchief in the purse she'd carried in with her. By the time Twyla had rooted it out for her, Lorna's sobs had pretty much subsided, the physical portion of her grief spent.

"Feeling better?" Twyla asked, handing her the hanky anyway.

"Yeah. Thank you, so much, Twy. I'm so glad you were here. I haven't had any friends to lean on for a long time now."

"I'm sure Lamar would be glad to give you a comforting embrace," Twyla said with a smile.

"Oh, no," Lorna said, grinning. "I mean, I'm sure he would, but . . . I wouldn't want to spoil Lamar's image of me, I guess."

"You mean 'Lorna Croft, Temple Raider'?"

"Yeah, but he knew me a long time before all that began. Back then . . . oh, I was still a flirt, Twy. But even then I tried to keep it light between him and me."

Twyla was relieved to hear that, but she wanted to be sure.

"He has feelings for you, you know. Not just 'friend' feelings."

"I know."

"Why did you invite him out here to Tar Forks?"

"I felt the need for some support, I guess. A little heroine worship. But I didn't *just* invite Lamar. We had another friend there, at the university. Harlan Webb. I invited them both, but I gather that Lamar must have got the message first and cut Harlan out of my invite, if he even told him I'd called."

"Oh."

"He's got a crush, I know. Any rivalry between him and Harlan for me is just in his head. I wish I could wipe that movie I did, that *'Barbarian Babe'* thing off the face of the earth. I feel like I'm still taunting him – and who knows how many other guys –through it. That's not what I'm about. Not anymore, at least."

"So, I take it you haven't told him about *El Santo y La Voluptua Contra Des Mujeres Vampira* then?"

Lorna blushed. "You know about that? Please don't tell him. I haven't. It'd be like I was leading him on, you know. And that's so unfair."

No problem, Twyla thought. "So, how many movies did you make in Mexico?"

"Just that one. It was during the period I was modeling, and I had an agent. My other movie had been really popular in Mexico, so this film company there contacted me, and I flew down. Actually, El Santo's been dead for years. But somebody came up with this idea that they'd do a new Santo movie by digitally transferring his image from his old movies into new footage, featuring me as his super hero girlfriend, La Voluptua."

"Like in *Forest Gump*?"

"Right. In fact, they even call the technique 'Gumporation.' How did you know about my Mexican movie?"

"Okay. That brings us to what I came here to talk to you about. Are you up to it?"

"Bad news?"

"Maybe. I'm not sure. But . . .yeah, probably. It's about April."

"What is it?"

"First, let me go back to the other night. I'm friends with a girl named Myra. She's always wanting to get me together with her friends . . ."

When Twyla got to what Miguel claimed April had told him, Lorna held out her hand, motioning Twyla to "stop."

"That's not right," Lorna said. "I mean, April may have said that she was afraid of her father, but he would not have killed her. He loved her. He's made the mansion a shrine to her. You saw him the night of April's vigil, right?"

"He looked sincere, sure, but that doesn't count him out. That Susan Smith was all tore up about her boys she drowned, remember? And there's more. When Tate had me, he told me Vernon Gurley got him out of jail to turn April off."

"*What?!*"

"And Mr. Gurley got me aside the morning I found April. He made it clear I'd better not try to connect him with her murder. He compared himself to John and Patsy Ramsey, and if that's not a damning comparison out of his own mouth –"

Twyla noticed that Lorna had slightly paled as she spoke.

"Are you okay?" Twyla asked. "I'm sorry, Lorna. You were already upset, and it was selfish for me to drop this on you, too."

Lorna waved her off. "No. It's only an accusation, right? And you just have Miguel's word on it, and your uncle, whose moral character wasn't exactly beyond reproach."

"We don't just have to take his word for it – or Miguel's."

"What do you mean?"

"I have the password into April's diary on her laptop. There's a good chance the laptop is still in the mansion, right across the hall from April's room."

"You want to go in and get it?"

"I want to go in and get a copy of it on a flash drive and find out who her psychiatrist was. He might know something incriminating. I hope I can use the diary to encourage him to go to the police and *they* can go get the laptop."

"You still have your key, I take it."

"Yes, but assuming the locks haven't been changed, the security code *has*. I came here hoping that you could disable it, or whatever you do when you're getting into the Mormon temple and high security places like that."

Lorna took a deep breath, then let out a heavy sigh. "Sure," she said. "I just can't discount that . . . April's father is a suspect. But we read what's on that flash drive first, before turning it over to anyone else. We don't bring up any accusation we can't back up, right? He's been through a lot already."

"I'm on the same page, Lorna. I agree exactly. So, what do we do?"

"We plan it out. We find out what hurdles we'll have to jump, and then we wait until its dark, and we go jump 'em. Can you make a little map of that part of the estate, and how the inside of the wing is laid out? Windows, side doors, other possible escape routes?"

"Sure. Yeah," Twyla said.

As Lorna got up to get the pen and paper, Twyla found herself looking at the end table where Ganesh no longer set.

"Hey," she called after Lorna. "What happened to the magic elephant god?"

"Oh," Lorna said, returning to the living room. "Mary has been chidin' me about my 'trophies.' For showin' off. Vanity makes me vulnerable, you know. Takin' time to put the Popes around a card table and stuff. So all my icons are in a back room now."

Twyla knew by "Mary" Lorna meant Albert Metz, and she hadn't yet mentioned his visit earlier, or his "message." But Albert wasn't Mary, his concerns were not in the same league as Twyla's – because, for one thing, *hers* were real. Still, she felt she ought to say something.

"Lorna, Albert Metz was here earlier, with Lamar."

"Oh?" Lorna asked, her eyebrows rising. "Was it Albert or was he channeling Mary?"

"That's what he claimed. He said he had an important message for you."

"Then why didn't he stick around until I got home?"

"He started yelling that he wasn't wearing any underwear, and he wanted to be naked and all that stuff. Lamar took him home."

"What did she say before Albert's Tourettes kicked in?"

"'She?'"

"*Mary*, Twy. Did she tell you anything about what she wanted to tell me?"

"That there's danger. Something about a door opening. Do you know what he could have been talking about?"

Lorna shook her head no, her eyes taking on a distant, searching look. "Did she say anything else?"

"Did I mention he said I'd ' shaken hands with the dark one?' I got the feeling she – he – doesn't like me."

Lorna didn't respond.

"What?" Twyla asked insistently.

"I didn't tell you everything, Twy, about why I didn't get in touch with you earlier. Everything I said before was true, but there was something else. Mary told me to stay away from you."

"What? And you listened to him?"

"I always listen to him. To *her.*"

"What about our friendship? Didn't that mean anything to you?"

"I invited you back, didn't I?"

Twyla sighed, and she reached out and gingerly patted Lorna's knee. "Yes, you did. I know," she said.

"Anything else to that message?" Lorna asked.

"He said that we were going to 'give her to them.'"

"Her? You mean April?"

"April's dead, Lorna."

"Yes. I know that, Twy. Was there anything else?"

"Oh, he wrapped it all up by making an 'L' and a 'V' with his fingers on his forehead, right before he started screaming about his lack of underwear."

"Wait . . . . *what* did you say"

"He started screaming for his underwear."

"No, no. An 'L' and a 'V.' He made an 'L' and a 'V' you said. Are you sure?"

"Well, what else?"

"You said Albert was with Lamar?"

"Lamar was taking him back to work."

"I'm gonna give Lamar a call while you're working on that map of the Gurley mansion," Lorna said, handing Twyla the paper and pen she'd brought.

Twyla began sketching it out, but she was half-concentrating on Lorna's conversation.

"Hi, Lamar? Yeah. Is Albert still with you? Wait . . . you're *where?*"

The tone in Lorna's voice halted Twyla's half-attempts at drawing. She stood up and walked over to her. "What?" she asked.

"What happened?" Lorna asked Lamar, waving Twyla back. "Uh-huh. *He* said that? Could it have been *her?* Okay. Stay with him. Give me a call when he comes around."

"What?" Twyla insisted as Lorna hung up. "Was there an accident? How's Lamar?"

"No, no," Lorna said. "There wasn't a wreck. Albert had a seizure in the car. They never made it back to Booger Grubbs. Lamar took Albert right to the hospital. He passed out and he hasn't come to, yet."

"What brought that on? Is it related to Albert's problem?"

"Lamar said that he was getting a lot of static on his radio out of nowhere. He went to adjust it, and Albert reached out and grabbed his hand and he had this fear in his eyes, Lamar said, like he hadn't ever seen before and Albert said, 'They're in the air; they've found me.' And then he went into a seizure."

Lorna had a distant stare in her eyes as she sat back down on the couch. "Twyla, did I ever tell you about Lucifer Vesuvius?"

"Yeah. Your mother said he was a demon that killed your daddy –"

"With radio waves. She said . . . she said he comes 'through the air.'"

"So you're saying Lucifer Vesuvius attacked Albert today, too?"

"'L' 'V,' Twy! It's what Mary came to warn me about!"

"Sug', I'm not trying to be mean, but you got to take into consideration your mama's mental state. Maybe your daddy's death was what caused her to lose her grip."

"Lots of people have emotional blows, Twy. I lost someone when my daddy died, too. It hasn't affected me that way."

"Sure, honey. You've done really good with your life, considering everything."

But after Twyla turned back to sketching April's wing of the Gurley mansion, she found herself looking up to watch a pacing, pondering Lorna. She didn't doubt that her friend had the skills to get them into the Gurley mansion, not one bit. But her quest, her belief that the Virgin Mary had called her to some heavenly mission – and that Albert Metz, of all people, was a . . . a Marian conduit?

Like mother, like daughter? Twyla hoped not. She really, really hoped not.

Chapter 41

By 8:30 PM, Lorna and Twyla had mapped out their attack plan and were sitting in Twyla's car, parked down the road a quarter mile from the Gurley mansion. Between them on the front seat set Lorna's laptop. Lorna now picked it up, opened it, and went to work.

"You're not taking time to check your email?" Twyla asked.

"Of course, not. I'm getting the Wi-Fi frequency at the mansion, so I can hack into the security camera's Wi-Fi feed. Ah, there it is!"

Twyla looked into the laptop's screen and saw the familiar Gurley mansion backyard through the lens of the security camera. Lorna continued working at her keyboard. "Now, without disrupting the feed, I'm going to create a looping image of what we're looking at." After a few minutes, she smiled. "Now I've spliced the loop into the feed. Okay, let me cut and paste the time stamp from the live feed into the looping clip, so, if anybody looks, it'll appear as though this spliced image is what is being recorded in real time."

"What do you mean?"

"We won't have to worry about being caught on camera. As far as security is concerned, this loop is the image of how the backyard looks now. And how'll it'll continue to look while we get this job done."

"So we'll be invisible!"

"Now, let me do the same thing for the camera at the door to the back gate. I'll check the one that was monitoring April's room, too, but I suspect that's no longer on since there's no need for it." She spoke over the rapid clack of her fingers on the keyboard.

"Wait a minute - how did you know there was a security camera in April's room? Did I tell you that?" Twyla asked

Lorna stared at the laptop screen, her hands hovering momentarily over the keyboard. Then she began typing again, keys rattling once more under her fingertips.

"No, you didn't tell me. Isn't that to be expected, though? Some kind of monitor on a patient, in case they get in distress? Especially someone like April who can't call for help."

"Well, yeah. I guess you've learned to think about all the potential angles," Twyla said.

"Turns out we don't need to worry about the camera in the room; it's shut down. Gate's taken care . . . . You ready girl?"

They had changed into dark clothes and Twyla now wore pragmatic slacks, courtesy of Lorna's wardrobe. Lorna carried only a pencil size flashlight; Twyla held her keys to April's door and the back gate.

"Ready," Twyla said, smiling to project a confidence she did not feel. *It'll be all right,* she kept reminding herself. *Lorna's experienced at breaking and entering.*

They exited the car and took a brisk walk to the back gate to the mansion.

Lorna immediately went to work on the security keypad, one gloved finger stabbing at the buttons.

"Lorna, wait," Twyla said.

"Hmm?" Lorna looked up, index finger hovering before the keypad.

"Shouldn't we try the old code first? Just to see? Maybe he hasn't changed it yet?"

"Sure. Good idea." Lorna pressed the button to cancel what she'd already typed, hit the reset button, then tapped out what Twyla told her and pressed "enter."

Immediately the digital screen flashed "Invalid Code."

"Nope," Lorna said, pressing the reset button. "Don't worry, Twy.

This is gonna be a cinch. Let's just hope your keys work, huh?"

"Yeah. What will we do, if –"

"Shhh, Twy. Let me think."

After a moment, Lorna began tapping out a sequence of numerals which showed up glowing green on the keypad's small digital screen: 090781.

Something familiar about that, Twyla thought. Before she could ask Lorna about it, there was a tiny beep from the keypad. The digital screen read "Access Granted."

"What I always do," Lorna said, sober-faced. "I'll find a way, and if there's not one, I'll make one. Trust me. If this doesn't work out tonight, we'll take another swipe. But maybe we won't need to. Give the gate key a try."

Twyla did, and the gate opened.

"Great!" Twyla blurted out loudly and immediately clapped her hand to her mouth.

Lorna didn't respond. She immediately took Twyla by the elbow and steered her through the gate's door, telling her to crouch low behind a large bush. Then Lorna quickly darted back to carefully *almost* close the gate, so that it would not appear open to anyone passing by, yet would be prepped to open when they pulled on it in case they were beating a hasty retreat.

That job accomplished, Lorna joined Twyla behind the bush. "Okay, Twy," she said. "Give me your key. I'll try the lock and if that one has been changed, I'll see what I can do to gain us entry."

"What will you do?" Twyla asked.

"Secrets of the trade," Lorna said, looking toward the door. Then, rising but keeping her back bent low, Lorna quickly made for it –

– as the light in April's room flashed on.

Lorna fell flat on her belly, halfway between the door and the bush that still hid Twyla, who watched eyes wide.

If whoever's in there comes to the door, that'll be it. Lorna'll be caught. There's no way –

But in the time it took Twyla to think, Lorna had rolled to the side, taken cover behind another bush. From there, she could see Vernon Gurley through the window as clearly as Twyla.

He paced back and about and when it became obvious that he wasn't coming out the wing door anytime soon, Lorna scurried on her stomach across the yard and back to Twyla.

"What do we do now?" Twyla whispered loudly at her.

"Stay calm, Twy. Maybe he's in there tonight just trying to feel close to his daughter, you know? Look, I should be able to get him out."

"What do you mean?" Twyla asked. "Are you going to slip into your bikini and start dancing around his swimming pool?"

Lorna waved Twyla off. "No. But you're right. He likes me. If I can just get back out of the gate without anyone noticin,' I'll just slip back out the gate, brush off my sweat suit and go ring the front gate. He should be glad to see me."

"Lorna, no!"

"He'll let me in. I can offer condolences and while he's distracted, you can get in there and copy April's diary."

"Lorna, what if he starts chasing you around the room, trying to feel you up again?"

"He's in mournin', Twy," Lorna said with a frown. "That won't be a problem. Now, listen to me. Get in there, and get the diary copied, and then get in your car, and don't wait for me. I want you to get home –"

"What? You want me to leave you stranded with that murderous letch?"

"Twy," Lorna said. "I've been handlin' men before I was handlin' a car, okay? Mr. Gurley is *not* going to rape or kill me. For the last time, he's grievin'. He's a broken man."

"But are you going to walk back to your home then?"

"I'll get a ride. That won't be a problem."

"How?"

"Cell phone, Twy," Lorna said. "I'll call Lamar."

"But what if he wants to know how you got to his house?"

"An old friend dropped me off. Look, trust me: he'll be so glad to see me that he won't care how I ended up on his doorstep. Now, you go home with that flash drive and wait for me to call you. Then you'll come over to my place, and we'll read April's diary together."

Twyla sighed and cast her gaze to the ground for a moment. Then she looked up at Lorna. "You're Lorna Croft, right? You'll be okay."

Lorna smiled and nodded her head. "You'll need to re-set the security code to the gate door when you leave. The code is 090781. Can you remember that?"

"090781. Right. Something familiar about that . . . ."

"And don't forget to press the 'enter' button as you leave, so the alarm will be activated. We don't want anyone to know this wing has been broken into, right?"

"Right. I'll remember."

"Now, you wait. Give me about ten minutes. Watch, and when you see Vernon leave the room, give him a few minutes to get out of the wing. Then try the door. Here," she said, passing the key back to Twyla. "If it doesn't work, just go home. I'll call you."

She looked at Mr. Gurley through the window. His back was turned and he was at the other side of the room. Lorna started to go, then turned back and handed Twyla her small, pen-size flashlight. "Tool of the trade," she said with a smile. "You'll probably need this."

Twyla took the flashlight, nodding her head in agreement. Lorna looked, saw again that Vernon Gurley's back was turned, and then made a quick crawl for the gate.

Chapter 42

Left alone by Lorna, Twyla now felt particularly vulnerable and obvious in her spot behind the bush. She tried to stay as low behind it as she could, risking the occasional peek to see if Vernon Gurley were still in the room. He was.

She checked her watch. It had almost been fifteen minutes now, since Lorna had gone, and she'd told Twyla to give her ten. Had something gone wrong? Not for the first time, she felt like bolting for the car, like getting out of there right now –

But then she took a deep breath and tried to take another, more calming perspective. Lorna had meant ten minutes as an approximation. And what had almost been fifteen minutes, had, more precisely, been only thirteen. Not enough time to assume something had gone wrong. Maybe it had taken longer than she'd thought she'd need to freshen up and look pretty for Mr. Gurley – a plan with which Twyla still wasn't comfortable. She hoped for Lorna's sake that her friend had rightly assessed his mental state.

Twyla peeked again from behind the bush.

The light in the room was out.

When had that happened? she thought. She checked the time. Fifteen minutes had now indeed passed since Lorna left. Thirteen had passed when she had looked away from the window to regard her watch before.

So, at the most, Vernon Gurley was two minutes gone. At the least, he could still be within earshot of hearing the door open.

Eyes on her watch, Twyla let two more minutes tick by.

Then, bending low, she scurried for the door.

Halfway there, Twyla wondered if perhaps Mr. Gurley had seen her crouching out there in the dark. In that case, he might think that he was about to be robbed. He could have called the police –

– and what would she say to Detective Grell this time? Already suspect in April's murder, now returning to the scene of the crime . . .

And there was another, more deadly, possibility: what if Mr. Gurley had weapons in the house? He might be waiting for her himself. That realization brought Twyla to a dead stop, right as she was about to put the key in the lock. She could be shot, maybe even die. She was giving Gurley another opportunity to kill her and get away with it. Was justice for April worth that steep of a price?

But Lorna was in there, adding a new factor to the equation. She would still be a major distraction for Mr. Gurley, Twyla was convinced, even if he did think he was being robbed. If that were the case, his major concern would be getting Lorna out of the house for her safety. Though he might *still* call the police – but even then she would have a window of opportunity, though one which could come down on her fingers while she twiddled them on the window sill.

She shoved the key into the lock, and was relieved to feel it turn. Then she twisted the doorknob, and gently pushed.

The door opened onto the dark hallway with April's room immediately to the right. Across the hall was Shametrice's office, where she had performed her website tasks. Its ajar door revealed it was empty.

Twyla sighed with relief and quickly stepped inside, closing the outside door. Immediately she began a search of Shametrice's office, but the laptop was no longer there.

"No!," she said under her breath.

Then she remembered Shametrice sometimes moved the laptop into April's room, for the occasional live chat room from April's bedside. Had she conducted one of those the day before April's death?

Hoping that was indeed the case, Twyla stepped into April's room, and began searching it. Afraid to turn the light on, she was compelled to use Lorna's pen light to probe the chamber.

The light played eerily over the icons of saints, the resulting shadows distorting their features as though with agony. Twyla wondered if they were silently moaning at *her*, wanting to drive her from the room as though they suspected her of after hours pilfering. The over-all spooky effect was heightened by the fact that the images still wept blood and dripped oil, and what had become routine for Twyla in her daylight visits was now extremely disturbing, especially under her already nerve rattling circumstances.

It's all in my head, she thought, spurring her concentration back to her search for the computer. *And besides, the saints would be on my side tonight: I'm here trying* to help *April, after all.*

Twyla shined the light under the table where Shametrice stored the laptop and found it there–

"Yesss," Twyla quietly hissed. She pulled the laptop out, dropped it gently onto the table, flipped the lid open, and said "thank you, Jesus" as she confirmed that this was indeed April's. Shametrice must have left it there, planning to return it to her office the next morning after her web chat. But the next day, April was dead, Demarcus was in jail, and Shametrice had apparently never come in for work.

Twyla quickly unwound the laptop's cord and plugged it into a nearby electrical socket. Soon the laptop was switched on and booting up.

Twyla pulled from her breast pocket the flash drive she'd brought for copying April's diary. *How's Lorna making out with Mr. Gurley?* she wondered, then realized "making out with Mr. Gurley" wasn't quite the way she should phrase that when she queried Lorna later about what happened between the two of them.

Now with the computer up and running, Twyla maneuvered her fingers over the keypad, pulling up the computer's menu. She suddenly found herself slammed against a wall she should have foreseen: which file was April's diary? If it was something she was trying to hide, she wouldn't have labeled it plainly. Twyla wondered if she was going to have to go through each and every file folder and see what came up. How long would *that* take?

Forcing herself to calm down again, Twyla clicked on the "My Documents" icon. She discovered the files there were all labeled "Prayer Requests 1, 2 . . ." and so on.

Twyla clicked on one and found its content to be just as described. Opening the second file revealed more of the same.

Maybe April had hidden her diary under one of these prayer request files? She kept clicking through them and finally, when she hit the seventh file, she found she was no longer looking at a list of prayer requests, but a computer window with the words "Password Required" and a cursor blinking in a blank field beneath the words.

"Yes!" Twyla pumped her fist once then and promptly typed in "Sangreal." The password was rejected, but Twyla had known the computer would most likely be case sensitive. So she took another pass – sangreal – and this time the file opened.

Twyla quickly perused the first lines, to confirm that this was indeed "it."

Feb. 1, 2008

Today I questioned God for the first time. More than that, I question myself –

"Whoa," Twyla said. "This is it, and that first line alone is potentially scandalous." She pushed aside the temptation to read more and began copying the information to her flash drive.

That done, she secured the memory stick back in her breast pocket, then quickly unplugged and folded up the laptop and returned it under the table. Twyla checked the hallway. Empty. No sounds from the direction of the main house, either. She again felt apprehensive about leaving Lorna stranded, but it *was* Lorna's plan, after all, and she seemed confident that all would go well.

So Twyla determined to stick to the plan and made for the outside door. She gained it with no problem and was soon making her way across the back yard. The gate was still slightly ajar. She slipped through it without a problem, closing it behind her, and locked the gate. Then she saw the security keypad. She'd almost forgotten. She typed in the numbers: 090781. Even though it wasn't the old entry code, there *was* something familiar about it.

She had no time to tarry there and figure out what, though. She pressed the "enter" button, and the system beeped affirmation.

Then Twyla ran – hard – for the car.

Chapter 43

Twyla was soon safely behind the wheel of her car. It was then she decided that she was going to deviate from the plan she'd made with Lorna.

She had Lorna's laptop. She couldn't just wait at home with the flash drive, having what might hold all the answers right in her grasp, and not read April's diary when she could easily pull it up. That first line she'd glimpsed on April's laptop screen –

Today I questioned God for the first time. More than that, I question myself –

– intensified her already excited curiosity. And there was no need to wait at home for Lorna to call her. She remembered where she had seen Lamar put Lorna's spare key to her trailer earlier that day. Why not go directly there? It would save time. Lorna would understand, certainly. Especially since, if Twyla had already opened the file, then Lorna herself would more quickly get the information herself. A win-win situation.

Her mind set on this slight alteration to the evening's itinerary, Twyla drove to Lorna's trailer.

Lorna's car was still where they had left it, and the trailer was dark. She wondered how long Lorna would have to stay with Mr. Gurley before she could get away without looking suspicious. Twyla figured she would probably not rush it; after all, for all Lorna knew, Twyla was still in the mansion, still needing time to find the laptop and copy April's diary.

Twyla got out of her car, found the fake brick with the help of the pin light and took out the key. Then she climbed the steps and unlocked the trailer door. Opening it, she stepped inside, shutting the door behind her. She flipped on the light, sat down with the laptop and plugged in the flash drive. Then she pulled up the file and read:

Feb. 1, 2008

Today I questioned God for the first time. More than that, I question myself. And since there is no one I can confide in, no one whose faith I wouldn't shake by admitting my doubts, I have only myself to turn to. I have begun this diary as a record of my personal quest for truth – the truth about myself, about my gift – and to understand how I could have failed someone who needed me so desperately.

Jennifer Peele wanted healing for her diabetic child. Her e-mail especially moved me, so I did something unusual. I sent her a bandage from my hand, urging her to touch her son with it. She took my sending the bandage as a sign to strengthen her faith, especially since I told her I felt impressed to mail it to her.

When her son went into a coma, Jennifer Peele held out for her miracle, refusing medical attention. And so her boy died. That is the concise version of her e-mail I read today, but it radiated anger and grief and despair. Especially despair.

I was so sure that Jennifer Peele's son would be healed! I know that in the past there have been requests presented to me to take before God which were not answered the way the petioniers desired. And to be honest, since this is just me, there have been times I doubted from the moment the initial request was made, but I felt full of faith in this case.

I have the wounds of God, I have the angelic visitations, but none of that seemed to count for anything. And while my wounds continue to bleed, Gabriel – someone who could actually do me some good by answering my questions – has not come again, not since I failed Jennifer. Am I being tested? Tried? My preacher said trials are a mark of God's favor, so should this be an honor? That a child's life was taken because I'm so valuable to God? But I don't want to be valued, not at that price. I never asked for any of this.

"The gifts and callings of God are without repentance." You can't hand back what God has given to you. But is this a gift of God? Is there anyway that it might not be? I intend to find out. It will be my private quest and this diary will be my secret record of it. No one else can know about my doubts.

"But you *did* share your doubts, April," Twyla said aloud. She wanted to read further, but she was looking for the name of April's psychiatrist, and reading anything unrelated, that she didn't *need* to know, felt like a violation of April's privacy. So Twyla began scrolling again down the screen – until she saw a name that brought her to a halt.

– name is Jenny Barefoot. We usually don't share our real names, in our group, but Miguel invited her into our private chat room, and said I wouldn't have to give up my identity, but Jenny volunteered hers. She has visitations, too, but hers are from an ancient Aztec warrior, Cuchotemac, who was tortured to death by conquistadors. And the thing is, Jenny has stigmatic wounds, too – corresponding to the wounds Cuchotemac suffered at the hands of his torturers.

She was telling me that it was all connected, her wounds and mine and Cuchotemac's and Christ's, but how can that be? I joined the Internet Support Group for People Who Encounter Non-Corporeal and Disembodied Entities, hoping there would be someone like me – other Christian stigmatics. I didn't expect a psychic surgeon who gets her powers from an ancient Aztec warrior.

That sort-of thing I've always been told was evil. And if we're the same, like Jenny says, then, what I always assumed was from God – is it evil, too? Am I?

Twyla really wanted to read further to find out what April had decided, if she had, but once again she felt she was trespassing into some place she should not go. So she started scrolling again, watching for any mention of "Daddy." But it was another unexpected name that brought her to a stop again before she caught any mention of Vernon Gurley:

– met Apotlette Shametric Prayer today –

"Whoa," Twyla said. "Back up." She didn't have any idea that Shametrice had known April before her accident. Shametrice had certainly never volunteered that information.

Twyla found the beginning of the diary entry that described their brief acquaintance.

April 8, 2008

I met Apostlette Shametrice Prayer today, a most extraordinary lady. She is a Pentecostal preacher, and the founder of Open Door Ministries. I remember her son Demarcus from school, not that we were ever friends, but he always seemed kind-of nice. She didn't elaborate when I asked how he was doing these days, and that was fine, because I really wanted to talk to her about me. About my condition. She's so assured, so strong. I didn't think I would shake her faith.

So I told her about Jenny Barefoot and her stigmata from the ancient Aztec warrior. I asked her if my own might be from the same source – a sinister source.

She told me not to trouble myself, and reminded me of the story of Moses, how he was able to cast his staff on the ground and it would become a serpent. It was a miracle from God. But then, the Egyptian wizards who opposed God turned their rods into serpents, too. "The devil can imitate God's miracles. Don't have your mind cast into confusion because of that," she said.

She then advised me to get out of that Internet group. I told her I pretty much already had. Except for Miguel.

Having eliminated a diabolical source for her miraculous wounds, April was still unsatisfied that they were necessarily of God. And so Twyla read of her research into secular explanations, her learning of *psychogenic purpura*, and cases of stigmata cured by hypnosis. Which led to her own secret psychiatric sessions after she had opened up to her mother. All just as Miguel had said.

As she skimmed over April's account of those sessions, much of the information was, again, what Miguel had paraphrased the other night. Though there was one bit that he hadn't related, probably because April, out of embarrassment, would have never told him. But here was the answer to the riddle Twyla had encountered each day that she'd changed the bandages of April's bleeding hands – and the diaper from her loins that bore no sign of menstrual bleeding.

Chapter 44

Today I finally got up the nerve to tell Doctor Hewitt that my menstrual cycle is nonexistent. When he asked me how long it had been that way, I told him I had never menstruated. His jaw almost hit the floor. Why hadn't I ever mentioned it? he asked. "Why do you think?" I asked him back. He wanted to know how it had escaped my mother's notice.

I explained that when I told her we had covered a woman's cycle in Health class, my mother and I went through the application of tampons so that I'd be prepared when my bleeding began. After that, she thought I just took care of it myself. I let her think that I was normal, and I went through Kotex when I thought it was about time, you know. But nothing ever happened. I was actually glad – I'd heard what I had to look forward to and wasn't anxious to start. I didn't say anything because I was afraid my parents would send me to a doctor, and he'd see to it that I began to menstruate.

I told Doctor Hewitt that I knew I should have said something, that it didn't seem healthy, but I was only thirteen when I began to suspect something wasn't normal, and I was thinking like a kid, you know. My palms had already begun bleeding about that time, which seemed like enough of a problem to contend with.

After I finished, Doctor Hewitt sat quietly, thinking. He then said he was going to recommend an internal exam with a gynecologist. "No way," I told him. "I don't want someone touching me there." He assured me I could make an appointment with a female gynecologist if I were uncomfortable with a man. "No gynecologists at all!" I *insisted. After that, he just looked at me for a long moment, as though he didn't know what to think.*

I tried to steer the conversation away from this impasse. I explained that I had always thought God had exempt me from normal womanly bleeding because I was called to a non-sexual life, one dedicated to His work. "Married" to Him you know, like the nuns. But Doctor Hewitt was interested in other possibilities.

At his suggestion, we tried hypnotic regression. He said that there might be something in my past, some singular trauma that had preempted my menstruation and began my stigmata. I told him I didn't know what that would be, and he said that I wouldn't if the memory were repressed. He said he thought that repression might be why my stigmata had resisted his efforts to cure it hypnotically.

There was something I still couldn't get by, not today. And then we were out of time. But next time. Next time, I think.

Then the entries jumped to one week later, the date of the car accident of April and her father.

April 18, 2008

Nothing to write about this week. Gabriel still has not spoken. No visions. No word from God. And after my session tonight, I feel strangely certain that there'll be no further need for speculation. That I will know. And Doctor Hewitt. And my mother.

And there the entries ceased.

"No!" Twyla shouted. "No, *no, no!*" Why hadn't she spelled it out? Was there even any use in the police seeing the diary? April had only mentioned that *her mother* would come to "know." Why not her *father* as well? Because she feared him, like Miguel had said? For the same reason she didn't want to be examined by a gynecologist?

Whatever April had found out at her final psychiatric session, she had never returned to record it. And Twyla suspected that Vernon Gurley was somehow responsible for that omission, that he had learned about April's sessions, that he had gone and interrupted her last one with Doctor Hewitt before anything that would disgrace him would come out.

Was he too late? Twyla wondered. Father and daughter had apparently left the doctor's office together that night. But wouldn't Hewitt have refused to turn April over to her father, if he'd just uncovered that the man had molested his daughter?

Perhaps April *had* remembered, but had not told her doctor before her father interrupted. Or perhaps her memory had not returned until they were on the way home. And if she had confronted her father with that memory, that could have prompted Vernon Gurley's losing control of the car. And April's subsequent coma.

And Vernon's getting the plug pulled on her, Twyla thought bitterly. But why had he waited so long? If he was afraid she'd come out of her coma and reveal his secret, why had he ever put her on life support to begin with?

His wife, April's mother Kyra, though dying, was still alive then and may have insisted on it. Given his wife's condition, Vernon Gurley probably couldn't deny her anything. And by the time Kyra died, the publicity of the miracles around her comatose daughter – considered as a sign that God wasn't done with April – would have made it very difficult for Vernon to pull the plug, at least publicly. He had gone on record, after all, as praying for her recovery. But was that just talk? And his plans for a multi-million dollar park to honor April and accommodate her devotees – just *more* talk?

He'd painted himself into a very public corner, one from which he couldn't extricate himself to follow legal channels to do away with his daughter without condemnation. So he had her murdered secretly.

But then there was the matter of the Saint Anthony statue missing from April's room. Why was that taken? Was either Gurley or his hit man Tate a secret disciple of Santeria who believed the icon meant Eleggua's protection of his victim? That seemed unlikely.

Further speculation would have to wait; she now had the name of April's doctor. That was something concrete, a *real* lead. That was the important thing. And besides, at the moment, Twyla *really* needed to break for the bathroom.

She had never gone at Lorna's home, so she proceeded uncertainly down the hall. The first door to her left was apparently locked; it didn't open when she turned the knob and pushed on it. But, fortunately, the bathroom was further down on the right, and the door was open.

When Twyla stepped back into the hall, she noticed that her efforts at what she'd thought was a locked door had evidently worked it open. At least, it was cracked now.

Curious, she pushed the door the rest of the way when she came to it, and peered inside.

She immediately saw the statue of Ganesh. So she realized that this was Lorna's "trophy room," where the "Virgin Mary"'s chiding had caused her to relegate what she'd collected during her temple raiding. Twyla was still creeped out a bit by that Ganesh statue, but she was curious to see what else Lorna might have in there.

Twyla stepped in. Her attention was first arrested by some statue of a woman with multiple arms erupting from her torso. Kali, she guessed, Lorna's latest acquisition. Apparently, it *did* bleed, too – . At least, Lorna had taped what looked like a sanitary napkin around its loins. Twyla wasn't about to test her theory, however. So she turned her attention elsewhere in the room.

Her vision touched on something that made her blink . . . . and then her hand was scurrying over the wall by the door in search of the light switch. The light she'd been using was dim, coming in from Lorna's living room down the hall, and she had to be certain.

She flicked the light on –

– and there was no longer any doubt. Twyla was looking at a statue of Saint Anthony. A *bleeding* Saint Anthony.

Twyla approached it slowly, part of her wanting to flick off the light, close the door, go back in the living room and wait for Lorna, as though nothing had changed.

But it had. *Everything* had. How many times had she seen this statue in April's bedroom, morning after morning? She moved in closer. There! There was a chip missing from one of Anthony's ears, the white plaster under the paint showing. This was *it*.

Still, she resisted the implications of its presence in Lorna's trophy room. This was *Lorna*, after all. They'd been good friends. They were becoming friends again. And what motive would she have? She could have gotten in the mansion, sure; she'd shown that this very evening. But motive?

Crazy. Like her mother.

Twyla flinched against that thought. But what other explanation was there?

Then Twyla heard a car pull up outside.

Lorna? Flicking off the light and closing the trophy room door behind her, she made for the living room. She felt very aware of how she wasn't supposed to be at the trailer now. Was that because Lorna only wanted her there if she could supervise her? Because she knew the lock on the trophy room was no good?

Through the living room window, Twyla saw Lorna getting out of the passenger's side of a non-descript car. She must have already seen Twyla's car and that the lights to the trailer were on.

Lorna had now come around to the driver's side of the car; a hand reached out from the window, beckoning. Now a man's head appeared momentarily. Lorna bent at the waist, to meet him. He withdrew into the car, and she poked her head inside after him.

For a kiss?

Lamar?

Then she was out and coming up the walkway, her ride driving away. She didn't look after the driver, or wave goodbye. She seemed intent on the house, though she didn't look angry.

"Not yet, anyway," Twyla said aloud to herself. Her fingernails were digging into the palms of her clinched hands as she stood erect, ready to bolt, facing the door that was about to open and bring her face to face with –

A killer? She bit her lower lip and waited.

Chapter 45

The door opened. Lorna stepped inside, frowning. "Twy," she said, closing the door behind her, "you weren't suppose to be here yet."

"I . . . knew where you kept the key, and I didn't want to have to wait to read April's diary," Twyla said. She was having trouble looking Lorna in the eye when she talked to her. But in the process of avoiding looking at her, she found herself instead casting a glance toward Lorna's trophy room, and for a moment, almost involuntarily, her vision fixed there, her eyes widened: the door had come back open. She quickly turned her head back around, and she saw Lorna was looking at the opened door now, too.

"What's wrong, Twy?" Lorna asked from across the room. She folded her arms across her breasts and gnawed her lower lip.

"I just . . . . I'm having trouble . . . I just can't believe what I've seen here tonight Lorna. I mean, how can you explain it any other way than what it looks like?"

"I can't," Lorna said, sinking into a chair with a sigh. "It's exactly what it looks like."

Twyla's eyes widened. "How can you just — you're not going to even deny it? You're just going to admit to it?"

"What else can I do? You saw us out at the car, right?"

Twyla hesitated, uncertain of Lorna's question. "Well, yeah," she said after a moment.

"And the way you're looking at me, you must have seen who I was kissin'." Lorna sighed again, tucking her head and shaking it slightly from side to side. Then she looked up at Twyla. "We knew it would come out eventually. But we didn't mean for it, yet. It's why I didn't want you here when I came back. I knew Vernon would insist on driving me back himself. He wasn't able to go with me to see my mama today, and he wanted to talk about –"

"Wait, wait," Twyla interrupted her. "*Vernon?*"

"Come on, Twy," Lorna said. "We're all adults now. I can hardly keep calling him 'Mr. Gurley.' Especially under the circumstances."

"You were kissing . . . ?"

"It's not a fling kind-of thing. We've been seeing each other for nine months –"

"Practically since you came back . . ."

" – and we've been secretly married for the last three."

"*What?!*"

"We've been keeping it a secret until his wife's been dead a year. Because you know how people would talk if he married a younger woman real quick without a mourning period."

Now Twyla collapsed into a chair across the room. "When did this happen? *How* did this happen?"

"You know I came back to Tar Forks to seek counsel from Mary, through Albert Metz. I had already heard about the car accident and April's coma. And then I found out Vernon's wife had died, not six months later. I saw him on the street. I could tell he recognized me, and he looked so forlorn, I couldn't just walk away from him when he came up to me.

"And we started talking. And after we'd chatted awhile and I was excusing myself, he offered to buy me dinner. Like I said, I felt sorry for him. I didn't have the heart to say 'no.'

"He was a different man. He even apologized for what he'd done, back when I was in high school. Sorry he'd selfishly chased away his daughter's only friend. Grief had changed him. I could see that. And, after that – well, we both needed somebody, Twy."

"Does he know about your temple raiding?" Twyla asked, still stunned, then realized: "He bankrolls your adventures, right? With his fortune?"

"That's right."

"And I bet you didn't need to override the mansion's security code last night. As the lady of the manor, you already knew the new code –." Twyla slapped her forehead. "I thought I recognized the numerical sequence: it's your birth date."

"Yes."

Twyla's brow furrowed. "That's your mansion in town, but you're not living together, you're in this trailer park, because you're keeping your relationship a secret. So, are you sleeping with him?"

Lorna actually blushed. "C'mon, Twy . . . we're husband and wife."

"So does he visit you here?" Twyla knew her probing wasn't appropriate, but she was getting at something else, something important.

"Never here. I meet him places. You know, nice places, out of the state – or the country even."

"What about at the mansion? Do you ever spend the night there? What about the servants?"

"He gives them time off. We have the residential wing of the mansion to ourselves, then, and I can use the mansion gym. But I'm mostly there at odd hours."

"Did you two love birds have the residential wing to yourselves the night April was murdered?" Twyla asked her.

Across the room, Lorna sat erect and looked at Twyla, her eyes partly hooded. "Yeah. We did. I mean, I feel terrible that *that* could have been happening while we were . . . together."

Twyla closed her eyes. Her stomach roiled.

So, no one but Mr. Gurley had any idea you were in the mansion that night. And if you knew there'd be no nurses with April for an hour and a half, then you had opportunity to kill her without ever coming under suspicion –

Unless someone could place you in the mansion that night.

And then it clicked for Twyla, who clutched her wrenched gut.

219

"Twy? Are you okay?" Lorna asked, rising.

Twyla waved her back as she tried to resist the realization that pressed in on her mind. It was an unwelcome scenario that fit the evidence of the Saint Anthony in Lorna's trophy room and inevitably implicated her in April's murder.

Vernon Gurley thought I saw you leaving April's room! That I'd recognized you! You're who he thought I might be protecting by keeping quiet, when he grilled me that morning.

You knew someone else was coming in on you, and you told your husband you may have been seen. If you told him April was turned off, he would have thought Tate had been there already. But what if it was Tate getting there late who saw you, not me getting there early?

Had you already done his job for him, Lorna?

Somehow during his acquaintance with Vernon Gurley, his time in the private family wing, Tate could have learned of your relationship with the millionaire. He could have even learned enough to know that you and I were friends. And maybe Gurley, who would have wanted as few people as possible involved in his schemes, had taken Tate deeper into his confidence. Tate did say he was the one who suggested getting rid of me by letting the fire extinguisher lapse beyond its expiration date.

When Gurley paid Tate for April's murder without question, Tate must have figured you hadn't confessed to your husband. So, he could have planned to try and blackmail Gurley later by threatening to reveal you as April's killer. That was why Tate said what he knew would hurt me, but could make him rich.

But Lorna, why would you?

Twyla's extended silence, and her nauseated expression as she regarded Lorna from across the room, made clear to Lorna the direction of her friend's thoughts.

"C'mon, Twy," she said. "You can't really suspect me."

Money to back your secret mission, Lorna? Is that what you wanted? Twyla thought. *You already had that. Did you need more for what you're trying to pull off? Maybe you thought Vernon Gurley was serious about channeling millions of dollars into a meditation park for April's followers. But if she died, he would reconsider that project. No one would be coming to see her and the miracles around her. And you could use your influence in the bedroom to gain those suddenly freed-up finances.*

Because you believe in this cause of yours. You traded yourself away to Gurley for it. Would you have felt justified in sending April on to heaven? Like you were doing her a favor? Lorna, have you really lost your mind?

"Twy, that's just crazy. April was my friend."

"You just said you were in the house when it happened. That makes you a suspect, Lorna," Twyla said. "And nobody knows that, do they? Except for your husband and he wouldn't tell, would he? Bring you under suspicion and reveal your relationship at the same time?"

"Waitaminute, Twy. What about your uncle's confession? What did you read on that flash drive? Did Vernon hire Tate to kill her? Please tell me he didn't."

"Stop it, Lorna! Don't try to turn the spotlight on them when you —" Twyla choked the rest of the sentence back.

"When I *what?*" Lorna insisted.

"— when you have in your 'trophy room' that Saint Anthony statue that disappeared from April's room the morning she was murdered!"

Lorna cocked an ear at Twyla and blinked. "What?" she asked.

"I just saw it, Lorna! Right before you drove up! Don't deny it when we both know it's in the next room. Are you stalling to come up with some story to explain that?"

Twyla *wanted* Lorna to explain it. But how could she? Would she even own up to being in April's room that morning?

Eyes tearing, Twyla asked Lorna, "Do you think if I look again the statue will have magically disappear —"

Twyla suddenly stopped and stared into space. "No," she said to herself after a moment. "Oh, no, no, no . . . ." She was trembling now.

"What is it Twy? Are you okay?" Lorna asked, walking oiver to her friend. She reached out to touch Twyla's shoulder. Twyla dodged her hand before she could make contact.

"'Disappear.' *Disappear!* You made yourself invisible to the security camera in April's room just like you did with the security cameras tonight."

Lorna tucked her head.

"You made that Saint Anthony disappear, too, didn't you?" Twyla said. "But I've seen it now anyway, Lorna. I know that statue in your trophy room is April's."

And then Lorna told Twyla a flat-out lie – what she knew Twyla would *know* was a lie:

"I'm not denyin' it's there," Lorna said. "But it wasn't taken the mornin' April was murdered. Lamar said he took it the day before, when you got him in."

Twyla started at this. "Lamar did *not* take the Saint Anthony statue!" she said. "He took a prayer card. The statue was already gone when we got there, and we were *not* there the day *before* her murder. It was the day of!"

"That's not what Lamar told me."

"So that's how you're going to defend yourself? You figure Lamar's so smitten with you, he'll subscribe to your version of this story that you've come up with just now, and it'll be my word against his? You're a married woman and you're still using your body to string Lamar along, using his crush to get him to lie for you. That's despicable! And he won't do it, Lorna! Lamar may follow you around like a puppy dog, but he won't help you get away with April's murder. Lorna, you . . . I don't know what to think . . ."

"Listen to me, Twy," Lorna said, eagerly leaning forward. "I know what's goin' on here. What's *really* goin' on."

Chapter 46

"What do you mean? You've got another lie you think I'll swallow more easily than your Lamar story?" Twyla asked.

"It's no lie. It's a theory I've been thinkin' about since before we left for the Gurley mansion this evenin'. Hold on."

Lorna walked across the room and picked up from an end table a couple of books she'd pulled from a shelf earlier, one of which was the Mystic Fez lodge handbook, *The Ancient and Accepted Tiresian Rite*.

Lorna sat down beside Twyla on the couch. Twyla immediately moved over to put some space between them. At once, she felt ashamed, wondering if she'd hurt Lorna's feelings. If she was offended, however, she didn't show it. In fact, it looked like she hadn't even noticed, she was so intent on the two books on her lap. She opened the one on top.

"What's that?" Twyla asked.

"Cross reference work on various deities of the world's religions. Look, I know you believe Miguel was faking about being possessed by Eleggua, but I want to ask you to keep an open mind, okay? I want you to consider the possibility that he *was* possessed."

"Lorna . . ."

"Please, Twy. Now look here." Lorna jabbed a fingertip at the entry on Eleggua. "Eleggua is known as the 'opener of doorways.'"

"I know that," Twyla said. "So?"

"This book cross references gods of the world's religions several different ways, but one is by motif. So, like, you look up Hermes and you're referred to the Roman Mercury, of course, but also the Egyptian Thoth and other messenger deities of various pantheons. Now, look. See the note here in the Eleggua entry. Baphomet is connected to him. Now . . . ." Lorna began to quickly flip through the pages, to another section of her book.

". . . under Baphomet, we have some speculation about the origin of his name. One occultist, Madeline Montalban, said that 'Baphomet' was derived from the word 'Bfmaat' which is ancient Atlantean for '"Opener of the door."'"

"Like Eleggua," Twyla said. "But what's that got to do with you having that Saint Anthony statue from April's room?"

"Just keep an open mind, okay, Twy?" Lorna put the first book aside and opened the Fez Lodge manual. "This is the only documented corroborating evidence I've found of him, and I wouldn't have had this if an old boyfriend hadn't been a Mystic Fez lodge initiate. But look at what it says here, Twy! Just look."

Twyla looked where Lorna was again stabbing with her finger. There she read: . . . *Baphomet, known and worshipped by the Knights Templar as Lucifer Vesuvius . . . .*

Twyla looked up at Lorna, who was smiling. "So, you're saying Lucifer Vesuvius, Baphomet, and Eleggua are all openers of doors."

"Not just that, Twy. They're all the *same* entity. When Eleggua possessed Miguel, it was Lucifer Vesuvius speakin' through him – the same bein' that's had a vendetta against me and my family since he killed Daddy with airwaves."

"Lorna, you're talking like your mama. Don't you see that? *Can* you?"

"Don't *you* see, Twy? Lucifer Vesuvius is manipulatin' all this! You're under his influence because you participated in that Santeria ritual! He's the opener of doors, Twy! How do you think you got into my trailer tonight?"

"I told you. I saw where Lamar got the key from the other day."

"Lucifer Vesuvius directed you to be there so you'd see it. So you'd be here tonight and it would come out about me and Vernon and put me under suspicion. Lucifer Vesuvius is framin' me. That's what Mary was tryin' to warn me about today. The 'L' and the 'V,' remember?"

Twyla felt her heart lanced by pity, despite every moment solidifying her conviction that Lorna was indeed guilty of murdering April. As much as Twyla had envied Lorna in the past, to see her friend's beauty and intelligence dissolve into madness was painfully saddening. She reached out and gently touched Lorna's cheek.

"Lorna, honey, you're sick. You need help."

"Yes! I need you to help me by believing what I'm telling you!" Lorna said, taking the hand from her face and placing it in Twyla's lap.

"But Lorna, why? Why would this Lucifer Vesuvius pick on you?"

"I got in his way, once, Twy. That's all I can say. I don't know why he killed daddy."

"Listen to yourself, Lorna . . ."

"You're helping him, Twy! Can't you see that? You're helping him get me!"

"You . . . you're starting to scare me, Lorna."

"I would never hurt you, Twy. I know you're just being used by a higher power."

You're going to give her to them.

Albert Metz's words came back to Twyla. He'd said that she'd 'grasped the hand of the dark one,' too. Eleggua? Lucifer Vesuvius? Could it be possible that she *had* opened herself up to his manipulation when she played along with Miguel's Santeria ritual?

Miguel, speaking as Eleggua, had promised to open the doors she needed to bring April's killer to justice. There were three. The key to one, he said he'd already given her: he, the finder of lost things, had taken credit for bringing her together with Lorna, and then Lorna, as it turned out, did have the necessary 'key' to turn off the Gurley mansion's security system so that they could enter. Then there was the password into April's computer diary. That was another key.

And yet one more door will I open for you Miguel, speaking as Eleggua, had said that as well. Twyla remembered how Lorna's trophy room had been locked at first – she *couldn't* open it – but when she'd come back, there it was, the door ajar . . .

No, she thought. *This is crazy. I can't be thinking this way. Lorna has the Saint Anthony from April's room. She lied about how she got it. I know that.*

"Look," Lorna was saying, "Tate said he did it, right? You were convinced of that before, and now you're just dismissing his confession."

"He changed his story toward the end. He said . . . he said he'd seen something that morning that would make him rich. But it would hurt me to know . . ."

"He saw you, Lorna, leaving the scene of the crime. He was going to bribe your husband with that knowledge."

She stood up as Lorna looked at her wide-eyed.

"Twy, where are you going?" she asked.

"I've got to tell what I know, Lorna."

"No, Twyla! My mission for Mary will be compromised. I have to be free. They want to stop that, don't you see? He's her enemy. Lucifer Vesuvius is Mary's enemy. It's an ancient enmity. It –"

"No, Lorna. *No!*" Twyla snapped. "I'm under suspicion too, okay? What if *I* go to jail? And get a lethal injection? Are you telling me *that's* what Mary would want?"

"But Twy, why would they suspect you?"

"The discoverer of the body is *always* a prime suspect, Lorna. And if it comes out that I lied . . ."

"What did you lie about?"

"I didn't tell them Lamar was there when I found the body."

"But Lamar was there the day before, when he got the statue."

"You're sticking to that story? You see – you would obviously lie if it was between you and me going to jail. But you expect me to help you, like I'm your fool."

"No, Twyla. That's not . . ."

A sound of gravel crackling under tires and the sweep of headlights through the living room window announced a new arrival.

Lorna rose, crossed the room and pulled back its window's curtain.

She smiled. "It's Lamar. Just wait, okay? He'll clear this up."

Chapter 47

Lorna sprang to the door and already had it open while Lamar was still getting out of the car.

"Hi," he said, smiling at the eager greeting Lorna was giving him as he walked up the steps and into the trailer. Then he looked over at Twyla, who sat hunched over on the edge of the couch, her head bowed.

He looked back at Lorna. "What's up?" he asked.

"I want you to tell Twyla what you told me, about how you got the Saint Anthony statue from April's room and *when* you got it. The day *before* she was found dead, right?"

"Don't put words in his mouth, Lorna," Twyla said, rising from the couch and walking over to where Lamar and Lorna stood. Then she said: "Tell the truth, Lamar. I've already told Lorna what really happened that morning. You just have to back me up."

Lamar looked back and forth from Lorna to Twyla, both women staring at him as his mouth worked mutely for half a minute. Twyla nodded at him, as if to nudge him in the right direction.

"The truth," he said finally. "This is hard. But, Lorna, I can't continue to lie. Not with Twyla standing right here. She knows."

"What are you sayin', Lamar?" Lorna asked, her eyes shining with tears. "You told me —"

"Yeah, I did tell you that I got the Saint Anthony icon the day before

April's body was discovered. Just like you said. It's just . . . I lied to you. I mean, it was embarrassing, how I ran out like that. I was a coward. That's not something you tell someone you're trying to impress, especially when you're trying to convince her you're the next Indiana Jones. So I removed my presence that day entirely. The truth is, I got the Saint Anthony statue the morning Twy got me in."

"Wait," Twyla said, unsure of what she'd just heard. "What are you saying? You didn't take the Saint Anthony. It was gone already, when we got there."

"What I'm saying," Lamar said, "is, 'no,' I wasn't there the day before April's murder, but 'yes,' I did take the statue the morning we found her."

The corners of Twyla's mouth turned down. "You know that isn't true. You know that *I* know that isn't true."

"No, you just didn't see me take it."

"What are you talking about? I saw you run out of that room and you were *not* lugging any Saint Anthony icon from behind April's door."

"No, no . . . ," Lamar looked at Lorna again. Twyla watched their eyes meet, saw Lorna tuck her head slightly toward him.

He looked again at Twyla. "What it was . . . you see . . . when I came running out, I glimpsed this Saint Anthony statue behind a bush. Near the gate. And then when I saw what it was, saw that it was bleeding, I knew it must have come from April's room. And it would be a lot more impressive if it looked like I could get that Saint Anthony out – more of an accomplishment than swiping a little prayer card, you know. So I picked it up and ran with it. It was a spur of the moment kind-of-thing."

"So it just appeared there?" Twyla asked, glaring at him. "Between me and you going in and you running out? That was all of what . . . five minutes? Lamar, why didn't *I* see it if it was near the gate? Are you telling me now that you did, but you just didn't mention it?"

"No, I didn't see it going in either. Like I said, it was kind-of behind a bush, there. And, you know, we were both intent on what we were doing . . . you know?"

"What I know," Twyla said, her eyes tearing, "is that you're lying.

For *her*. You're taking the long shot of a chance that she'll reward your devotion with her love. That'd be funny if it wasn't so pathetic."

"Twyla, don't –" Lorna said.

"Ask her why she didn't invite you to her wedding," Twyla said. Then she pushed by him and was running out the door, running for her car. No one tried to stop her. She got in her car, backed out onto the road, and tore through the trailer park, pressing her gas pedal to the floor, regardless of the park's 15 m.p.h. sign.

She ended up at the Tar Forks water front, around the corner from Pope's Seafood, where she and Lorna had waitressed in high school. It seemed so very long ago now. So much had changed, and so much was still the same. Lorna was still the same. All of her talk about this mission, this "divine call," but she still played the same games to get what she wanted – from Mr. Gurley and just now from Lamar.

But now that Twyla had had some time to cool down, she had to question her conviction of Lorna's guilt. How much of her anger had been raised by Lamar being willing to discard her to stay in Lorna's favor? Did she have such resentment for her friend that Twyla *wanted* to believe she was guilty?

But personal feelings aside, the statue was *there*, in Lorna's trailer. She'd lied about how it got there. And Tate *must* have seen her fleeing the murder scene and consequently found April already dead – what else could he have discovered that morning that could make him rich? What other millionaire did he know other than Lorna's husband?

Lorna was guilty. She had lost her mind; that was the only explanation. Like mother, like daughter. Lorna's undoing was in the "charmed" genes that had given her so much beauty and intelligence. But more than her DNA template, Lorna's mother had passed on to her the shape of her dementia, and even supplied a character resume: Lucifer Vesuvius, power of the air.

And there was more: Lorna's own Marian vision and the communal delusion she shared with Albert Metz, who believed he turned into the Virgin Mary from time to time. Maybe Lorna could call him – as Mary – to the stand as a character witness. It was almost funny – or would be if it wasn't so tragic.

So, Twy, she asked herself, *what do you do now? Let's say you go to Detective Grell, and tell him you found the statue and who has it. What happens then? Tate, the actual witness who could put Lorna on the scene, is dead. Lamar could account for the statue's presence at Lorna's, but if Lamar told everything, Grell would know for certain that I straight-face lied about that morning. How could he trust my word again? Lorna could still get away with it, and I'd end up under more serious suspicion.*

She needed some counseling. And she certainly couldn't get it from her mother, not in this situation. But there was someone else –

Shametrice. Twyla had found guidance from her before. Of course, she was going through problems of her own. Maybe they could help each other.

———————

Twyla mounted the steps to Shametrice's house and rang the door bell. After a long moment of silence, she thought she heard a rustling from somewhere inside. She should have called Shametrice first, she knew, to see if she were home, before coming out to this part of town at night. But she wasn't going to be able to sleep or concentrate on her job until she'd reached some kind of decision, and she was afraid, at this hour, that Shametrice might put her off if she'd phoned ahead.

Twyla held her finger over the doorbell, peering inside the house through a window in the door. There was a small amber glow at foot level in the recesses of the house, what could be a night light, but no sign of movement. From the porch, Twyla looked over her shoulder. Across the street, the convenience store, with its bars on the windows and door, had closed. Two men who appeared to be loitering were smoking in front of it.

She quickly turned back around to look again through the window. She jumped, startled by someone looking back at her. At first there was uncertainty in the face of the person inside, but then both Shametrice and Twyla realized who the other was.

Twyla smiled with relief. "I'm sorry," she said through the door's glass. "I should have called, I know, but can I come in?"

Shametrice paused, still hesitant to open the door. This sent a fresh wave of discomfort through Twyla. Was she going to be sent away?

But then Shametrice was turning locks and pulling the door inward.

"C'mon in, hon," she said.

Twyla stepped inside, smiling with relief. Shametrice seemed embarrassed – perhaps at the frayed bathrobe she wore. Was that why she'd hesitated to let her in? But then Twyla realized that Shametrice wasn't hiding her attire, but her *hands* . . .

"What happened?" Twyla heard herself asking, her eyes still riveted on Shametrice's hands as the woman crossed her arms over her breast, trying quickly to tuck her hands into her armpits. But Twyla had already seen that both were rolled in bandages.

"Shametrice – how did you get hurt – was there an accident or was it Demarcus? Or –"

Or was it what had immediately popped into her mind, something she could barely believe –

"It's the stigmata, sug'," Shametrice said. "I've taken over for April."

Chapter 48

"When? How?" Twyla asked as she and Shametrice were seated in the living room.

"A couple days ago," Shametrice said. "Since you last saw me. I woke up one morning and there was blood on my sheets. And on my hands. I thought it was a nosebleed at first, or I'd scratched myself while I was sleeping. Then I got this sick feeling, and I wondered if Demarcus had come back and cut me. We had a bad argument the night before.

"Well, when I started cleaning up the blood I found it was seeping from my palms. When I tried to staunch the bleeding, it wouldn't stop. And then I remembered. I'd dreamed of April the night before. I don't remember the details. But I remembered enough that this bleeding in my hands made sense.

"April passed it on to me."

"Can stigmatics do that? And after they're *deceased?*" Twyla asked, thinking of what she'd learned of *psychogenic purpora*, that stigmata resulted from emotional trauma. Well, Shametrice *had* been through a lot recently. She'd always been so strong before. But everyone had a breaking point, she supposed, and she believed Shametrice's had triggered her stigmata. Still, she didn't challenge Shametrice's more mystical account of her bleeding's origins. "I've never heard of someone passing it on," was all she said.

"I never heard of it either. But there you are. I think it was her way of sayin' –" here Shametrice's voice choked, and her eyes teared.

In a moment, Twyla had left her chair and was on her knees before Shametrice, who'd bent over. Twyla reached out and embraced her. "It's okay, sug'. I understand," Twyla said. "You think it was her way of saying she wanted you to carry on the ministry."

Shametrice said neither "yes" or "no," just continued to cry. After a few more moments, she'd gotten herself together and withdrawn from Twyla's embrace, sitting up straight now in her chair. Twyla sat down on the floor by her and continued to gently stroke Shametrice's arm on the chair's armrest nearest her. She'd come to get support from Shametrice – *knowing* she had her own problems with her son as well as April's loss – and now Twyla felt so incredibly self-centered.

"You and April went back further than I knew," Twyla said. "I didn't know you'd known her personally. I mean, known her before the accident. You were a great help to her, the guidance you offered her about her stigmata."

"How did you know about that?" Shametrice asked, her eyes suddenly squinting a bit at Twyla. "I never told anyone –. Girl, are you operating a gift of discernment?" Shametrice shifted her weight in the chair, as though one of her legs had gone to sleep.

"No, no," Twyla said. "I've seen April's diary. She mentioned how you'd helped her. You told her about those two Egyptian wizards that imitated Moses' miracle of turning his staff into a serpent. That you had to be careful because the devil could imitate God."

"Oh, baby," Shametrice said, emotion in her voice. "I didn't know to take my own advice. When it counted, I didn't know."

"What do you mean?" Twyla asked.

"I let Demarcus bring the devil into this house. I let him practice his witchcraft right here under my nose."

Twyla remembered Demarcus returning to Miguel the Santeria objects which he'd believed would ward off the police and protect him. That paraphernalia included the Saint Anthony statue that had stood behind Shametrice's front door.

And then an unwelcome idea came to Twyla's mind, a suspicion from which she found herself flinching, but was nevertheless compelled to ascertain.

"What do you mean, Demarcus practiced witchcraft here?" Twyla asked Shametrice.

"He brought in those Santeria charms: colored beads and such."

Twyla strained around as though to look back toward the door she'd come through to enter the house. She was going to make a leap here.

"You used to have a Saint Anthony statue here, didn't you? Behind the door? Like in April's room?"

Shametrice's eyes narrowed. Her mouth opened slightly and for a moment the tip of her tongue appeared, as though gingerly trying a sore place on her lower lip. She didn't speak.

"I mean, wasn't that Saint Anthony supposed to keep the evil away?" Twyla pressed on.

"'Keep it away'? It was evil itself. But I couldn't tell," Shametrice said. "I mean, Saint Anthony is holding the baby Jesus in his arms. What could be purer – holier – than that?"

"But it wasn't," Twyla said.

"No! Behind the door like that, Saint Anthony represented some Santeria demon. It had been there for months, and I didn't know. I *still* wouldn't of known – 'cept when I saw the beads and things in Demarcus's room that he said were black magic, and I told him they had to go, he just got all sassy. He asked me if I knew so much about what was evil, why did I let him put one of the Santeria gods downstairs, behind the front door?"

"So, you had to throw Saint Anthony out, too?" Twyla asked.

"Yeah," Shametrice said. "I made Demarcus take it away. Even though it looked like a saint. You can't compromise. I had to make a clean break. I had to make it clear to my boy, especially after the way he'd challenged me – I had to make it clear that there is a difference between good and evil in this house. So I made Demarcus get rid of the Saint Anthony with his other things of the devil."

"This confrontation with your son, was it the same night the law caught Demarcus?" Twyla asked.

"Yeah. He blamed me for it when I went to see him in jail that morning – because I'd made him throw out his 'protection.'"

"That was the morning I discovered April's body. Except for Demarcus, you'd have been there at 7:15 in the AM, sharp – as usual."

"Yes."

"But *you* were there earlier, weren't you Shametrice?"

Shametrice's eyes widened. "Girl – you *are* operating a gift of discernment, aren't you?" Her voice was small as Twyla stood to her feet and stepped away from her.

Twyla didn't answer her friend's question. *Let her think that*, she thought, *if it'll make her open up. Maybe it is divine discernment; I don't really know that it's not.*

"Twyla?" Shametrice said.

"Sometime after you made Demarcus get the Saint Anthony out of your house, you thought of the one in April's room, still behind her door, still invoking the presence of evil. And you couldn't let it stay there, now that you knew, not a moment longer, could you?"

"No," Shametrice said. "I couldn't rest when I realized what was in there with innocent April. It had hindered my prayers, I was sure. I thought if I went and got it out I could pray again, and this time my prayers would take. I'd greet her daddy and you girls that morning with a revived April, raised to the glory of God!

"So I went back to the mansion. The first step was, I got that statue out the house. I took it out the door and threw it behind a bush. I didn't want anyone noticing it – that might raise questions. And I couldn't have no one interrupting my prayer, bringing that Saint Anthony back with them, not before the Lord and I were through. That demon wasn't going to be a problem anymore, and Saint Anthony wasn't going to get any credit for *this* healing."

C'mon, Shametrice. Twyla thought. *Tell me someone* else *had already turned off her life support when you got back.*

And who do you want that to be, Twyla? she asked herself. *Lorna?*

"And then, on the way back to pray for her, a voice spoke to me,"

Shametrice was saying. "It was more than just a 'feeling,' understand? This voice said to me, 'you're throwing out the statue, but that's only part of the problem. If you really had faith that I could raise her, you would have turned off the life support a long time ago.'"

No Shametrice, Twyla thought. *No!*

"Then a scripture came to my mind: 'I have set before thee an open door, and no man can shut it.' This was the moment, it was clear to me, now. If I'd tried when you girls had been around, someone would have interfered. At least, that was what the voice said I'd always told myself. But there was no one else, now. No humans with good intentions, no demons with evil ones. Just me, and April, and the Lord in that room – but I was wrong.

"I was headed back to inside the mansion, but I'd only taken a few steps when I thought, 'You know you can always lose faith while you're trying to raise her and plug her back in. You can't give place to the devil to be tempted to exercise that option.'

"'I had taken away Demarcus's wire shearers he was using to cut through chain link fences and barbed wire and thrown them in my trunk. But I'd never gotten around to throwing them away. Now I knew why. I needed to cut the cord in two so I couldn't be tempted to plug it back in.

"First, though, I took out the alarm's battery, then the respirator's back-up battery, and finally I unplugged it from the wall and cut the cord. And I prayed, Twyla, I prayed, all the time, believing she'd start to breathe on her own and wake up. And even when I didn't see her reviving. I kept hesitating. Putting the battery back in would have been a lack of faith. So I didn't. And then it was too late."

Twyla sat down hard on a chair to which she'd been slowly making her way while Shametrice talked. "Oh, Shametrice . . . honey . . ."

"I only realized, then, that it wasn't the Lord who'd been talking to me. I'd lost my own discernment, you see? I'd already opened the door to the deceptions of whatever thing was in that St. Anthony back when I let it be placed in April's room. By now, I could no longer tell the difference in the Lord and a devil *imitating* the Lord.

"It was like when Satan tried to prompt Jesus in the wilderness to turn stones to bread, or make a show by floating down from the top of the temple in front of everybody. You don't put God to the test; that's not how it works, and I was tempting God by cutting April's air off. I see that *now* —

"I know I should've turned myself in right then. But Demarcus was up to something bad. He'd gotten into witchcraft, and he needed my guidance more than ever. I couldn't stand the thought of going to prison, not being able to be there for my child. So I couldn't risk getting caught. I ran. I was in such a panic, I didn't take time to wipe the door knobs clean of my fingerprints. Once I was outside the back entrance, I did reset the gate alarm. I thought that was smart, but I wasn't thinking! I'd just left more fingerprints.

"But what did any of that matter? I couldn't do anything about that monitor camera in April's room; it would have recorded everything I did. But when the police never came for me, it was a confirmation that I'd made the right choice: the Lord hid me from sight in that room!"

Not the Lord . . . Lorna, Twyla thought. *Even though Lorna wouldn't have known Shametrice was there. When Lorna had spliced a loop into the surveillance feed so that she wouldn't be recorded in April's room, she had unwittingly covered Shametrice, too.*

"The Lord already knew Marcus was in jail again," Shametrice was saying, "that my boy needed me. The Lord wanted me to be here for him."

"But it wasn't the right choice, Shametrice," Twy said in a small but firm voice. "You know that now."

Shametrice began to sob. Twyla hesitated, then stood up, walked across the room, and sat down beside her friend. She hugged her. "You have to turn yourself in, Shametrice," she said.

"My *baby*, though, Twy! If he's held on to anything good it's because he still respects me. He counts on me to hold up the standard, even when he's letting it down. This could destroy him, destroy any hope I have of him turning back around."

"You can't make things right by hiding a crime, Shametrice. You can't expect God to bless that."

"But my boy —"

"You're going to have to turn him over to the Lord, Shametrice. And yourself to the authorities, if you want to have any effect from your prayers for him."

Twyla felt Shametrice's body heave in her arms, smelt her breath from her sigh. "Yes. You're right," she said after a moment. "I know that now. But I want to be the one to tell him, okay? I don't want this dropped on him by the news or him walking up and seeing the police take me away."

"Sure, sug'," Twyla said softly. "I can let you have 'til tomorrow night to turn yourself in before I'll say anything."

Twyla continued to hold Shametrice, who made no move to disengage herself from the embrace. But Twyla was getting antsy. She had to get back to Lorna and tell her that she knew she was innocent. She couldn't really tarry here. Still, she didn't want to just up and drop her distressed friend.

In the end, she was at the Prayer house for about a total of thirty minutes. And those thirty minutes, she would reprove herself later, were enough to change everything.

Everything was about to get worse.

Chapter 49

Driving back to Lorna's, Twyla put the pieces in place. The reconstructed scenario, she figured, had unfolded something like this:

Gurley had gotten Tate out of prison to unplug April. But Shametrice beat the hit man to it. Between Shametrice and Tate, Lorna had arrived in April's room. She must have known April would be alone for an hour and a half, and took the opportunity to visit her old friend, Lorna and Gurley's secrecy about her presence in the mansion and their relationship having made it difficult to pay her respects.

She had no idea she would discover a corpse.

Lorna had fled when she heard someone entering the wing. That would have been Tate, come to murder April. Though he was unseen by Lorna, he recognized her as she was slipping away. When he subsequently discovered April was already dead, he must have believed Lorna was responsible. He was determined that he get the credit, and the money, and so would have taken the respirator's back-up battery, its alarm battery, and that piece of its cut power cord to Vernon as evidence *he* had carried out the deed.

Though he was no doubt instructed to make that evidence disappear, Twyla bet he planned to use it in a future attempted blackmail of Vernon Gurley with what he believed he knew about Lorna. That's what he meant when he croaked out of his burned mouth that he knew something that would make him rich. The way Gurley had set him up in the private wing of the mansion, he could have had opportunity to have seen her, even seen her being affectionate with Gurley in an unguarded moment. Maybe he had even asked Gurley directly about his relationship with Lorna. Surely, Gurley wouldn't have revealed their marriage, but perhaps he let Tate believe Lorna was only his mistress. Even so, she was one so stunningly desirable Tate would have believed the millionaire would surely be willing to pay high dollar to protect her.

Gurley would have thought Tate was bluffing, that Tate couldn't tell on Lorna without running the risk of incriminating himself. But Tate would have had no discernable motive for murdering April (Gurley certainly couldn't reveal that *he* had hired him to unplug his daughter), and he would have believed he could count on Shametrice for a character reference.

And, should Vernon have continued to resist Tate's demands, *then* Twyla suspected he would make Gurley aware that the police might get a tip that April's respirator's batteries and electrical cord had shown up in the mansion's residential wing.

Of course, Tate never got around to telling Gurley that he had caught Lorna fleeing April's wing. And when a distraught Lorna had told Gurley that morning that April was dead, her life support cut off, he would have assumed that Tate already had done his job as planned.

Since April was already dead when Lorna came to her room, Gurley would have believed his hit man to be good and gone by then, instead of having just arrived *after* Lorna (Tate apparently figured, since he had almost an hour and a half to murder the comatose girl, there was no need to hurry). Gurley expected Twyla, whom he believed would be in at 6:30, to find the body. But when Gurley discovered that Twyla had been on the job earlier than usual, he believed only *she* could be the one whom Lorna had heard inside the wing. In which case, there was a chance she could have recognized her old friend. Hence Twyla had become a "threat" to Gurley's plans for himself and his new wife.

A threat to be eliminated.

"Well," Twyla thought as she turned into the trailer park, "I'm still here; I only hope Lorna's not in danger from Vernon Gurley herself, now."

For the accusation she'd leveled at Lorna could have sent her friend to confront her husband. Although Lorna had been initially hesitant to consider him a suspect, he would be the most likely one in Lorna's mind – especially if she had read April's diary, which Twyla had left on Lorna's computer when she'd stormed out. Lorna could have filled in the blanks the same way Twyla had.

When Twyla pulled up to Lorna's trailer, she noticed immediately that Lorna's Dodge Omni was gone.

This did not bode well.

Twyla ran from her car to the trailer and rapped a quick staccato against the door.

"C'mon, c'mon, Lamar," she mumbled insistently.

Lamar opened the door after only a few seconds. He started at Twyla's appearance.

"Where is she?" Twyla demanded, pushing her way past Lamar and into the trailer.

"She didn't specifically say," Lamar said, following her inside. "When I wanted to talk to her about what you'd said, about her being married, she promised to explain everything to me later, but she had to read that flash drive you'd brought over right now. So, I just hung around, thinking we'd talk when she was through with it, but then she took off. She wouldn't let me go with her, said I'd get in the way. But it's trouble, huh?"

Lorna's computer was still up, and Twyla quickly crossed over to it. She could see on the monitor where Lorna had last been reading; it was where April's entries stopped.

"I'm afraid so," Twyla said. "And when she confronts him, I'm afraid it won't matter that they're married."

"*What?*"

"Mr. Gurley's her husband, Lamar. C'mon!"

Twyla quickly led Lamar to her car and in a moment they were speeding through the trailer park, onto the state road and to the Gurley mansion outside town.

Twyla pressed the accelerator to the floor. Lamar grimaced, stretched his arms out before him and pressed the heels of both hands into the dashboard to brace himself as she ran a stop sign.

"Take it easy, will you?" he said. "Us having a wreck isn't going to help Lorna out, okay?"

Twyla decreased – slightly – the pressure of her foot against the pedal. "Lord, don't let us be too late. Help us to help Lorna," she prayed under her breath.

Finally, after what seemed like one red light after another, she pulled up to the mansion's rear gate.

She tapped Lorna's birthdate on the keypad, and she and Lamar passed through the gate. She still carried the key to the door of April's wing, so they entered easily. They were moving ahead at a brisk pace, though Twyla was aware that they had no idea where Vernon Gurley and Lorna were, or what she and Lamar were going to do exactly when they got there.

And then what sounded like the explosion of a small canon paralyzed them. The ebullition seemed powerful enough to bring down the mansion –

Followed by the fading reverberation as the walls and ceiling remained in place –

Twyla remembered how she'd wondered just a few hours ago if Mr. Gurley had weapons in his house. Now she had the sickening answer.

In the next instant, she felt the weight of Lamar's body crashing against hers, knocking her to the floor and pinning her there.

Chapter 50

Twyla's breath was jarred from her and while she lay unable to move, unable to breathe, she wondered if Lamar had been hit by the bullet – if he, in fact, were dying while she lay helpless beneath him, at the mercy of Vernon Gurley.

"Lamar, are you okay?" Twyla was finally able to gasp out. "Be okay, please."

"I'm all right. How about you?"

"Lamar, could you get off me?"

"He could start shooting again."

"And we're right here in the open, you see? C'mon."

"Okay, just keep low, all right?"

Twyla felt Lamar's weight lift from her; then he grabbed her hand, pulled her up, and dragged her into what turned out to be a side bedroom.

"You're not hurt?" Twyla asked. "Why did you jump on me like that?"

"I was trying to shield you from getting shot."

"You were?" Twyla asked, touched by his clumsy heroics. For a moment. Then she noticed there were no more bullets forthcoming and realized with a fresh wave of horror that if neither she nor Lamar were the ones being fired on, there was probably only one other person in the mansion at whom Mr. Gurley would be shooting.

"Lorna!" she said to Lamar, and then bolted out the door.

He was right behind her, and saw her draw up short where the hallway opened on the den Vernon Gurley had led her through days ago. Lamar, too, came to a stand still at what he saw:

Lorna lying on the floor; one hand clutching above her left breast. Blood on her; blood on the floor. And standing over her, holding a gun, was Vernon Gurley.

He looked up at their entrance, his mouth dropped open, and he waved the gun their way.

Twyla grabbed Lamar's hand and pulled him with her. They dropped down behind the liquor bar.

"Twyla?" she heard Mr. Gurley ask, his voice breaking.

"What have you done, Mr. Gurley?" Twyla asked from where she and Lamar huddled. "*What have you done?*"

"I didn't mean it to happen this way –"

"Then why are you standing around? Why don't you call 911!"

"Twyla . . ."

It was Lorna's voice, and it prompted Twyla to raise her head from behind the bar.

"Lorna?"

"It's my shoulder, Twy," Lorna said, still lying where she was, but turning her head in Twyla's direction. "He didn't mean for it to happen."

"Then why's he still waving the gun around? Why hasn't he called an ambulance?"

"I think he's in shock," Lorna choked out.

"*He's* in shock?"

"You have to understand," Mr. Gurley said. "She was *looking* at me –"

"You shot her because you didn't like the way she looked at you?" Twyla said.

"– her eyes – just like my baby's."

"April's?" Twyla asked.

"I never meant to hurt her," Mr. Gurley said. "And I thought she'd forgiven me for doing . . . *that* to her. Coming back from the psychiatrist . . . the look in her eyes. So betrayed, and angry, and disgusted. Just like *she* " – he nodded toward Lorna – "like she was looking at me. Sayin' the same thing, that I couldn't touch her ever again. It was just like that night in the car."

"So you tried to kill Lorna when she rejected you just now – just like you tried to kill April in that car wreck," Twyla said.

"No!" Vernon Gurley shouted. "I didn't try to kill her. *I* wanted to die. Not April. Not Lorna. *Both* times . . . don't you understand? The *scandal* would ruin me, what my family built over generations. I couldn't live with that. Both times . . . I meant to kill *myself*."

"You weren't trying to kill yourself when you hired my uncle to unplug your daughter."

"If April ever woke up . . . it couldn't come out. Not after I'd rebuilt my life. See, I would have had Lorna, and April would have her mother."

Silence for a beat, a pause as he looked pleadingly at Twyla, as he seemed to realize for the first time the evil of which he was capable, of which he had justified himself.

What does he want from me? Twyla thought. *Absolution?*

She had none to offer.

Beyond forgiveness, Vernon Gurley quickly thrust the handgun's barrel into his mouth, made yet another attempt on his own life.

And this time he did not fail.

Chapter 51

"Lorna!" Twyla shouted, grabbing a towel from the bar and running toward her friend. Seeing Lamar was following, she shouted out to him, "Call 911!"

Twyla landed hard on her knees beside Lorna, and used the towel to try and staunch the bleeding of her shoulder. She raised her friend's head, and cradled it in her lap. "Oh, Lorna, I'm sorry. This is my fault. I shouldn't have accused you. That sent you over here to confront him."

"It's all right, Twy," Lorna said. "I knew it was dangerous. I just had to know."

"So he admitted raping . . . ?"

"Once when he was drunk. He molested her. Once. She never talked about it afterward and he never did; he was ashamed when he sobered up. He wanted to forget it, and when April never said anything, he thought she'd forgiven him. He said he meant to spend the rest of his life trying to make it up to her.

"But when he heard about her psychiatric sessions, he was afraid his secret would come out. He interrupted her final session to stop it. She hadn't told her analyst yet, but she confronted Vernon with the rape on the way home, and he wrecked the car. He *was* tryin' to end his *own* life. Like just now. He was goin' to shoot himself. I tried to get the gun away, and I got shot."

247

"Lorna," Twyla said. "I know who murdered April. It was Shametrice Prayer."

Lorna's eyes narrowed. "I thought your uncle . . ."

"No. It was Shametrice. She confessed to me."

"The preacher who ran April's website . . ."

In the distance, the just discernible sound of an ambulance siren . . . .

"That's right," Twyla said. "But don't say anything. I told her I'd give her a day to settle things and turn herself in."

"Sure," Lorna said. "You're a good judge of character."

Twyla nodded at Lorna, on the floor with a bullet in her. "Apparently not."

"It looked bad, I know. My fingerprints were all over everything, so to speak. I *was* in April's room that morning. I always spent my time in the mansion in the privacy of the residential wing, since Vernon and I were keeping our relationship secret. But when he told me about the hour and a half time period that morning that April wouldn't be supervised, I saw an opportunity to visit her.

"Naturally, I couldn't let myself be recorded in her room on the monitor's hard drive and risk breaking the secrecy we were still trying to maintain. So, before I went over there, when I was still over in the residential wing, I did to the Wi-Fi feed to the security camera in April's room what you saw me do when we were breaking in the mansion." She smiled and squeezed Twyla's hand. "You had me figured out back at my trailer. Not that I dared admit it then."

"What you didn't realize," Twyla said, "was that you'd set it up so that there'd be no record of Shametrice's visit to April's room. She was in and out between your splicing in that video loop and your getting there," Twyla said.

"Once I actually got in her room, things went south pretty quick," Lorna said. "She was dead, and I could tell it had been long enough that there was no bringing her back. Then I heard somebody else in the wing –"

"Tate," Twyla said.

"– just as I noticed that the Saint Anthony statue was missing. That's why, when Lamar told me he had taken it the day before, it made sense. But I didn't dare say anything more to you. Your judgement was clouded. You were –"

"Jealous?" Twla said, coloring.

"I notice I seem to bring that out in a lot of women," Lorna said and smiled against her pain. "Even when I'm not tryin' anymore. Hi, Lamar."

Twyla looked up to see Lamar squatting down by them. He was a bit pale.

"It looks worse than it is, honest," Lorna said, holding out a hand to him. He grasped it.

"You're gonna make it, right?" Lamar asked. "You can hold out 'til the ambulance gets here?"

"Relax, Lamar," Twyla said. "It's just her shoulder. No vital organs hit or anything."

"Honest, I'll be okay," Lorna said. "But I want to apologize to you, Lamar. I should have never invited you to Tar Forks, not with me bein' a married woman and all. It wasn't fair to you; selfish of me."

Twyla looked at the body of Vernon Gurley then back at Lorna. "You're not married anymore," she said quietly. "You're a widow now."

Lorna's brow furrowed and she tried to turn to see the body. "Are you sure?"

Twyla reached out and gently guided her head back away from the sight. "You don't need to see that. He's dead; no question," she said.

"A widow," Lorna said. "It seems unreal. The whole marriage seems so unreal right now."

"But it *was* real, right?" Twyla asked. "I mean, you did all the paperwork, made sure it was legal?"

"It was 100 per cent legal. Documented."

"Then you're not only really a widow, you're a really rich widow. Probably one of *the* richest in the state when it's all sorted out."

"Yeah," Lorna said. "But I'll bet there are some other family members out there who won't be thrilled with me gettin' that inheritance, who'll think I'm just another Anna Nicole Smith or somethin'. I don't think . . . I'll fight 'em."

249

"What do you mean?" Twyla asked. "I know material stuff doesn't mean anything to you personally, but what about your mission?"

"My mission," Lorna said softly. "Lamar, is Albert going to be okay?"

"He came out of his seizure all right. They said it was probably related to his Tourettes."

"It wasn't the Tourettes," Lorna said. There was a hard set in her eyes that Twyla had never seen before, a look that was light years away from the coy, playful ones Lorna had been given to back in high school.

It made Twyla uncomfortable, a sense of impending loss rushing over her. *But why?* she wondered as the loudness of a siren outside announced the rescue squad had arrived. Lorna was going to be okay. The danger had passed.

So why did she have to fight to smile encouragingly at her friend as they wheeled her out to the ambulance.

"Twyla, what's wrong?" Lamar asked. He tentatively reached for her, and Twyla, seeing his hesitance, fell against him and began to sob.

"Nothing. Everything. I don't know. Just hold me."

He did.

Epilogue

Myra's marriage to Miguel ended up being heralded in the same issue of the *Tar Forks News* that belatedly announced Lorna's nuptials. Of course, Lorna's wedding was not on the society page. It *was* front page, though, while the announcement of Myra's wedding was regulated to Section C, just a copy column or two across from the "Buy one; Get one Free" coupons for the local Wriggly Piggly grocery store.

The brief article, however, did not account for the bandage the groom sported on his nose. It was the result of an injury incurred while Miguel was searching for Chupacabra spoor with his friend Jamie down on Booger Grubb's Ostrich and Emu Farm. There Miguel encountered Albert Metz, who unexpectedly struck Miguel in the face as the migrant was passing him. Albert's attack was attributed to his Tourettes syndrome. As he lashed out at Miguel, he was heard to scream, "THIS IS FOR THE FREQUENCY! THIS IS FOR THE FREQUENCY!"

However, in Tar Forks no one was very much concerned about any altercation out at Booger Grubb's, anyway. No, the townsfolk were focused on the secret union of the town's richest man with a former local beauty queen – the news of which had erupted with bloodshed into the public consciousness.

The deaths of Vernon Gurley and his daughter, only a few days apart, were of more than mere local interest, of course, and the cable news networks, CNN, FOX NEWS and MSNBC, picked up the story for national coverage. It was sensationalistic material to begin with, and it only became more juicy when the public learned that Vernon Gurley's suicide was witnessed only by his much younger wife, whom he'd secretly wed mere months earlier, and two of her friends. Very convenient it all seemed and Lorna fell suspect. Had she been responsible for her husband's death – and April's as well?

These suspicions persisted despite community pillar Apostlette Shametrice Prayer turning herself in as April's murderer. There were those who couldn't accept it, even given the tell-tale scarlet lettering on Shametrice's stigmatic palms. One popular rumor was that Lorna had convinced a desperate Shametrice to take the heat. In exchange, Lorna used her new financial resources to get Shametrice's criminal son Demarcus out of the country with a virtually bottomless bank account from which to draw.

Demarcus had indeed suspiciously disappeared sometime between April's murder and his mother's confession. His whereabouts remained unknown, and thus Lorna remained under suspicion in many minds –

– especially since any motivation for Vernon Gurley committing suicide was never made public. All that was known was that Lorna, who had retained a lawyer, met with the Gurley family and their lawyer behind closed doors. Less than thirty minutes into this tête-à-tête, those doors opened and the Gurley family reappeared with pale faces.

The agreement they had reached was summed up thusly: "Give her whatever she wants."

Whatever Lorna wanted, it *wasn't* residency in the Gurley mansion, but it offered her security from the paparazzi that her mobile home could not. And so she was at the mansion, recuperating, when Twyla came to visit her.

"You're looking good, girl," Twyla said, greeting Lorna as she sat in the sun by a pool that needed skimming.

"I don't feel so good, Twy," she said.

"Wound left you sore, huh?"

"*That* I can work out. The gym here, that Vernon put together for me, is excellent." Lorna frowned. "You know, he did all this stuff for me, and then he killed himself because I was gonna leave him. But what else could I do, Twy? After all he'd done?"

Twyla seated herself on a beach chair and reached out and placed her hand over Lorna's. "Sug', Vernon Gurley is responsible for his own self. I mean – you got shot trying to keep him *from* killing himself. It's all *his* fault. If *he* hadn't of messed up April's life because of one night's drunk, everything would of been different. She'd never of been traumatized and started her stigmata. There would've been no car 'accident.' He took any chance of his daughter having a normal life away from her. But for him, she'd probably still be alive today, married and a mom, I bet."

"His gettin' drunk that night cost a lot more than the price of his liquor, didn't it?" Lorna said.

"Like when someone drives drunk and kills somebody – what Vernon Gurley did was no different in my book. So don't feel bad about using that gym or continuing to use his money to take care of your mama, if you're feeling bad about that, too."

Lorna patted Twyla's hand on hers. "Thank you, Twy. Mama is goin' to be well taken care of. The best. And why I'd rather not be livin' here, lookin' like I'm what everybody thinks, some black widow that's livin' in ill gotten gain – the fact is that I *do* have security from the press here, I can use a gym without goin' public, and I just don't need the hassle now. Not *now* of all times."

"You're talking about your mission, aren't you?" Twyla asked. "Lorna, what is it?"

"Twy, I can't –"

"I know. Look, whatever it is ain't important. I mean, after all that's happened, can't you just let it go, now? You wouldn't have ever got in this mess if you hadn't married Vernon Gurley, and you wouldn't of done that if you didn't feel you needed his financial support for this quest of yours."

To Twyla's surprise, Lorna actually seemed to be considering what she was suggesting. For a long, silent moment, Lorna gently gnawed her lower lip and stared into the distance. Then she slowly shook her head "no."

"C'mon, Lorna," Twyla said, leaning toward her. "I mean, we only just got back together after so long. I've spent the last twelve years resenting you – it was wrong, I know. But I could make it up to you. I could be your friend again."

Lorna's eyes had begun to brim while Twyla spoke. "Twy," she said after a minute. "I can't be your friend."

"*What?*"

"I can't be *anybody's* friend."

"But . . . why?"

"Because Shametrice Prayer may be the one sittin' in a cell, but I'm the real reason April Gurley's dead."

"What . . . what do you mean?"

"The Virgin Mary came to see me yesterday."

"You mean Albert."

"I *mean* Mary. And she explained to me what she was tryin' to tell me, to tell you, that day at the trailer."

"Lorna, please don't tell me you're starting up about Lucifer Vesuvius, again. Can't you let that go?"

"Not when I'm responsible."

"*How* exactly are you responsible?"

"April died because I took that statue of Ganesh from his temple. The demon in the thing was worshipped like a god, and I humiliated it by stickin' it in a white trash trailer park and makin' it do parlor tricks. So he wanted to get back at me, but his situation in my mobile home sort-of restricted Ganesh. He appealed to Lucifer Vesuvius. Who didn't need to have his arm twisted to set me up. He used poor Shametrice to murder April because they knew I'd be in the house, and I could come under suspicion."

Twyla found herself thinking of the voice Shametrice claimed had spoken to her, that prompted her into turning off April's life support. Shametice had said it was the devil's – at least, she said that *now*. More likely that Shametrice was trying to justify her actions to herself, to account for behavior that her conscience couldn't own up to.

Still, Twyla couldn't help but note that Lorna was making a point *not* to say that she would never have been in danger of suspicion if Twyla hadn't discovered the icon of Saint Anthony in her trailer. Had she indeed opened herself up to demonic manipulation through participating in Miguel's Santeria ritual? Twyla shook her head, shaking off the notion.

"Something has shadowed me, Twy, all my life," Lorna said. "And I can't be friends with anyone until I've resolved whatever it is. Call it Lucifer Vesuvius or whatever. It all comes down to the same thing: people I care about end up in danger if not outright dead."

"So, what are you going to do?"

"First thing, I'm returnin' Ganesh to his temple. And then, I think I'm goin' to be by myself for a while."

"You'll let me know, won't you? When it's safe again to be friends? Because I'll be waiting."

"You'll be the first to know," Lorna said. Seeing tears stand in Twyla's eyes and feeling them well in her own, she leaned toward her old friend. Twyla met her and the two women embraced.

"Give me an e-mail address or something, so I can keep up," Twyla said as she withdrew. She wiped her eyes with the back of her hand. "By the way, I plan to be out of my mom and dad's house as soon as I can."

"And how soon is 'as soon as you can'?"

"Well, actually, the middle of August."

"What happens in August?" Lorna asked.

"I'm taking the cat and going to finish nursing school where you were getting your doctorate."

"When did you decide that?"

"Well, I been planning to start back at the community college. But, State, well – *you* know." Twyla tucked her head and half-covered a smile behind her hand. "That's where Lamar works."

Lorna crossed her arms and smiled. "You and Lamar, huh?"

"Well, he can *talk* the Bible, even if he's not a regular church attendee. Mama's impressed."

"He's already met 'mama,' huh? Sounds serious."

"Well, I sort-of stepped that up, because Mama was questioning my romantic choices and Lamar, you know, he's a nice guy."

Lorna reached out and touched Twyla's arm. "Well, I hope it works out for you two."

"And I hope – I hope you find out what you're looking for, Lorna; I hope you're able to do whatever it is you're supposed to do."

As she walked away from the Gurley mansion for what could be the last time, Twyla paused to look at the window that opened on what had been April's room. She thought of the rumors of angels there, and how they no longer had need to remain, since April had at last been set free to join them. Still, Twyla again thought she saw a flickering of wings in that very special place, and she hoped that the angels might linger as long as Lorna had need of them.

End

Notes

Notes

Made in the USA
Columbia, SC
10 November 2018